P9-BYA-300

PRIZZI'S
MONEY

Novels by Richard Condon

The Venerable Bead
The Final Addiction
Emperor of America
Prizzi's Glory
Prizzi's Family
A Trembling upon Rome
Prizzi's Honor
The Entwining
Death of a Politician
Bandicoot
The Abandoned Woman
The Whisper of the Axe

Money Is Love
The Star-Spangled Crunch
Winter Kills
Arigato
The Vertical Smile
Mile High
The Ecstasy Business
Any God Will Do
An Infinity of Mirrors
A Talent for Loving
Some Angry Angel
The Manchurian Candidate
The Oldest Confession

Other Books by Richard Condon

And Then We Moved to Rossenarra

The Mexican Stove/Ole Mole
(with Wendy Jackson)

PRIZZI'S MONEY

RICHARD CONDON

CROWN PUBLISHERS, INC.

New York

Copyright © 1994 by Richard Condon

All rights reserved. No part of this book may be reproduced or transmitted in any form or by any means, electronic or mechanical, including photocopying, recording, or by any information storage and retrieval system, without permission in writing from the publisher.

Published by Crown Publishers, Inc., 201 East 50th Street, New York, New York 10022. Member of the Crown Publishing Group. Random House, Inc. New York, Toronto, London, Sydney, Auckland

CROWN is a trademark of Crown Publishers, Inc.

Manufactured in the United States of America

Library of Congress Cataloging-in-Publication Data

Condon, Richard.
    Prizzi's money / Richard Condon.—1st ed.
       p.   cm.
    1. Organized crime—United States—Fiction. I. Title.
  PS3553.0487P75 1994
  813'.54—dc20   93-8983
                                        CIP

ISBN 0-517-59695-4

10 9 8 7 6 5 4 3 2 1

First Edition

For two well-loved and
loving daughters

PRIZZI'S
MONEY

ON A HOT summer afternoon, while he was roaring his cigarette boat across Long Island Sound about four miles off Bent Island at the eastern end toward the open sea, Henry George Asbury, "adviser to presidents," was kidnapped. When it happened, he was standing at the helm of the 42-foot powerboat, flanked by one armed security man and an engine crewman who was trimming the twin 440-horsepower turbo engines.

Asbury wore black-trimmed racing goggles and leather racing gloves. The winds were strong. As they headed into heavy seas, the boat smashed into the waves, each hit making the men grunt as if they had been punched.

The security man was ex–Secret Service, a former presidential bodyguard, one of a set of four who had gone over the boat with bomb-and-weapon scenting dogs and had run hand-held buzzers over the two engine crewmen, even though they had been with Asbury for nearly six years. The bodyguard aboard, Dick Gallagher, was equipped with special emergency communications gear.

The tremendous noise of the engines made all four men wear

noise suppressors over their ears. It was impossible for anything to be heard.

Asbury was large. He was five feet eleven, forty-two pounds overweight, barrel-chested and thick-armed. He was wearing, illegally, a U.S. Navy captain's cap. His lifetime trick was that he never thought of anything except himself, and of advancing himself to where he had all the attention. People said, as he moved himself along, that he had a hunger for power. But power is just another tool for getting attention. Four days before he disappeared, he had had a nurse give him an enema in a bedroom crowded with his wife, lawyers, a lady journalist, and three blaring television sets while he yelled orders at almost everyone in the room. He used everything to get attention: lavish praise, bribes, elegant double-talk, barnyard language, cruelties, lies, bullying, and conduct so gross that now and then it bordered on the aberrant.

Everyone on the horrendously ear-splitting boat, alone in the water for miles in each direction, was looking straight ahead at the empty sea when the kidnapping happened. There was not another craft in sight, port or starboard, fore or aft. A shaft of brilliant sunshine had just broken through the clouds gathered directly ahead.

The bodyguard had no chance of protecting Asbury, because whatever doctrinaire security plans might have existed to prevent an abduction from a boat moving at sixty-eight miles an hour were seriously damaged by a stun bomb dropped from a helicopter to explode at a hover position twenty-three feet over their heads. Neither the bodyguards nor the crew could have heard the approach of the helicopter. The relative speed of boat and helicopter made it possible that fragments of the stun bomb fell into the sea, out of the reach of subsequent FBI forensic teams. The bodyguard, the engine crew, and Asbury were rendered unconscious by the stun. The boat began to run slowly in a wide, random circle.

A bulky man rappeled down from the helicopter to the deck of the cigarette boat. It was a tricky operation that required skilled piloting by the helicopter pilot and impressive physical coordination by the athlete who came down the rope. He silenced its engines. The boat came to a choppy halt while the helicopter waited overhead. The man unwound a loading net from around his waist, dumped Asbury into it, then closed the net with a clamping hook. The two of them were winched into the fuselage of the chopper, which flew off across the Sound thirty miles offshore to the open sea.

Eleven minutes later, the helicopter landed on the pad of the *Benito Juárez Bennett,* a container ship, where Asbury, still unconscious, was extricated from the cargo net and taken below. The container ship made a course due north by northeast, moving at a leisurely speed toward the United Kingdom.

The speedboat, with its unconscious cargo, lolled on the Sound for almost twelve minutes before its passengers, one by one, regained consciousness and, unmanned by the discovery that their patron had vanished, took groggy command of the boat. Dick Gallagher, the bodyguard, called up the security station on Bent Island.

The distress call raised the security guard on the island, who rushed the message to Emmaline MacHanic, secretary to Mrs. Asbury. Shaken but steady, she hurried from room to room until she found Julia Asbury doing a crossword puzzle on a terrace overlooking a well-ordered garden.

"Mrs. Asbury!" she blurted.

Mrs. Asbury held up a hand to still Miss MacHanic long enough to finish writing a word into the spaces identified as 24 Down on the puzzle.

"Yes, Emmaline?"

"Agent Gallagher just signaled from the boat. Mr. Asbury has been kidnapped."

"*Kid*napped? *Hen*ry? How could that *be*?"

"That's just it, Mrs. Asbury. They don't know. No one knows. They were all standing in the boat. It was speeding. Mr. Asbury was singing. Then—the next thing they knew—they woke up and he was gone."

"Woke *up*? *Gone*? Gone *where*?"

"That's just it, Mrs. Asbury. No one knows how or where he went."

"This is terrible."

"Shouldn't we call the police?"

"Yes! My god, yes, call the police!"

Miss MacHanic rushed out of the room. Greatly troubled, Mrs. Asbury put finishing words into the crossword puzzle.

Inevitably, the telephone operator at the local police station told her sister on the Montauk newspaper about the kidnapping and, within the hour, the story had leaked to the wire services and, within two hours, a raucous mass of the news media swarmed over the Asbury compound on Bent Island: reporters, television crews, news photographers, feature writers, and radio commentators.

One of the most powerful men in the country, an "adviser to presidents" (an appellation which validated his enormous contributions to the "campaign funds" of both political parties), had disappeared from his powerboat on open water as if he had been demonstrating the Indian rope trick. The news media reacted like small boys on Christmas morning. It was a story made in heaven: a locked-door mystery, a *National Enquirer* scoop made kosher and fit for the *Wall Street Journal* and the *New York Times*.

Henry George Asbury had stood shoulder-to-shoulder with President Noon, making history with clean-air proposals that included special provisions promoting three automobile fuels: ethanol, natural gas, and reformulated gasoline, all products of several different Asbury companies. When Osgood Noon released the federally subsidized water which enriched Asbury's agri-industrial holdings in California, it was the result of a large, over-generous "campaign contribution" from Henry Asbury. Even though they seriously weakened wetlands protection, the Administration-backed real estate tax shelters went through Congress from the Noon White House like a shot because Henry Asbury believed in paying his share for good government; in his case (through several of his companies)

$1,439,560. His relations with Osgood Noon's "vision thing" were so good that one of his executives had been invited to join the President's pleading expedition to Japan, where Asbury had landed four lucrative deals for the company.

Henry Asbury had arrived on the American financial scene in the late 1950s. He was a native Texan, although without any trace of a southwestern accent, had a framed diploma from Southern Methodist University at Dallas (which had a thoroughfare called Asbury Avenue leading at right angles from it) and the Wharton School of Business in Pennsylvania.

Upon graduation with an MBA, he had thrived on the turmoil in the credit and securities markets. His legend was by now puffed and daily recounted to the world by his considerable public relations department: the stories of his almost psychic insights, his fifteen-hour working days, and the force of concentration with which he had built a medium-sized Boston brokerage firm—and turned it into what was to become the giant Asbury & Company, investment bankers—dealing with riffraff instant millionaires and raising billions of dollars for television networks, publishing conglomerates, and computer software geniuses with junk bonds. Where he had found the capital to do all this was, as usual in all these cases, mysterious, but then the genesis of great sums of money will always remain mysterious to the citizenry.

Asbury's action, more and more, had shifted from the deck of his yacht to his *palazzo* in Rome to a chalet in Gstaad to his compound on his own Bent Island. He had played a major role in closing the gap between public and private market values during the piratical Reagan years, as the Dow Jones Industrials climbed from under 1000 to nearly 3000 and several (rapidly depreciating) trillion dollars was added to the net worth of both consumers and investing institutions. During those years he had added an investment bank to his string, and at first gradually then rapidly acquired 137 interlocked companies, some enormous, some merely huge. The oddity which no one bothered to be curious about was that it all had happened so fast. But that was the American way. The good book of gigantic success said that if you had the best mousetrap, people with large amounts of money beat a path to your door and forced the money on you. Hadn't they all been poor boys with a vision? Hadn't they all awakened one morning with an endless line of credit? The rest of the people took that for granted and waited beside the phone for an opportunity to call back.

He had met Julia Melvini, his wife, while she was employed as secretary at the Executives' League. During the period of liaison between the League and Asbury prior to conferral upon him of its Executive-of-the-Year Award, Asbury, a lifelong bachelor at forty-two, had been impressed by the thrift and efficiency of the young woman if not at first by her most striking beauty. But, to Asbury, thrift was an "always" quality while beauty was just another evanescent advantage. He spent fortunes on buying houses around the world but he melted down small slivers of soap and poured that into new bars. He wore quite clean but ragged underwear. He made sure that the odometers on his automobiles showed mileage which matched the proven miles-per-gallon capacity of his cars. His drivers did not pad Henry Asbury's gasoline accounts.

This thrift-induced admiration for Miss Melvini had begun during a heavy rainstorm when Asbury, at his office, insisted that she accept taxicab fare to return to her own office. Miss Melvini had refused the offer, saying that taxis were an extravagance; she had her raincoat and her umbrella. She thanked Mr. Asbury but was firm in her refusal of his kind offer. She was so resolute in her refusal that Asbury stopped overlooking her as just somebody's stenographer. His admiration of her stoic thrift opened his eyes, permitting him to see her as a distinct, healthy young woman who had developed, quite suddenly he thought, a thrilling voice—soft, clear, and persuasive; superb carriage; excellent taste in clothes, considering what she must earn; and began to believe more and more, as he invented reasons for meetings with her in the four weeks of preparation for the awards dinner, that she was a singularly, even uniquely beautiful woman of such intelligence and respect for the value of money as to make it desirable to convert her into an Asbury asset.

These unconscious evaluations might have been the essence of "falling in love" if they had been happening to an ordinary man, but Henry George Asbury, adviser to presidents, had been seriously involved with every mirror he had ever met, and whereas "ordinary men" found passion and fulfillment with a woman or women, Asbury had sublimated all that in the relentless pursuit and capture of money. This conditioning muted, without blunting, his responses to qualities in Julia Melvini which he found to be more and more desirable, so it was not until after there was no longer reason for them to meet to discuss details of the awards night and his acceptance speech that Asbury found himself staring at Julia's absence wherein, except for his marking her tendency toward thrift, she had merely been an expediting convenience provided by her employers, his sponsors.

Miss Melvini, in truth, was not a thrifty woman at all. On the contrary, she had been using family connections to acquire a parrot-importing business to support her tastes for larger, more expensive, and more elegant things. She had refused the offer of taxi fare only because she had planned to shop at Saks Fifth Avenue when she left the Asbury offices at the RCA building. A taxi would have been an inconvenience.

Belatedly and in an alarmed state, Asbury did what he always did when it had become necessary to evaluate a deal: he drew a dividing line down the center of a pad of lined legal foolscap, listed the reasons for and against his attitudes toward Julia on separate sides, discovered that the only negative he could think of was her job, a simple secretary-stenographer probably earning a pittance a week, while on the positive side of the dividing line he was shocked to find that he had enumerated two and a half foolscap pages of reasons why she deserved his further attention.

By the time he had reached the conclusion that it was possible that he was responding to this young woman in the manner that any average, foolish male might respond, i.e., that it was possible that he was allowing himself to undergo something as banal as "falling in love" with her, three weeks had passed, summer had come, and Miss Melvini was on her annual holiday from the Executives' League, and had taken one of those cruises to the Caribbean.

Unable to cope with himself, Asbury had flown to Grand Cayman Island in one of his companies' jets to be able to greet the cruise ship as it arrived for a twelve-hour stayover. He boarded the ship, bribed the purser with a hundred dollars, and was escorted to Miss Melvini's cabin, which she shared with three other young women.

At the sight of him, Julia produced a thrilling manifestation of the actor's art: astonishment, gratitude, and touched adoration all in one mute, compelling response. Few professionals could have achieved the effects she called up before the besotted Asbury. As she dazzled him with technique, she gloried in the realization that here, at last, was the forever escape from her sweat-stained father, from Brooklyn and President Street and his whole grotty environment; from wise guys, from hustlers, from the depressing, endless parade of hoodlums, principal of these being her brutalizing, heartless wop of a father himself, which was the most important escape in the entire repertory.

She saw Asbury as a healthy, well-washed, deliciously respectable, Anglo-Saxon, extraordinarily rich man, her dream of a great golden gate swinging open to reveal the promised land. It would take the power of respectability of Henry Asbury, she knew, to get her over the wall.

Four days after Asbury had overtaken the cruise ship in the Caymans, they were married by a Methodist minister at the Asbury estate in Palm Beach on a perfect day beside a pavonine ocean. Her twin brother, Allan, flown in from New York, was principal witness. With Asbury's reluctant consent, Julia remained chaste until their wedding night.

"You may call me Henry," he said after their union was consummated. "And I shall call you Julia."

"Yes, Henry—dear," she murmured in reply.

Henry George Asbury, now a married "adviser to presidents," was one more in a huge population of legendary Americans, another shadow who was passed from *People* magazine to *Sixty Minutes* to Senate hearings to Oval Office meetings, all the while straddling an enormous conglomerate of diversified companies, to be counted a household word, a Croesus, a myth among myths, a true owner of the Republic.

RICHARD GALLAGHER, the Asbury bodyguard who had been standing beside Henry Asbury, adviser to presidents, when he vanished, was grilled mercilessly by the FBI and the news media; the engine crew was hammered at; but none of them was able to explain how they could have been knocked unconscious while Henry Asbury had gripped the helm, singing.

The man from the *New York Times* insisted on knowing what Asbury had been singing. Gallagher said it was "The Night Maloney Landed in New York," an old favorite of Mr. Asbury's. Gallagher said emphatically that whatever had knocked *him* out certainly had to knock out Mr. Asbury, because he had been standing directly beside Mr. Asbury, but whatever it was, however it had been done, Mr. Asbury was gone when the rest of them came to.

"How could you hear him sing with that engine roaring and the noise suppressors over your ears?" the *Times* man demanded.

"I couldn't actually hear him," Gallagher said, "but we were trained to lip-read when I worked in the Noon White House."

Walter Sidyen, Assistant Director, FBI, had flown to Bent

Island from Washington aboard a fighter bomber because the Director had had an urgent call from the Attorney General, who had been jostled very emotionally by the President. When he reached Bent Island, a team of six FBI agents was already on the scene. They were irritated that the news media had overtaken the story so abruptly, and had herded all the journalists into the main room at Flag House, one of the eleven buildings in the Bent Island compound.

The complex of buildings around the main house had been placed on the highest hill on Bent Island, overlooking the rolling terrain of white oak and the waters beyond. The interior of Flag House was a large single-unit area which combined the architectural memory of ancient Rome and Etruria with the neoclassicism of Robert Adam. It rose for three storeys, was plated with nine different complexions of Italian marble: yellow broccatello on a splendid spiral staircase which lead nowhere, pink and apricot across the north wall, and in the expansive area where the news media had been gathered, an aquatic deep-green and turquoise. It was only a part of a country house compound but it reflected the dignity of its owners. The room had many hundreds of books, or (clearly) the spines of many books, but no television set.

American flags, hallowed national flags, battle flags, and historically significant flags, whose sight had once made Osgood Noon, President of the United States, break down with emotion, were hanging from the walls which surrounded a long, oak table in the center of the room. The fireplace in Flag House had been modeled on the fireplace in *Citizen Kane*. It was eighteen feet high. A moving van could have been parked inside it.

"What could they do with a fireplace that size?" the *Chicago Tribune* man asked his photographer. The photographer shrugged. "Maybe toast marshmallows," he said.

The great table was removed. ABC, CBS, CNN, and NBC television cameras and crews were able to set up. Expediters from Asbury Industries public relations departments moved everywhere with background information on their leader. News photographers lugging gear and somber self-conscious

Sunday morning television correspondents sat ready to bring comment and meaning to the scene. Celebrated anchormen had been rushed in from world capitals to sop up reality; wire service and newsmagazine people and FBI and police photographers were packed into the room along with FBI, local police, state police, and IRS representatives, as well as three Asbury footmen who circulated with trays of hot coffee, cold beer, and sandwiches.

The *Wall Street Journal* staff were everywhere, looking panicked. Lifting Henry Asbury was a market story equal to rushing the money changers out of the temple.

The noise was horrendous. Everyone seemed to be talking at once, to each other, into walkie-talkies, to law enforcement people, or into portable telephones. The media, collectively and separately, interviewed everyone, including each other, from the bodyguards and the crew to Miss MacHanic, to a staff masseur, and to car drivers as well as kitchen and household staff.

The crew and the bodyguards took the worst of it. The FBI team took on the bodyguards first, then the crew, passing them along to the ravenous media people.

"How can you say you were knocked out, that you don't remember anything before or after, when you were guarding a man who was driving a boat that was going almost seventy miles an hour?"

"I say it because we were knocked out, that's what happened."

"Something puts you to sleep and Asbury disappears?"

"That's what happened. He was standing beside us, at the wheel, then he was gone. That's all any of us remember."

The *Wall Street Journal* man was the most insistent, almost hysterical in his questioning, but no matter how many times or in how many different ways they were made to say it, the four men always told the same story.

The *Washington Post* front-page, double-streamer headline the next day read

ADVISER TO PRESIDENTS VANISHES INTO THIN AIR THREE MILES FROM NOWHERE

Walter Sidyen, Assistant Director of the FBI, somber, stern, and concerned not only because he would be in charge of the case but because of the extent of Henry Asbury's political clout, confirmed the kidnapping officially and gave a scanty wrap-up of the details as far as they were known. He vowed to bring the criminals to justice, then introduced Julia Asbury.

The victim's wife, more pregnant than Piero della Francesca's *Madonna del Parto*, was bursting at the seams of her $3700 frock, which seemed, because of her extraordinary gravidness, more ample than a tropical night and embracing her as completely. As if to draw eyes away from her ballooning condition, she wore an antique cabochon sapphire necklace threaded through with skeins of sapphires within a baguette diamond ribbon. She was an altogether splendid-looking woman, of an age young enough to surprise and interest everyone; looking more, however, like a condor than a wren. She had the kind of legs which, if they had been photographed in a bathing suit during World War II, would have been pinned on every barracks wall and footlocker in the United States Army. She had a chest which created an instant mythology among the assembled members of the Fourth Estate; a tall woman, a statuesque grabber, with cheekbones as high as the heads on Mount Rushmore. Her glossy, blue-black hair was arranged flat against her head, like a flamenco dancer's, over large, dark, steady eyes like *periaktos*, those triangular revolving prisms used as scenery in the ancient Greek theater, eyes which seemed to mock the men in the huge room for somewhere taking the wrong turning.

Staring at her with admiration from the third row of journalists, the correspondent from the *Times* of London, who had spent most of his career as a science reporter, marveled that such a sublime creature could have descended from the wormlike comodont, the first vertebrate from which the human race had sprung. The reporter from *Time* magazine, a born-again Christian, rued the lust he was feeling in his trousers and in his heart.

Every man in the room fell into hushed silence as the gorgeous hunk of womanhood began to speak.

"They tell me my husband was kidnapped but no one can tell me how or why," Mrs. Asbury said directly into the CNN camera. "All I know is that he is gone. He could have been murdered."

She choked back a sob. That sob and her engrossing pregnancy trembled every heart in the room. "All I am sure of is that there is no rhyme or reason to any of this. But I want whoever did this thing to guard his safety as if it were their own." She paused, staring hypnotically into a camera lens. "I don't know what you expect to get out of this," she said directly into the camera lens with a voice like heavy opium smoke, intimately, as if she were talking sex with the kidnappers, "because my husband meant no harm to anyone. We have to get this thing settled. Just tell me what you want and you will get it." She bought a tiny handkerchief to her face and sobbed into it.

The man from the *Wall Street Journal* asked what effect her husband's disappearance was going to have on the stock market.

Mrs. Asbury answered bravely. "I haven't had time to reflect on or to deal with my emotions," she said, "much less to think about such things as stock values. But I do recognize that we have an immense responsibility to thousands of employees, shareholders, advertisers, consumers, and suppliers. I am aware that any large business built up over decades is more complex than a corner grocery store."

Staring tragically at the red light under the ABC camera lens, she wept for all women, not noisily or in any way vulgarly, but with a slow, hesitant cascade of large, wet tears rolling down her beautiful cheeks, whose thrilling pallor was the work of Albert of Warsaw (salons in thirty-one principal cities). Having done her part, she turned away from the cameras and left the room. News media people tried to talk to her but they were stopped by state and local police.

Walter Sidyen, the FBI team leader, followed Mrs. Asbury out. When he caught up with her he said, "Mrs. Asbury, please do not—repeat not—make any mention of ransom arrangements to anyone at any time."

"I don't understand."

"You just said—on the air—that if the kidnappers will tell

you what they want that you will get it for them. Kidnapping is a federal crime, Mrs. Asbury. All contacts and arrangements with the kidnappers are in our hands and only in our hands."

"I will discuss the matter with my lawyer." She wiped her eyes carefully with yet another handkerchief. "Be clear on this, Mr. Sidyen. I must be apprised of every contact you have with my husband's kidnappers—everything, no matter how small. Will it be necessary to have the Director of the Bureau tell you to do that?"

"No." He looked as if he were deciding whether to punch her in the mouth.

"I want my husband back and that is going to take money, not federal statutes. Keep remembering that this is a matter of personal concern to the President, the First Lady, and the entire administration. Now leave me, please."

The evening news on all television networks ran footage of speeding powerboats, including tapes of President Noon recreating— as the White House handouts put it—at the helm of his cigarette boat surrounded by Secret Service men, a crew, six chase boats, mostly $230,000 cigarette boats manned by Customs agents and the Secret Service, a Coast Guard cutter carrying a squad of combat marines, and a guardian Huey attack helicopter hovering overhead; 147 security people to make sure the President could relax, or recreate. There were diagrams, clips of Henry Asbury at work and play against a narration by the network anchor telling how it was physically impossible to have done what the crew and the bodyguards said they couldn't remember having been done. CNN ran a segment out of London with a famous writer of "locked room" mysteries speculating on how the Asbury kidnapping had happened. "I would not rule out a submarine," he said. "A kind of attack periscope could have sprayed a gas upon the occupants of the powerboat, then, as they lay unconscious, the submarine could have surfaced, boarded the craft, and made off with the victim."

A desperate reporter from *Women's Wear Daily* came up with a yarn about five passengers from two sailboats which had been lolling on the Sound at about the time Henry Asbury had disappeared. Pressed, persuaded, cajoled by the reporter, one of them thought he remembered a helicopter flying around in the general direction of where the powerboat's crew had said it might have been. The story, having its outlandish side, was ignored by the rest of the news media.

In the course of the long, subsequent siege of waiting for a signal of any kind from the kidnappers, Julia Asbury received two tentative offers from two literary agents and five inquiries from film producers asking if she would consider authorizing movies on the Asbury experience. She had no intention of accepting any such offers but she wondered, if she ever did accept a movie offer, who would play her.

FIVE DAYS after the Asbury kidnapping, there had been no word from the kidnappers, but the prestigious *New York Herald*, under the byline of Nuala Counihan, revealed a fraud investigation into a $117.5 million loan to an Asbury company by a leading Hong Kong bank. At the urging of the *Herald*, under the Counihan byline, the newspaper conjectured whether Asbury companies had been seeking refinancing of heavy debts.

Each edition of the newspaper had a negative effect on the values of the stocks in Asbury companies. Prices fell, though nothing crashed. Experts were rushed in to explain and persuade. There was some market deterioration in Asbury shares but, with the exception of the stocks in the companies under investigation, the line held.

Eight days passed without any word from the kidnappers.

The news media had reduced its death watch to a skeleton force at Bent Island, then to a pool of a cub reporter from a local paper and a free-lance photographer. The thundering editorials across the nation had been silenced. The television and radio people had long since gone to pursue a story that President Noon was about to insist that homosexuals be recruited for the U.S. Forestry Service.

All telephones on Bent Island were tapped for recording and all incoming mail and faxes were carefully examined by the FBI before the addressees saw them. The FBI had reduced its resident staff on the island to one special agent and a gofer. Walter Sidyen had returned to Washington and was now entangled in interstate automobile theft violations.

Julia Asbury had lost weight in her face and on her arms and legs, making her seem more bulkily pregnant, and as if that were possible, she *had*, rather quickly, become more pregnant. She was pale, faintly red-eyed, never leaving Bent Island in case the kidnapper's call or letter or whatever came in.

In the study of the main house on the first Monday of August, she met with her twin brother, Allan John Melvin, a partner in the Wall Street law firm of O'Connell, Heller & Melvin. They were not identical twins; two people could hardly have looked more dissimilar. Allan John had dropped the ultimate vowel from his name long before (mainly as a protest over being a son to a sort of father who simply did not conform to the son's standards), although his sister had stuck with their family name, Melvini. He was blond, what the Spanish would call *muy suave*, a well-contained man who dressed in the most expensive English manner. No stranger would have believed that he was a Wall Street lawyer, rather a young duke among the fishmongers, but his law practice was well established and respected. He had one blue eye and one brown eye, the same sort of aquiline nose and Eskimo cheekbones as his sister but, of the two, he was of softer stuff. That is, he was softer than his sister, which still left him as soft as a quarry of Vermont granite.

"We are at an impasse, Al," Julia Asbury said to her brother.

"The world has forgotten Henry. No one cares. Why haven't they contacted me? I'm so *worried*."

"You'll hear from them, babe. They are after big money."

"I can't just sit here and pretend I believe that. We have to force their hand. We have to keep this thing alive. Everyone must see that we are doing absolutely everything to force the kidnappers to contact us and tell us what we must do to get Henry back."

"Jesus, hon. What more can you do?"

"I am going to fly to Rome to get the advice of the Pope. He will have, to say the least, an objective view. In his wisdom, he can tell me what I must do."

"Well—"

"I have one question."

"A question?"

"Should I invite Barbara Walters and an ABC crew to go along with me?"

"Walters?"

"Yes."

"I hardly think the Pope would consent to a network inter-view show."

"No, no. Just me. On the plane over and back. And around Rome. Very serious."

"Julia, believe me, exposure with the Pope will be more than enough to revive the national interest in Henry. Anyway, if it doesn't, you can always do Walters when you get back. And Oprah. All of them."

Arrangements were made with the Vatican. Mrs. Asbury flew to Rome three days later in one of her husband's planes. The news media was given ample time to cover the departure from JFK.

Flying to Kennedy from Bent Island in the family helicopter with her brother, Mrs. Asbury asked him to make a few notes. "First," she said, "tell the Nuncio that I will have a check for the Society for the Propagation of the Faith immediately after the audience."

"Will do."

"Did you talk to Arpad Steiner in Gstaad about staffing the *palazzo*?"

"All set."

"What a stroke of luck that he was still closing the Swiss house. God, if I only had a *clue* about how Henry is bearing up."

"Henry is a very tough bird."

"The FBI have done nothing, absolutely nothing. I have talked to the President twice, and to Oona I don't know how many times, yet they seem utterly powerless. Oh, Al! I'm so *worried!*"

"But just the same I am certain that there is a design behind all this. I just sense it."

"How do you mean?" his sister asked sharply.

"The people who lifted Henry know they have a big money-maker on their hands. They don't want to rush things and maybe make mistakes. You'll see, Julia," he said, patting her hand, "it will all work out."

"You'll need to talk to Steiner about opening the *palazzo* in Rome."

"Sweetheart—I've *done* all that."

"Just have him bring along one footman, a cook, a house-keeper, and a driver—Italian-speaking, please. I'll travel with my maid and a secretary. I don't expect to be there more than three or four days."

"What will you bring the Pope?"

"Oh, dear. I hadn't thought of that. Ah! I know. There are some relics of the fingerbones of St. Irenaeus in Henry's collar drawer—he died about 202 A.D. so he'll have real status with the Vatican."

"Was he Polish?"

"Polish?"

"What did he do to be sainted?"

"Father Passanante says Tertullian called him a careful explorer of all doctrines. He was also an authority on St. Polycarp."

Brother and sister were different, each to an extreme. He professed to see something funny in everything, behind a deadpan mask; even things which, if they were funny, could have been funny only to him. She was incapable of seeing anything funny in anything, although she always made a point of laughing a great deal.

When she stepped down from the helicopter to the apron at JFK, gripping an attaché case which had three safety locks, the news media people were there, although in a somewhat reduced force (compared with the early days of the kidnapping) of nine, including only one CNN television camera crew, no network coverage. Julia regretted not inviting Barbara Walters to go along; that would have brought out an ABC news crew but—all in all, considering everything—Allan had done an excellent job by turning out this many and she was going to see that the Pope blessed some rosary beads for him as a coming-home surprise.

"My husband has been missing without a word for almost six weeks," she said to the single television camera and the assembled print press. "I simply can't go on like this. I need calm, sound advice. I must know God's will."

They asked her all the same questions, taking up almost a half-hour until Allan insisted that she must board the Jetstream. They wanted to know all over again if she had had any word from the kidnappers, if the FBI was still actively on the case, when the baby was due, if her husband's businesses had suffered inasmuch as the stock market reaction to the kidnapping had been drastic at first but had restabilized, and if the Church had invested in Asbury enterprises.

Mrs. Asbury answered that she had had no word from the kidnappers, that in any case, the baby was not expected for at least another month, and that "I would like to assure stockholders and employees that there have been no crisis meetings at any of the Asbury companies. None of the public companies is seeking the refinancing of any debt. We have been meeting our bankers and the meetings have been well organized."

She was finally able to get away, knowing that she would be on the evening news across the country and (probably) around the world.

NUALA COUNIHAN'S strength as a newswoman lay in the way she noticed things. At the first media overrunning of Bent Island she noticed the heavy Chas Addams makeup on the victim's wife and how she made all her moves on camera as if she had been rehearsed by an expert. She noticed how the big tears had come out of her eyes after she had pressed the handkerchief to her face, as if the handkerchief had contained some chemical—or an onion maybe?—which would bring on big tears. She noticed how Mrs. Asbury was red-eyed before she wept, as if she had been weeping, which would have been the natural thing to do, but only the rims were red, as if they had been rouged, the eyes themselves as clear as any movie star's. In the two days that followed, Mrs. Asbury had seemed almost gay about the whole thing. That bothered Nuala. She was a short, professionally pugnacious woman with gorgeous legs and a great complexion. Six years earlier she had been elected Miss Overseas Ireland in an Innisfail Ballroom contest.

She didn't know why she did it because everything was hunches and flashes, but when she got back to town she talked to Hughie Pickering, the financial editor of the paper, and asked him to run down state-of-the-art on Henry Asbury. It was all routine stuff but, just the same, she thought there was something fishy about the setup.

Pickering checked around, then told her that aside from holding too much real estate around the country (and in Asia, Europe, and South America) and being undercapitalized and overextended, all of the kidnapped man's other holdings such as shares in the 137 Asbury companies, including a large investment bank, were on solid ground as far as any outside evaluator could see. He had an overload of real estate: everything from empty office buildings to foreclosed farms and factories was the current financial disease being suffered by bankers and big operators. Pickering told her there could also be a market reaction to the Asbury kidnapping and the value of Asbury holdings might dip temporarily but they would probably stabilize. So Nuala got nothing she could use.

Stymied, she decided to check out Julia Asbury, which took her to Julia's former parrot-importing business, which took her to the present owner of the business, a Mr. Peppino Aprile, who turned out to be a soldier in the Prizzi crime family. That knocked Nuala right on her ass. What the hell was going on? Mrs. Henry George Asbury and a Prizzi button man? How would Julia Asbury even know a bum like that?

Painstakingly, even painfully, Nuala put it all together as if the random pieces of the woman's life were part of a jigsaw puzzle. Julia Asbury, wife of an "adviser to presidents," a man who dined out on being a direct descendant of the first Methodist bishop in the United States, had, before she had married Asbury, been the owner of a wildly offbeat parrot-importing business and had, with all the buyers to whom she could have sold the business when she married, sold it to a Prizzi button man. That brought her to the enigma of why a Prizzi soldier would want a parrot business.

The light bulb came on over her head when she checked out Julia's background. Maiden name, Melvini. Then came the nuclear bomb: Mrs. Henry George Asbury's father was a *sotto capo* on the heavy muscle end of the Prizzi family. He was also a second cousin of Corrado Prizzi, *the* crime boss, a *capo di tutti capi,* and her mother was a Sestero, which was the married name of Corrado Prizzi's daughter. Then—holy shit!—it developed that Angelo Partanna's late wife was a Sestero, the married name of Corrado Prizzi's daughter, and Partanna was *consigliere* of the Prizzi family. Something was *very* fishy, so Nuala dug deeper. And got nowhere.

She talked it over in bed on a Sunday morning with her live-in companion, an NYPD homicide lieutenant named Harvey Zendt. He spent four days talking to buddies and checking around. He told Nuala that, whereas nobody had ever been able to prove anything, it was very much on the *emmis* that the parrot business was a front for cocaine importing from South America.

Nuala was all over him to find out how it worked, but Zendt didn't know how it worked. If they knew that, he said, they could break the whole thing up. Unless, he added, there were a lot of people on the pad. So Nuala didn't know anything except she knew what she knew, and what she knew was that practically *everything* about the Asbury snatch was fishy. What she didn't know was where to go next, so she talked it over with her boss, Eddie Markel, editor of the paper.

"You're saying Asbury set up his own lift so he could pay himself the ransom? Why?"

"It would be tax-free money, Eddie. Like maybe fifty million dollars or whatever, tax-free. This guy is in so far over his head in skyscrapers and real estate that the next time a loan comes due, the next time he asks the banks to cooperate, the whole thing could fall on him, so what he's tryna do is come up with a nest egg for himself."

"Isn't that a little Byzantine?"

"Byzantine? A heavy hitter like Asbury disappears in the middle of four witnesses out in the open air? Almost two weeks and nobody hears anything? *That's* Byzantine."

"What can you prove? The mob connection with the wife is just hearsay. You're never gonna prove it. And, since you brought it up, how come no ransom demand if his finances are that close to the brink?"

"That's a good point, Eddie. But it's gonna be any day now, and all I'm saying is that, when it happens, we gotta be the ones who pull the chain."

5

MRS. ASBURY'S decision to fly to Rome to seek solace from the Pope was announced in the morning newspapers and carried on all the morning and evening news shows. Her declaration of faith seemed to draw her closer, not only to the American people but to people in all parts of the world, of every religious denomination, a massive congregation that had been moved by the tragedy of the Asbury kidnapping and her pathetic pregnancy. They responded with letters, faxes, telegrams, greeting cards, and gifts—nothing lavish but each richly sensitive to her suffering: recipes for mahimahi, mezuzahs, lucky hair locks mounted in brass holders, rosary beads, bronzed baby shoes, portraits of Mother Teresa, Elvis, and John Wayne; scapulars, Ouija boards, autographed baseballs, and a replica of the Sacred Heart of Jesus done in silver and ruby-colored bugle beads, with assurances that she was, at last, on the right track toward finding her husband by putting herself in God's hands.

It was a smooth flight to Rome. Rosie Curry, her personal maid, made up the large double bed and she slept like a lamb all the way. There was nothing to fret about. O'Connell, Heller & Melvin, her brother's law firm, had made all the necessary arrangements with the Vatican. Arpad Steiner, the best butler in the known world, would take full charge of her at the Rome airport, and she knew, from what Monseigneur Coggins had said about him, that she was going to *adore* the Pope. After an excellent dinner that had been put aboard from Lutèce, she slept almost all the way to Rome.

Julia Asbury was now thirty-four years old, educated at Manhattanville College with a major in Romance languages; and at the insistence of her mother and to the dismay of her father, at the Università per Stranieri at Perugia and at the Sorbonne in Paris. She was a serene, collected woman with a compelling passion, even an obsession, for high luxury. She had been married to Henry Asbury for twelve years. Before she met her husband, in order to live in the advanced luxury to which she had always aspired, she had imported parrots from South America. She had not married Asbury for his money per se but rather for the really developed sense of comfort that he could give her, with his many houses in several countries, his staffs of perfect servants, his planes, his yachts, and his generosity.

The parrot-importing business, with its connections both to South America and to her parent's relatives, had lent a clean front for the relatives' cocaine-importing business, which had gone unsuspected by the DEA for the years it had been in operation. Julia's dad, Alberto Gino Melvini, aka The Plumber (because of his signature threat to flush recalcitrants down the toilet), had been a longtime aide to successive *vindicatores* of the Prizzi crime family.

After her marriage to Asbury she had sold the parrot business to a peripheral member of the Prizzi family. It had been producing a steady $300,000 a year for her, mainly tax-free, but she had earned a substantial sum for the outright sale of the business to the friends. What she had earned—and what she possessed—was not much when compared with Henry Asbury's fortune and wide-flung holdings, but it enabled him to view her as something of an equal even if she was a Sicilian and a Catholic who had come out of small business.

Her husband still thought of her as being thrifty, a mistake made possible because she had invested every cent of her profits from the parrot-importing business in sound securities, not bothering her husband for advice so he never really knew that she had comfortable assets of her own. He was proud to shower her with jewels, houses, servants, and a place in society; proud that as a little stenographer she had come so far.

Although Henry Asbury was twenty-four years older than she, the marriage was still as close to being a love match as either of them might have wished.

Arpad Steiner had the 1911 Rolls-Royce Silver Ghost parade

car standing by for her at the airport; silver with French blue leather, with a fully collapsible top. Henry Asbury had picked the car up from a collector in the Saudi ruling family. It had 7490 miles on it and was worth as much as any car on any road, about two million two. The driver, Laszlo Lowenstein, who *was* Rome to Julia, met her at the Customs & Immigration gate. He was a small man with a pleading voice and eyes like fried eggs who was fearless when he had a gun; always.

A gathering of Italian, European, and American news outlets, including the five U.S. television networks as well as Italian, French, Polish, and Irish television, filled out the assembly of print reporters and photographers. Mrs. Asbury undertook to perform separate interviews for television, in English, Italian, and French, because she was gratified to see that the story was still very much alive.

She looked very brave, confident that an audience with His Holiness would make the defining difference to her peace of mind, she told the press. Wearing a smart Mother Hubbard by Chanel, in black from head to foot, and a *bon chic, bon genre*, black ballibuntl hat with a saucy half-veil, she answered all questions with serene grace until, before the media was finished with her, she withdrew, stepped up into the enormous Rolls and, with an American Embassy representative seated on either side of her, was driven off to Rome. Curry, her maid, was in the front seat. Miss MacHanic, Julia's private secretary, was still at the airport coping with the eleven trunks, bags, and cases.

She was comforted once again by the cool peace of their home-away-from home in Rome, the Palazzo Melvini, in a street called St. Agnes in Agony, one of the tangle of ancient streets beyond the Piazza Navona, just across the river from St. Peter's and the Vatican. The *palazzo* was a magnificent example of Early Renaissance architecture begun in 1514 for a nephew of Sixtus IV. Henry had been able to pick it up for a song and then name it for her family. (Her dad seemed to be ready to burst with pride when she told him.) The real charm of the place, Julia thought, was that Michelangelo had taken over as its architect when Antonio da Sangallo (the Younger) was canned. Michelangelo had added the big window, the molding on the façade, the third floor of the court, and the fountains.

The place was loaded with frescoes by Carracci and Domenichino, names that Julia hadn't been able to recall right off but who she knew were very big.

Being the *governatora* of one of the great palaces of the ancient city, while it had not exactly opened all the doors to Roman society, had, in a way, established her as something of a hostess, even if the guests were mostly American movie people or clients of her husband. But no matter how many wonderful parties she gave at Palazzo Melvini, no matter how much publicity Henry's PR people got for them, the provincial Romans kept calling the house by its former name. Not that Julia cared; she had her all-new American plumbing installed, her silk sheets, a really great cook, and Arpad Steiner, so let the rest of the world knock itself out.

The papal audience, in a reception room facing the Piazza San Pietro, was a *total* success. Italian was spoken with an occasional shift into English. The Pope was comforting, with very sound advice that she must find patience somehow because her suffering was in God's hands and, as mysterious as were His ways, His eye was on the sparrow. Graciously, he blessed the beads for her brother Al but it almost broke Julia's heart to discover that she had left St. Irenaeus's fingerbones back at the *palazzo*. She made a promise in her heart to send them to the Pope for Christmas.

After the audience, Beniamino, Cardinal Camardi, prefect of the pontifical household, saw her through several passages into a magnificent high-arched gallery. As they walked slowly toward the distant end she passed him a check, neither ostentatiously nor with any attempt at humility. "For the Society," she murmured. The Cardinal nodded courteously, glancing at the check before he slipped it into his pocket. "How generous, signora!" he said, and she was pleased. At that moment a young priest came out of a doorway on the right, darted to Cardinal Camardi, and whispered in his ear.

"Ah," the Cardinal said, "there is a telephone call for you, Signora Asbury. This way, please."

"A *telephone* call? For *me? Here?*" she said, as if with shock, but the Cardinal had begun to lead the way, half walking backward, beckoning her to follow him.

He left her in a (relatively) small room decorated with paintings by Caravaggio, one of which, Julia felt certain, had to be a portrait of Orazio Gentileschi's daughter, Artemisia. She worshiped Caravaggio because he was so cinematic.

A telephone receiver lay off-the-hook on a taboret. She picked it up slowly. "Henry?" she said softly.

"Hello, sweetheart. You okay?"

"Just fine. Are we ready now?"

"On schedule. And everything is coming up orchids. You have the letter, I sincerely trust."

"Oh, yes."

"Have Laszlo drop it in a postbox so you will have it in the mail tomorrow. Then have Arpad call in the press."

"I'll feel better if I mail it myself."

"Good thinking, dear. Everything will be riding on your performance at the press conference. And—no worrying about the FBI. You'll only be doing what a frantic, loving wife would be doing and you're probably out of their jurisdiction anyhow."

"Probably?"

There was a chuckle. "Good luck, baby. Bye." There was a soft click.

Laszlo was waiting with the Rolls outside the Vatican building, which jutted out into the Via Angelica. They drove along the *corridi* into Borgo San Angelo and crossed the Tiber on the Vittorio Emmanuele bridge. There was a short stop at the Piazza Navona while Julia got out of the car to mail the ransom note. They were at the *palazzo* in seventeen minutes.

6

SHE HAD a bad night. When she did get to sleep, which seemed to take hours, she had nightmares in which she was modeling prison uniforms for a crowd of men who, when they turned away from her, had FBI lettered on the backs of their jackets in large letters.

She was awakened by Curry with a breakfast tray. The ransom letter was on the tray with the other mail. She sipped coffee while Curry fussed with opening the curtains. Julia opened the ransom note. She screamed appropriately. Curry wheeled, crying, *"Madam!"*

Julia said in a low, shaking voice, "It is a letter from the kidnappers."

"Madam! Is Mr. Asbury safe?"

"I don't know. I must get some advice." She reached for the telephone as Curry left the room to spread the word throughout the staff. Julia called her brother in New York. The call went through instantly.

"Al? Julia."

"Julia? Jesus, what time is it?"

"I just got the ransom note."

"Ransom note?" It was three-thirty in the morning in New York. He had been asleep for four hours. "How much do they want?"

"They didn't mention Henry. Not a line."

"But how much do they want?"

"Oh, God, Al. They want seventy-five million dollars."

"That's outrageous!"

"Al, I'm going to London—today—to work in the city to raise the money. I'll be in the flat at Arlington House. Wish me luck."

"Raise money—how?"

"I'm still trying to figure that out, but what you don't know can't hurt you. Stay outta this one, Al."

*   *   *

After that, to Julia, she seemed to be trapped inside an emotional kaleidoscope. Police, paparazzi, the press, pandemonium. She had to move on what she and Henry had planned because if she didn't she would be giving up the kind of a life which meant more to her than just existing the other way. She had to have the servants, the houses, the freedom to feel safe from the mediocrity of living the kind of a life that her father lived or even the way Allan lived. Al was alone, lived alone, and didn't want to change that. Her father had his cockroaches. She had to have people and beautiful things around her. She and Henry, in their way, had filled each other's days. She knew forever that it wasn't enough just to have some money, the way Al did, the way her father certainly did. Al had a couple of million. Her father probably had about five. What was that? He couldn't spend it anyway because of the IRS and RICO. It could just blow away. To experience freedom you had to have more than anyone else, you had to let it lift you and carry you away in safety and true happiness. She had never cared about power. What she had always wanted and had finally got was perfect servants, beautiful clothes, elegant food, effortless transportation on land, sea, and in the air, and glorious changes of glorious houses wherever she went.

Henry's world was tearing itself into shreds. If they didn't do what they were doing, everything Henry owned would crash down upon them. Asbury Industries were about to collapse and turn to dust. They were facing bankruptcy and debt. They would have to sell everything; so when Henry had told her of the inevitability of what was going to happen, she had reacted almost instantly with this plan, this salvation through kidnapping and tax-free ransom.

She had gone over the plan in somber detail, sparing Henry wherever she could, improvising, inventing, always creatively bent toward realizing the great possible fortune out of the wreckage that Henry's companies had become. In the triple-locked attaché case that she had always kept by her side since leaving Bent Island were detailed plans for what she must do to loot the 137 Asbury companies so that she could accumulate the ransom money that they would be paying to themselves. There were lists of approved brokerage houses and banks in seven countries through which she was to conduct the operations. Henry had set things into motion with all of these so that she could operate by number, not by name, and only by telephone. It had taken him many months to build this intricate back-channel network. Julia knew that she must follow it as if it were the blueprint of a delicate machine.

On her own, without bothering Henry, who, heaven knows, had enough on his mind with needing to be kidnapped, Julia developed an intricate plan to realize an even greater amount beyond the ransom money because she, more than Henry, knew that although $75 million *sounded* like a lot of money, it actually went very fast. They were dependent upon living in luxury and no one could have too much money for that. To build a proper nest egg she had instruments and powers of attorney and iron-clad authorizations to sluice money out of the 137 Asbury companies silently, moving it around and through banks around the world until any trace of it was lost, then to funnel the money out of that bewildering chain into untraceable number accounts in the banks of eleven countries. She had calculated that the right kind of milking of the companies should yield about $800 million.

Then, when the companies were partly milked and sufficiently weakened to cause a reaction in the stock markets, to borrow against shares from the companies which she would sell, from London, at exceedingly good prices. As rumors of short-selling became known to the world markets and the values of the stocks held in the Asbury companies crashed, she would buy the same number of shares at much lower prices in order to repay in kind the Asbury companies that had provided the original stock. The profit from repaying the shares bought at the bargain basement prices would pile up in their family account. She was to finance the first purchase of the stocks with a loan of $20 million, already arranged for by her husband, her partner who had woven the intricate financial scheme by which they would escape the impending collapse of the Asbury companies. Through milking of the companies and the series of short-selling transactions, the Asburys calculated that they would make a profit of close to $250 million. She and Henry had gone over each step of the way, again and again—some of the steps were Henry's; others, which had occurred to Julia after the kidnapping, were entirely hers—until she could have executed the whole thing almost by reflex.

Julia transferred all of her husband's holdings worldwide—$826 million in stocks, bonds, tax liens, mortgages, real estate, holdings in precious metals, agricultural properties and production, minerals, personal holdings in public companies that Henry controlled—to a trustee, in the name of her brother, Allan John Melvin, who was entirely unaware that he had been named as a trustee; but Julia retained an option to buy them back for the amount of $100,000, because she felt Allan was entitled to some profit on the transaction for having unknowingly accommodated Henry and her. She placed all these assets in a Panama holding company called Jemnito Limited.

It had all become one substance like a genie out of a lamp: the Italian police, television crews, a heavy smell of tobacco, barking men who were like street dogs asking questions, but she made a good show of seeming to be overcome by all of it, by the ransom letter and the invasion by chaos. The news pictures the next day of a beautiful, very pregnant woman in despair caused admiration whenever men gathered to read newspapers. The television pictures were ravishing whether seen on a screen over a bar on Third Avenue in New York or in a souk in Marrakech. She was grateful, when she looked at the tapes, that she had had such difficulty sleeping the night before because it had produced a certain sublime haggardness, a rather lost, waiflike quality, she thought, which conveyed a sort of helpless hopelessness as she read the ransom letter to the rabid newsmen.

"This letter was on my breakfast tray this morning," she said directly into the CNN camera. "Curry, my maid, brought it with whatever other mail had arrived. I opened it without any particular curiosity because I certainly had not expected to receive such a message while I was in Rome to seek the counsel of His Holiness." Her voice broke admirably. The men in the room, particularly the Italian men, felt an overwhelming willingness to comfort her, each according to his own aberrations.

Julia recovered her dignity as eight or nine journalists shouted in several languages, "What did the message say?"

"It said," Julia replied, "and I will state it in English and Italian so that you will not ask me to repeat it—and photostatic copies of the demand have been made and will be distributed to you as you leave—it said that if I want to see my husband again, a ransom of seventy-five million dollars must be paid."

There was a tremendous reaction while three dozen men and women repeated the words "seventy-five million dollars," then again in lire, francs, zlotys, pounds, and pesetas, in totally shocked tones. Someone recovered enough to shout over the rhubarb at Julia, "How is it to be paid?"

"The letter did not specify," Julia said. "It said they would contact me again."

---

❼

NUALA COUNIHAN stared intently at Eddie Markel, her editor. "Eddie, lissena me," she said, "this guy had a hundred and thirty-seven companies in twenty-three states and nine foreign countries. They are interlocking companies, so where the profits or losses do or don't come from is like peeling an onion. You dig?"

"Where did Asbury's money come from in the first place?"

"Who knows? Like Abe Lincoln he started as a poor boy for all I know. Now he has this giant setup of financial and industrial combinations—eighty-one private, thirty-five public, with ninety-two thousand employees and assets of sixty billion—on paper. Besides real estate, he's into fast food, insurance, publishing, banks, mining, car rentals, movies—but mostly real estate, the loans and interest and depreciation on which is tearing him apart."

"How, fahcrissake?"

"He's too highly leveraged. He takes an equity investment in a holding company and parlays it into more equity in other companies in what is an avalanche of leverage. When the equity markets are healthy, when corporate profits are solid, the avalanche approach works. But—and this is the kicker—when all that doesn't happen, what *does* happen is that there is a cash shortage. And that weakened the Asbury companies' capital base."

"But—"

"And that ain't all, Eddie. This is what two of the largest money managers downtown told me: they avoided investing with Asbury because they couldn't figure out the setup, even after forty years' experience. The things Asbury does with those companies are not things you can follow up and down a ladder. The banks he owes are getting more and more nervous. Asbury can't find buyers for about one billion eight in unsecured short-term loans. Worse, his own bank—his bank, the one he controls—is wounded by other people's shaky real estate loans and its debt rating has been lowered twice in four months."

"But does it look as though Asbury himself has lost big money or is about to lose big money?"

"My sources say his paper losses, his estimated personal losses, before the kidnapping, have been about six hundred and fifty million. Now that he has disappeared, there could be a real crash."

Markel sighed. "Then you better open it up. Write the story."

FROM HER flat in London, Julia worked with brokers and banks in the markets of New York, Tokyo, London, Belgium, Luxembourg, and Liechtenstein, the Cayman Islands, Panama, Bahrain, and Zurich to prepare the liquidation of her husband's privately held companies and short-selling the public companies. She earned $76 million in the first two days of short-selling, greatly assisted by the Counihan exposés in the *New York Herald* that had been driving the stock prices down.

Julia was annoyed that her brother had not flown from New York immediately to give her his counsel and support. He knew a lot about Henry's companies that could have helped her. Henry paid Al's law firm a $175,000-a-year retainer against some pretty wild hourly fees so, as if it weren't enough that he was her brother and that she was under terrific stress, he stood to make a dollar out of just flying in and holding her hand. Who else could she trust?

Allan John Melvin had troubles of his own. He had been summoned to the office of Edward S. Price, CEO of Barkers Hill Enterprises. In all of the years of his law practice, because Barkers Hill was a principal client of the firm, Price had been handled by Francis A. O'Connell, Jr. Allan knew, straight from his father, what Francis A. O'Connell did not know—that Edward S. Price, lawyer, philanthropist, arts patron, and *conglomerateur extraordinaire*, was not as legit as he sounded.

Allan John Melvin entered Edward S. Price's seventy-ninth floor office from a private elevator into which he had been guided by the driver of the limousine that had picked him up at the entrance to his office building far downtown on Broad Street.

The limousine had delivered him to an underground garage beneath the Barkers Hill office building. The elevator that carried him aloft was decorated in true Renaissance style with fine gradings of plinth and cornice based on harmonious proportions of elevation, exemplifying, in walnut, the molding and carving of the great fifteenth-century Florentine craftsmen. Melvin had the sensation of rising rapidly, then had entered directly into the large office that had been modeled on the inner office of the late Benito Mussolini. It was a long, long walk from the elevator to the heavily carved seat in front of Edward S. Price's desk, under Price's iron stare that spread fear upon him as from an infected laser.

Allan made it to the single chair facing Price, who was as separated from him behind the enormous carved ancient Florentine desk as if there were the deck of an aircraft carrier between them.

"You have been a bitter disappointment to me," Price said without preliminaries.

Allan was sure he hadn't heard Price right.

"What?"

"We make you a partner in our law firm, we make you rich, we give you a place in the world, then, when we are in danger, you seal your lips and leave us facing ruin."

"Made *me* a *partner?* In *your* law firm?" Allan thought he knew all about Barkers Hill Enterprises but he had believed that O'Connell, Heller & Melvin was simon-pure.

"You are Henry Asbury's lawyer! There was nothing he would conceal from you! His wife is your sister! Did you think you could strip us of millions of dollars and walk away unharmed?"

Melvin began to feel that he was in serious trouble. "I don't understand," he said.

"Your sister is shorting the markets of the world with our stocks! She is selling our companies down the river! She thinks she is safe in London behind the false front of a bereaved wife who is scrambling to get seventy-five million dollars together to free her husband—and you let this *happen?* You, the man's own lawyer, the brother, the man who is privy to all of it, *you* let this happen to *us?*"

Everything Edward S. Price had learned about hosing fear on people, fear that turned blood into cement, was penetrating Allan's imagination. His hands began to shake.

"Mr. Price, believe me," he said, "I think I know what you are talking about. I mean, I have a vague idea who you are. My father told me, but this is—"

"We are talking about a fraud."

"Lissenna me," Al said, "I don't know what you're telling me about shorting stocks. I know my sister is in London. She called me yesterday. But if shorting is what she's doing, what else *could* she do? She wants her husband back. That's the only way she can get the money to pay the enormous ransom."

"To pay? To pay whom? Who do you think lifted Henry Asbury?"

"I don't know, Mr. Price. Nobody knows."

"We did! The Prizzi organization! It was my father's own plan. Henry Asbury came to me with some garbled idea about disappearing. I talked it over with my father and he came up with the entire plan. Asbury just did what he was told."

"What? This is preposterous! Henry Asbury is an adviser to presidents!"

"Henry Asbury has been our man in the White House through four administrations."

"Your people *kid*napped him?"

"Your own father, The Plumber, was in charge of the operation. He and his people did the physical work."

"Please, Mr. Price, you're telling me more than I need to know."

"You were his lawyer. You had to know all this."

"I was the lawyer of a man I thought was a legitimate business leader!" Allan was dazed. In any ordinary course of events it would have seemed right and natural for his father to be given such an assignment for the Prizzis but this wasn't ordinary. His own father's son-in-law was involved, his daughter's husband, and no matter how anybody looked at it, his daughter was being moved toward some big trouble.

"Why do you think we waited all this time to send that phony ransom note? We needed time to stabilize the value of the Asbury companies—to help them regain their value after the initial shock of Asbury's disappearance. Now your sister has undone everything we had planned to do and she'll be paying us our own money she got from the short-sales, except that somebody else, not us, will have bought our companies for ten cents on the dollar."

"Holy shit!"

"Watch your language, Mr. Melvin."

"Sorry. But as Asbury's lawyer, I knew nothing about any of this."

"Who cares? You've got to stop your sister while there is still something to salvage. We are going to Brooklyn for a meeting with my father right now. My father will give you your instructions."

"There is really nothing I can contribute."

"So that there may be no misapprehension, I think it is advisable to warn you that any display of any inclination on the part of you or your sister to intrigue against what we see clearly as our most devoted interests will not be regarded by us with complacency. Therefore, on your visit to your sister in London, you will be accompanied by my father's representative, Charley Partanna."

Allan was sure he was going to be sick right there on the fabulous Aubusson carpet. His father worked for Charley Partanna. Charley Partanna was the *vindicatore* of the family and he only handled the important hits.

He realized then that he should have made a pal of his father. He should have listened when he sensed that his father had been trying to tell him something. He had remembered snatches, here and there, but just loose ends, instead of concentrating on putting it all together in one piece and learning where the bodies were buried, like the stark fact that although Edward S. Price had never been publicly identified as a Prizzi, he was Corrado Prizzi's eldest son.

When Edward was a lad of twelve his father had had the shape of his nose adjusted away from the Arabic-Sicilian shape that so marked the men of the Prizzi family. Abraham Weiler, the most renowned plastic surgeon of the day, who did the work on Eduardo, had re-formed his face from its saturnine cast into a replica of the face of the late George Nathaniel Curzon, 1st Marquis of Kedleston, Viceroy and Governor General of India, later Chancellor of Oxford University and Leader of the House of Lords.

From age seven, Edward S. Price had suffered through intensive instruction from outstanding elocutionists until his diction sounded far more like William F. Buckley, Jr., than that of a Brooklyn-raised Prizzi. He had been sent away to the Groton School when he was twelve years old, after years of private tutoring, with a clear understanding of his mission in life. A part of the American aristocracy, he went on to graduate with honors from Harvard University and Yale Law School.

From the beginning he understood that he was to prepare himself to construct a giant laundry for Prizzi money: the great, leaping rivers of tax-free money from the family's great work in public service that provided gambling, building construction fraud, loan sharking, extortion, narcotics, labor racketeering, pornography, prostitution, fraudulent bonds, and recycled postage stamps to a great nation. The stamps were Corrado Prizzi's own idea. "People throw away the envelopes with the canceled stamps. We put the chemicals on the canceled stamps, the marks come off and they're like new. At thirty cents on the dollar it makes us a nice steady seven million five a year."

Gambling, which produced $6 billion annually, was a ritual that came naturally to the family. Like all aboriginals, they knew that metaphysical forces governed gambling as well as war and extortion (which were associated with gambling) and besides there were so many millions of airheads willing to be taken. The management of prostitution and pornography, like narcotics, sprang from the forces of nature. People yearned to be different from what they seemed to be and it cost money. The law stood in the way of all these things that the people had to have. It was the Prizzi family's duty as a service organization to get it for them.

All of the hundreds of millions of dollars from these good works were reinvested by Edward S. Price's tentaculiferous conglomerate, Barkers Hill Enterprises, in baking, insurance, electronics, real estate, cable television, brokerage and underwriting companies, undertaking parlors, car rental companies, food manufacturing and importing enterprises, savings and loan associations, fast-food chain franchising, motion picture production, photograph records, videocassettes, newspapers, book and magazine publishing, four law firms (New York, Washington, Los Angeles, and Zurich), eleven hospitals, a flower farm, 117 hotels, and three old-fashioned wet wash laundries in Brooklyn, Miami, and Vegas that Price's father's organization used as operating bases. Interlocked with Barkers Hill Enterprises were 1122 companies, all, as far as the economic life of the nation was concerned, independent operations. The 137 companies that were formally controlled by Henry George Asbury were among them.

The political and law enforcement life of the nation was not overlooked. "Foreign policy," after all, was stressed again and again by all candidates for any and all political offices, to divert any possible public interest in the skullduggeries at home. While the country went bankrupt trying to bail out corrupt savings and loans, President Noon vomited on a dinner dais in Japan helping to keep any thought of this national bankruptcy out of the public mind. Political Action Committee funds controlled by Barkers Hill Enterprises reached the vital 24.7 percent of the 497,697 elected officials in the eighty thousand-odd governments of the United States: federal, state, county, and municipal. Barkers Hill Enterprises was the nation's most generous contributor, in various forms, to the financial well-being of the 537 elected positions of the national government: president, vice president, 100 senators, 435 representatives. It was equally openhanded with the 18,134 elected officials of the fifty state governments and the 83,185 county, municipal, township, school district, and special district governments.

However, for every dollar invested, Barkers Hill, through its patrons, the organized crime families of the country, got $117 in profit. Narcotics, gambling, pornography, construction fraud, and recycled postage stamps alone brought in sixteen times the $535 million invested each year to ensure political and police cooperation.

The country was filled with small crime families: i.e., non-Prizzi families who didn't have either the muscle, the capital, or the attention to detail to keep the RICO enforcers in charge of official window dressing at bay, but Barkers Hill was a government in itself, so it dealt with federal, state, and local governments on equal terms. The Prizzis were *the* American service organization, after all.

Edward S. Price defined his family's financial destiny with the words Lord Curzon had used to define the British Colonial Service: "The message is carved in granite; it is hewn out of the rock of doom—that our work is righteous and that it shall endure," just as his father's motto, which was emblazoned upon his every smile, was "Fear was the first creator of gods in the world."

DON CORRADO PRIZZI'S house, with a garden that rolled down almost to the East River, was at the foot of Brooklyn Heights below an area that used to be the center for the society churches of Brooklyn, at a singular viewing point directly across from the eerie, alien skyline of lower Manhattan Island, which the don had not visited since 1957. It was a large red and pink Victorian house of Brooklyn, the last great Victorian city of the nation, a house that echoed the ringing sonorities of Henry Ward Beecher, once a close neighbor. Winston Churchill's mother had been born not far away in Cobble Hill.

The interior of the house had sliding oak doors, walls covered with bibelots and gilded picture frames, rooms paneled with dark wood surrounding some very serious, heavy furniture, and closed curtains because it was a house used for serious things: meeting and eating.

Edward S. Price, with his brother, Vincent Prizzi, who was the boss of the family's street operations, Angelo Partanna, *consigliere* of the family, and his son, Charley, the family's *vindicatore*, as well as Allan John Melvin, sat around the large table that had a basket of wax fruit at its center, with lighting made necessary by the closed curtains at the windows, light falling from a central hanging lamp that had a red silk shade with peach-colored fringes. Each man, with the exception of Allan John Melvin, wore a black suit, white shirt, dark tie, and shined shoes. Their permanent expressions, with the exception of Allan John Melvin, were blank.

Vincent Prizzi was built like an oversized fireplug. He was a serious man because of his digestion, his psoriasis, his urological problems, his high blood pressure, severe bouts of gout, and a marked tendency toward hernias. Vincent had a totally closed face, like a bank vault shut impenetrably by a system of time locks. Somewhere, hidden deep within his past, there was a boyish openness that had not been seen by anyone for over sixty years because, through carelessness, the combination to the shut vault of his expressiveness had been lost, somewhere in his preternatural resentment of everything that moved. He was a compulsive hummer, mainly of television commercial jingles with the occasional chorus of "You Made Me Love You (I Didn't Wanna Do It)." Technically, Vincent was boss of the Prizzi crime family, except that his father was his boss. Before his father had abandoned the day-to-day operation, Vincent had been the family's enforcer.

Vincent ran an active body of about seven hundred working troops that were about a third of the available *soldati*. He was assisted in the work by an underboss, Charley Partanna, and three *caporegimes*, Rocco Sestero, Salvatore Prizzi, a nephew, and Tarquin Garrone. Together they handled all gambling from casinos to street betting. Narcotics, loan sharking, interstate car theft, counterfeiting (bonds and currency), prostitution, pornography, organized labor suborning, extortion, political fixing, the Garment District, and recycled postage stamps. All told, Vincent's operation did a tax-free gross annual business of $92,000,000, all of which was deposited in foreign banks, then made available to Edward S. Price for legitimate reinvestment that produced additional annual income for the Prizzi family of $2,486,000,000, a generous percentage of which was shared with the two major political parties, the U.S. Congress, and with law enforcement leaders at federal, state, county, municipal, and precinct levels.

Due to a formal misunderstanding years earlier between Charley Partanna and Vincent's elder daughter Maerose (a calculated misinterpretation by Vincent blamed Charley for Maerose having dishonored Charley), Vincent was less than cordial to Charley, an aberration that everyone overlooked. Despite his prejudice against Charley, Vincent and Maerose and his father, Don Corrado, and the entire environment considered that Charley and Maerose were still formally engaged to marry, and had been for six years. This was despite the family punishment by which Maerose had been banished from Brooklyn, and set up in an interior decorating business in Manhattan. She was allowed to return only for funerals, christenings, and weddings.

Edward S. Price barely tolerated his brother Vincent, whom he viewed as a common ruffian. Silently, he objected to Vincent's constant humming. He detested the necessity for these infrequent meetings but, because they were the source of all of his money and his power, and because he had been ordered by his father to attend, he accepted them.

Angelo Partanna was professionally neutral in all things until it came to the crunch when he always came down on the side of Corrado Prizzi's interests, which was what he was employed to do; he undertook all counseling and reviewed the family's important bribery and other day-to-day intimate work with politicians and police departments. He was a smallish man with a jockey's hump at the top of his spine, coffee-colored skin, and a nose not quite as large or as colorful as a keel-billed toucan's. He was an entirely dapper man. His tailoring and haberdashery were more elegant even than that of Edward S. Price. When necessary he could be more polished than an actor's dentures.

Angelo had the lame title of *consigliere*. In all other crime families the *consigliere* had less access to the boss than the boss's chauffeur, the position of real power. The title *consigliere* had been invented in the 1930s by Lucky Luciano, as an intermural public relations gesture. The job was supposed to be that of an ombudsman who would settle family disputes and act as negotiator with other families. But Angelo Partanna had been a boyhood friend of Corrado Prizzi. They had both been born in the same village in western Sicily and still considered Agrigento a big city.

The don had sent for Angelo within the first year of settling in Brooklyn and, for fifty-three years, Angelo Partanna had been his counselor, bringing a trusted point of view to the problems Corrado Prizzi had faced through the years in his dedication to serving the public.

At thirty-six, Charley Partanna, Angelo's son, was a large, muscular man with a voice like grinding taxicab gears. In fact, if taxis wore clothes they would resemble Charley. He was large in all directions without ever giving the impression of being overweight. By heritage and as a result of long, demanding rehearsals he was able to confer fear beyond the most outrageous dreams of world-class masochists. Early on, when Charley was entering his teens, his father, understanding the career that Charley had ahead of him, had made the boy practice projecting fear, standing in front of a mirror for forty minutes a day, practicing the hardening of the eyes and features, the terrible, terrible blank look; all the postures and casts of face that promised far worse than death and torture until, when the boy was only twelve years old, the time when other boys were ready to join the Scouting movement, Charley had been able to intimidate and terrorize legendary *capos* with a glance.

By temperament Charley was a dreamer of irrelevant dreams, balancing information and opinions that he had accumulated from reading national women's magazines while he waited until he was told what to do. In fact, most of his off-course information had been gleaned from magazines; a mixed bag but one that he had kept earnestly filled. Also, Charley was possibly the most romantically susceptible man since Adam and the anecdote about the apple. The cause of his euphoria, when he had achieved the state known as "being in love," was the coincidence of all his infatuations with an abnormally high production of the chemical phenylethylamine, produced by the human brain, a natural amphetamine known as PEA. Charley's production of PEA when he met an attractive woman was so massive (and so continual) that most of the time he lived at two levels above ecstasy.

Certainly he was not an easy mark for all women, but there seemed to be a certain kind of woman, whose overmastering attractions he could not even have identified precisely, who rendered him helpless, mindless, and pole-axed until she did something to reverse all the wonderment. At one time he had been ready to give up his work, his place in the family, in fact all of his life as he knew it in order to win an out-of-town woman named Arlene McNally, a parking meter attendant in midtown Manhattan. He had proposed marriage. They had chosen a small cottage in her home city of Hackensack, New Jersey. He was absolutely wild about her. Then she had pre-ceded him up some stairs and he had noticed that the seams of her stockings were crooked. That had wrecked all of his dreams. He was finished with her.

Allan Melvin sat just as silent as the rest of them, dreading what was going to happen to him and his sister, unable to comprehend how he could be in the same room with such an assortment of violent people. His father's career had been one thing, but the idea of a mover and a shaker (and a direct de-scendant of the first Methodist bishop in the United States) such as Henry George Asbury being what practically amounted to a soldier in the Prizzi family was more than he was able to take in. His father, The Plumber, was what he was because he was a Sicilian and he had grown up and had been trained in his work as an assistant *vindicatore* and a heavy-muscle worker. Even Edward S. Price was a hoodlum in his heart but that was a natural thing; he was a Prizzi. Henry George Asbury had been a client of Allan John Melvin's law firm. But the law firm and Asbury had turned out to be owned by the Prizzis. He was in his father's business as if the Melvinis had never left Sicily. He began to wonder if his sister had known about this all along.

They all sat and waited around the table. No one spoke.

The solid sliding doors were opened. Don Corrado, age eighty-six, tottered into the room on the arm of his daughter, Amalia Sestero. Everyone stood. He waved them back into their seats while allowing Amalia to lead him to the armchair at the head of the table. He sat down, nodded to her to leave the room and, when the heavy doors had slid shut, said, "Eleven o'clock in the morning is a nice time for a meeting. Who is this young man?"

He stared at Allan Melvin. It was such a flat, lizardlike stare that Allan's mind went blank. Don Corrado didn't pour any fear on him intentionally but even the most normal glance of curiosity from this fabled avenger of injustice, real or imagined, was so unnerving that Allan believed he could hear his bowels creak as the freezing effect spread from his stomach in both directions: up to his heart and down to his trembling toes.

When Corrado Prizzi had emigrated with his little family from Agrigento to Brooklyn sixty-three years before, he was already a made man in The Honored Society. From the day he arrived, and for the rest of his life, he left Brooklyn only three times—to organize a whiskey bourse surrounding police headquarters in Manhattan during Prohibition, to attend the Cleveland meeting of the principal crime families of the country in 1928, and to attend the Apalachin convention of leading *mafiosi* in 1957.

He was a power in the federal, state, and municipal governments of the United States. He, more than anyone, had made organized crime the indispensable service organization that it had become for all Americans. He had created the oiled machinery that had gotten them booze in Prohibition, clean broads at any time, all the narcotics and bookies they could use, off-course banking, bigtime extortion, and a ruined labor movement. He gave them bent politicians; weirdo presidents and pliable senators. He took over the management of big-city police departments for them. Whatever they had to have which the laws said they couldn't get, Corrado Prizzi provided for them in return for tax-free income in the billions with which his son Eduardo could buy up the legitimate businesses of the world.

"This is Mr. Melvin, Poppa," Edward S. Price said. "He is The Plumber's son. You remember The Plumber?"

"A good worker. Why are we meeting, Eduardo?"

"The Asbury thing."

"Ah. Is the wife still making trouble?"

"Yes, Poppa. The wife is the sister of this man." He indicated Allan John Melvin.

Don Corrado gave Allan John that impersonal look again and Melvin felt like a mongoose who was being considered by a cobra. Corrado Prizzi had been *born* with the gift of bestowing fear on all people.

"Are you the lawyer?" the don asked pleasantly. As Allan nodded numbly the don said, "The Plumber told me once his son was gonna be a lawyer."

"We need to move on the Asbury thing, Poppa," Edward S. Price said briskly.

The don closed his eyes slowly, held them there, then re-opened them in the style of an iguana. "They are trying to take my money," he said so quietly that it was as though he were thinking aloud, making every one of them a part of the shame that was being poured upon Corrado Prizzi. They all leaned forward to be certain to hear him. "So what we gotta do, while the wife is shortchanging us with the stocks, we gotta give her a little room. She's gotta have a chance to get the money. Then the wife will lose the seventy-five million to get her husband back, then Charley will negotiate with her for the pay-over of the profits the wife made on the short-selling and we will buy back all the Asbury companies for a nickel on the dollar."

"That's absolutely brilliant, Poppa," Edward S. Price said.

"And while we gave her a little room, Eduardo's people have to move on looting the pension funds of the Asbury companies."

"Everything's arranged," Edward S. Price said. "I've pooled all the Asbury companies' pension assets, about a billion four. We've formed a company called Quantitative Investment Management and I've appointed as directors some very reliable people. QIM controls the pension investment policy. The trustees of the individual pension funds can no longer know what is happening."

"Just make sure that it looks like Asbury did it, then ran with the money."

"I like it," Angelo said, "but we need a gimmick to make sure that all the Asbury stock prices will hit absolute rock-bottom."

The don shrugged sadly. "So we gotta do the job on Asbury. After the wife pays the seventy-five million to get him back. When they know he's dead, everyone in the market will sell. Rock-bottom."

"Too bad," Angelo said. "I remember when we first found him, a pool hustler with a talent for numbers."

"Henry had the knack for making the right decisions. He was a very capable executive," Eduardo said. "But he never figured out that his wife was a part of the environment. And I think he would have lost his lunch if he knew that his wife was The Plumber's daughter, he thought she was like some kind of society princess."

"Henry didn't need to know that," Allan said loyally. "Why should she tell him a thing like that?"

"I remember Asbury," the don said with relish. "He was a man who always seemed to be sitting outside himself to admire himself, to taste every word he could hear himself saying. It made him happy. He was never lonely because he always had himself."

"How do you want Charley to handle the wife?" Angelo Partanna asked.

"Yeah," Charley said. It was the only word he spoke at the meeting.

"First she gives him the seventy-five million payoff for the husband," Don Corrado said. "Then she gives him the money she's been making on the short-sales. Then he does the job on her."

"No!" Allan yelled. Everyone in the room stared at him. "We can negotiate this!" he said frantically. "She's been a victim of this whole thing! What is the use of zotzing her after she hands over all that money? With the pension funds you are going to make over two billion dollars on this deal. And my sister will be handing you a big part of it! Be reasonable, Don Corrado. You never know how a smart woman like that can be useful to you again."

Corrado stared at him blankly. He shook his head slowly. He was like a glacier that had grown with each year's snow falling on top of ice from the year before. As the gelid layers had accumulated, the pressures of power had caused the deeper layers to turn into solid ice, locking in details of the climate that he created around him.

Allan stood up. He put both hands on the table and leaned forward toward the don. "She is the daughter of Alberto Gino Melvini," he said. "A man of respect."

As at the center court at Wimbledon, all the heads turned away from Melvin to look at the don.

"You are right," Corrado Prizzi said slowly, realizing that it had almost appeared as though he had been about to violate *omertà*, the sacred oath of manhood of the Mafia with which, among other things, he had pledged in blood that he would never violate a woman of the family of a *mafioso*.

Everyone in the room knew that *omertà* was only a myth, something observed by the people who wrote newspaper stories and movies. But he was expected, as a *capo di tutti capi*, to pay solemn lip service to it. The don knew that everyone in the room knew that if he ordered the death of this woman, daughter of his own soldier, The Plumber, this would be considered a violation of a bullshit code, but what could he do? He couldn't help it if he was an old-fashioned guy. However, he made an invisible mark upon his inexorable memory against this man for exposing him to such an embarrassing possibility. The man had offended him grossly, and when the time came, he would pay.

"There could be other papers to sign—transfers, liquidation orders," he said slowly. "She could produce her husband's suicide note if we needed it and she's good on television. So just talk to her, Charley, no rough stuff."

The don got up slowly, taking Vincent's arm on one side and Edward S. Price's arm on the other. Angelo Partanna slid the doors open and the slow-moving procession moved out of the room. Allan moved to stare out of a window, lost in fearful thought.

Angelo turned to Charley. "Whassamatta, Charley?"

"Nothing. I just don't feel so hot."

"Your eyes are all red, you look like you got a fever, and how come the cough?"

"I'm okay, Pop."

"Just the same, we're goin' over to see Doc Lesion on the way home."

The doctor hit Charley with the book. "You're going into Santa Richenda's for a week, ten days of bed rest," he said.

"I can't, Doc. I gotta go to London."

The doctor looked at Angelo. "Measles are serious at any age, Mr. Partanna, but at Charley's age they could lead to pneumonia and encephalitis."

"So you're going inta the hospital, Charley. No arguments."

"Then what's gonna be in London? You can't send The Plumber, he's onna boat somewheres. Anyway, how can he put the fear on his own daughter? Besides, he outta town. How can he scare the shit out the brother?"

"We'll send Pino Tasca. It'll be all right." Tasca was an associate enforcer who worked under The Plumber who worked under Charley.

"Pino is smiling alla time to show off his teeth. Where is the fear there?"

"Pino can fill in for you, Charley. He's a good worker and you ain't goin' noplace."

THE PRICE limousine returned Allan to his office building on Broad Street. In the lobby, Allan went into a public telephone booth beside the cigar stand, gave the operator his sister's telephone number in London, reversed the charges and waited. Julia came on the line.

"Jule? Al." He had the dread feeling that the line—a cigar stand phone booth—was tapped. How could it be tapped? Because he was getting so paranoiac that he knew that any cigar stand in any building filled with Wall Street lawyers had to be tapped by the Prizzis, the FBI, by Mu'ammar Qaddafi, and probably the Royal Canadian Mounted Police—but he had to warn her.

"How come you reversed the charges?" Julia asked. "It's deductible."

"Because I don't carry five bucks wortha quarters with me," he snarled. "Julia, lissenna me. Go out of the house. Find a phone booth and call me back at this number."

"What the hell is this, Al?"

"Please! Would I fuck you around?" He told her the number of the phone booth. "You got it? Write it down."

"I wrote it."

"Say it to me."

Julia repeated the number.

"Okay. Now do it."

It took Julia twelve minutes to find a phone box. Al answered.

"Okay, Al. What's going on?"

"Where are you?"

"The Ritz lobby. What's going *on*?"

"I just left a command performance with Edward S. Price— you know who I mean?"

"I know. Well, sort of."

"He told me that not only did the Prizzis handle the whole snatch but that Poppa is in charge of the operation."

"Poppa? *Whaaaaat?*"

"Now they are steaming because you are doing what they were supposed to be doing and they are not only very, very pissed off that you are going to be paying the ransom for Henry but that you'll be paying them with their own money."

"But this was Henry's scam. How did the Prizzis get into it?"

"Listen, Julia. This isn't going to be easy. Henry, it turns out, has been in with the Prizzis since he made his first dollar."

"Whaaaaaaat?"

"I'm sorry, baby. They dragged me into a meeting with Corrado Prizzi and the Partannas, all of them, including Edward S. Price."

"I'm going outta my mind!"

"Henry was good with numbers so they gave him his chance and he went right to the top. Ed Price runs the business side for the Prizzis. Henry was their man. Price said straight out to me that Henry was their man and had been through four Republican administrations, which comes out to almost twenty-four years."

"How could that be? Henry was such a—such a Methodist."

"He needed their help to set up the kidnapping, so he did what the Prizzis told him to do. Then they laid out what you had to do to get the money for them."

"Get *them* the money?"

"You and Henry were supposed to get the ransom. That was it. Now, they get everything. The ransom, the looted companies, the pension funds—everything."

"Well, fuck them for a start!"

"That isn't all, Jule. Price is sending me to London tomorrow morning on Concorde. I'm supposed to talk you out of what you're doing in the market."

"But—"

"That still isn't all. Price is sending Charley Partanna with me."

"Partanna? Partanna is their *vindicatore!* Why? Why Partanna of all people?" She sounded ready to weep with fear.

"I know."

"Poppa will never hold still for this. You gotta lay this out for Poppa!"

"Poppa is with Henry somewhere. Who knows where?"

"What am I gonna do?"

"Well—there's only one thing *to* do. You better have a coupla checkbooks ready. I gotta go." He hung up.

Julia raced out of the public telephone alcove at the Ritz Hotel and half walked, half ran down Arlington Street to the block of flats, stunned by her husband's past. Jesus, she thought she had traveled a million miles yet all the time she had never left President Street. She had married a man who was just like her father and he had betrayed her because that was the way all hoodlums thought. The adviser to presidents, the patron of the arts, the all-around champion businessman-industrialist, the direct descendant (it said on his wrapper) of the first Methodist bishop in the United States—except that all the while he had been nothing but a hoodlum. The knowledge was as crushing as if she had been dropped right on her head from a bomber flying over enemy territory at sixty thousand feet.

She caught an idle elevator and was back in her apartment within six minutes of ending the call with Allan. She had accumulated a billion, $257 million, give or take a million, in the eleven numbered accounts in the banks around the world she was feeding from the telephones in her living room, working with brokerages operating in the London, Tokyo, New York, Paris, and Milano stock exchanges, so she had to admit to herself that Henry had done *some*thing right. He had piled up all that money in the first place and, in his thrifty way, he had been pretty generous with it. The whole exercise was taking on a new meaning: she was taking the Prizzis for the only thing they valued in this world or the next, their money. Now she realized she was taking their money as the price in revenge for what they had done so unnecessarily to Henry; they had made a deal with him and now they were out to screw him out of his share.

She was almost unable to do all the things she had to do if she was going to survive. How could Henry force her out on the limb like this? He was her husband, she had thought she knew him, that she knew what he thought and how he thought. What a pack of shit this was! She knew nothing! Henry had been just another Prizzi hoodlum like a stickup man doing a stand at a gas station at two in the morning. Henry! Henry George Asbury! That big, genial, rosy-cheeked man who was so determined to be the head honcho wherever he was had been just another Prizzi *shtarker* in a gray homburg. Still, she thought, with everything he could have had going against him, he loved her, and what was the sense in faulting a man for that? What she couldn't forgive was what chained her like a bony dog to the cellar at President Street with that lump of an immigrant wop father upstairs. She could have forgiven Henry anything except that.

She had a leeway of roughly twelve hours before Partanna could maul her around. He couldn't leave New York until tomorrow at half-past nine, Eastern Time. The Concorde got into Heathrow at six-ten in the evening. It would be seven-thirty before they got into London—and she wouldn't be there.

She packed a bag with light traveling clothes and the important jewels. She told Curry to begin to pack as if they were going to New York that afternoon. When that was finished and Miss MacHanic had booked the air tickets she shooed MacHanic and Curry out of the flat and off to the airport, then hit the phones, almost breaking her fingernails because she was dialing so frantically until she had made herself understand that Partanna and Allan were still in New York; she still had time. She instructed brokerage after brokerage to transfer all credits to numbered bank accounts that Henry Asbury had opened for her in Zurich, the Cayman Islands, Hong Kong, Lagos, Nassau, Liechtenstein, Singapore, Panama, London, Belgium, Bahrain, and Capetown. She canceled all trading orders with all brokerages, thinking with certain sadness that this would probably mean the end of poor Henry but the Prizzis had forced her hand. She knew that, in their disappointment over losing all of that money, they would zotz Henry but there was nothing she could do about that if she were to be able to preserve her way of life. She wasn't going to let a bunch of Sicilians talk her out of her rightful share that she had worked like a dog to earn. That was the weakness of those people. They always fell back on muscle.

Henry had had a good life. He had packed so much into those fifty-seven years that he might as well have been a hundred and ten, she thought. Now it was her turn. This time she could have her billion-odd in banks where neither the Prizzis nor the IRS could find it.

She had about $43,000 in traveler's checks and cash; enough for traveling money. She would disappear, beginning the long dodg'em ride through three airports in three different countries. She was carrying two sets of forged passports: one set originally intended for Henry in the names of John Kullers and Gordon Manning and one set for her in the names of Denise Grellou and Eugenia Tylt. Henry had provided them in case of just such an emergency—the kind that would have them needing to loot all of his companies.

Protesting that Madam should not be left alone in her delicate condition, Miss MacHanic and Curry surrendered the keys to the flat and were rushed out to ride to Heathrow in a hired limousine with an estate wagon following them with the luggage.

Julia Asbury locked herself into the flat, went up the long staircase to her bedroom, pulled down blinds even though she could not possibly have been seen, and undressed herself, clearly and possibly gloriously pregnant in the bright fluorescent light.

She stood, not quite nude in front of a full-length mirror; not entirely nude because of the unusual packing that had been applied to her central section. She unwound yards of wide elastic bandage from around her bulging waist so that she could remove a large piece of foam rubber padding from the front of her abdomen. It came off easily.

She stood free of the large, commanding promise of motherhood. She folded the bandages carefully and took them, with the foam rubber padding, to the house incinerator shaft and disposed of them. She had insisted to Henry that she seem pregnant to pump up great waves of sympathy from the press and from television viewers around the world when the time came to announce the kidnapping. "We want them on our side, sweetheart," she said to Henry. She could kick herself; all that to make a billion dollars more for the Prizzis but the thought of it made her set her jaw; when she got through with this operation there wouldn't be enough left for the Prizzis to buy a pizza.

She showered, dressed, put on her makeup, checked her watch, comforted to see that she had at least a twenty-four-hour start on Charley Partanna, and left to descend the graceful curving staircase that led to the entrance hall. She was on her way to a new life, with a new name and a couple of tons of new money.

At the head of the steep staircase, she caught her French heel in the carpet and toppled headlong down the steep stairway, fracturing her left ankle, her right forearm, and three ribs. She lay in a helpless heap on the floor directly in front of the front door. She was found by the service maids who let themselves in to clean the apartment.

NUALA COUNIHAN walked into Markel's office at the *Tribune* with a heavy file.

"Look at this, Eddie," she said. "Asbury's wife is in London, raiding the markets from here to Tokyo. She's gone so short that very soon no one will be able to find the companies."

"You're sure?" He took the file from her and began to shuffle through it.

"And that ain't all. Someone else—I can't find out who—has begun to milk the Asbury company pension funds."

"No kiddin'?"

"She could be ripe. If we don't do it, one of the other blats is going to jump on her."

"You want to take her on in London?"

"What else?"

"It could be a wild-goose chase."

"Never. She has trained herself to think that she has the media eating out of her hand. She holds press conferences, fahcrissake."

"Well—it's worth a shot."

"Concorde?"

"Tourist only takes a little longer."

"But suppose somebody else has the same idea?"

"Tourist. And maybe it would be a good idea to talk to the brother before you go."

"The lawyer? Asbury's lawyer?"

"That's the one."

Nuala went back to her desk, flipped open a telephone directory, found Allan's number and called him. His secretary wasn't sure he was in when Nuala identified herself.

"Please tell him that I will be flying to London tonight to see his sister."

Allan took the call. "Miss Counihan?"

"I wondered if you'd have time to talk to me late this afternoon or early this evening."

"No, that won't be possible."

"I won't take more than a few minutes."

"It can't be done."

"Perhaps when I get back from London. I'll only be there for the day."

"I hope we can do that. Please call me."

Nuala had a long farewell dinner with Lieutenant Zendt, her longtime companion from NYPD Homicide, who armed her with a note to a Superintendent of Police at Scotland Yard because he knew all the good restaurants. They ate a last supper at the airport so she could be sure to catch the plane. He asked her to bring him a bottle of aftershave from Truefitt & Hill because he was convinced it was a powerful aphrodisiac.

"Listen, you smell great without it."

"You don't remember? It turned up in the Christmas loot about two years ago? You flipped your wig over it? So bring me back a boddle."

On the way to the departure counter they picked up a bull-dog edition of the *Daily News.* The headline, covering the entire front page, said

ASBURY WIFE LOSES BABY
FALLS DOWN STAIRS
TO MULTIPLE FRACTURES

"Holy shit," Nuala said. "There goes my exclusive."

"Maybe you don't even need to go," Lieutenant Zendt said.

"Are you outta your skull? Even if she broke into little pieces she's the story of the year. What hospital? Does it say?"

Harvey studied the news story. "Princess Grace, it says."

JULIA had lain on the floor of the entrance hall to the flat for almost two hours before the service maids had come in. She couldn't crawl on her left side because of her broken ribs and ankle. She couldn't crawl on her right side because her broken forearm couldn't support her to drag her forward, but all the doors leading to the hall were closed so there was no-place to go anyway so she lay there. She hadn't had so much time to think since she had had the mumps when she was eleven. She wasn't used to this kind of thinking—steady, monotonous, reflective thinking.

She knew she had lost everything—her husband, her money, and if she knew anything about the Prizzis, probably her life. Partanna would strip her of every dime she had but maybe, because her father worked for him, he might give her an airline ticket back to New York but no more. She would have the ticket and the $43,000 in traveling money in her purse and her houses—if they didn't make her sell the houses, the cars, the boats, and her jewels to get the money that would bring.

She had to have a plan or she would be out on her ass on the cold, wet stones. She had to get out of here somehow and get under the protection of a hospital so that when Partanna came for her he couldn't touch her, just lay the fear on her. While she had him alone in the hospital room, she had to work on him. He had a longtime reputation for being girl-simple so she had to take her best shot at him. She had to make herself look beautiful and helpless, then she had to negotiate, using her body as the stakes, like she had never put a lock on a man before. She had to convince him to let her keep the money or a large part of the money—like sharing the money with him so they could disappear together and, after a while, she could have him zapped, in exchange for convincing him that they had been made for each other. She shuddered. Her one haven had been that she had believed that Henry George Asbury was a militant Methodist, a cultivated college graduate, and more legitimate than Abraham Lincoln. The way things were going he would probably turn out to be a wop hoodlum named Johnny Bigshoes. She tried to force herself to think of how she was going to handle Partanna until she fainted again from the discomfort.

When the maids found her they called the hall porter on the house phone, started to move Julia to a sofa in the living room until her moaned curses and outright screams of pain forced them to leave her where she was until the hall porter came and immediately telephoned for an ambulance.

ANGELO took Pino Tasca to the airport so he could intro-
duce him to Allan John Melvin. They found him in the
Concorde lounge, sipping tea and reading the *Wall Street
Journal.*

"This is Pino Tasca, Al," Angelo said. "He'll be traveling witchew. He's been Charley's assistant for almost a year, like your
father only not so experienced."

"Your son isn't going to London?'"

"He got the measles." Angelo shrugged. "Forty years old.
The measles."

"Your father is a legend," Pino said to Al. "It is an honor to
be chosen to fill his shoes."

"My father wasn't home very much," Al said.

"I never been to London," Tasca said to Angelo. "If I can't
get the tools past the security check here, what am I supposed
to do?"

"Someone will bring everything to the hotel. But don't take
it until you need to do the work. They are very rough about
that stuff over there." He watched Allan as he talked because
he was establishing the consequences if neither Allan nor his
sister cooperated.

"Do the work?" Allan said. "On who? The don said my sister
was out-of-bounds for work."

"It's okay. We want you to think of Pino as your bodyguard.
And for your sister."

Pino Tasca wore the kind of suits that were advertised on
television for sixty-five dollars with two pairs of pants. He was
a tall, thin second-generation Sicilian. His father had emigrated from a village near Sciacca and had found work as
heavy muscle with the Prizzis, rising to the post of assistant
intimidatore in labor organizing. When he passed away as a
result of a turf dispute with the Bocca family, he had become

a legend in the garment and building trades. Pino had followed in his footsteps but, due to physical characteristics which were opposed to effective intimidation, he had studied uses of the gun and garrote and had set out to make a place for himself. He lived quietly in Bensonhurst, scored as many non-Sicilian girls as possible each week because he didn't feel he was ready to marry, and had spent a considerable part of his savings on his teeth, two rows of large, gleaming dentures.

He had been a preliminary fighter before switching to contract work for the family. The Armory fighting had cost him his teeth. The new teeth had been done by Dr. Pincus of Beverly Hills and they were an improvement over his original teeth, which had been spacey and dingy. But these were actors' teeth, maybe a little too white and too even, but that could also have been because they were set off by his Mediterranean complexion. They were expensive custom-made teeth, so he smiled a lot. He was a good-looking man with a long, olive-and-pink face under black curly hair and hazel eyes.

At those times when Charley had been too busy to do the work, or maybe out of town, or when the contracts had been on insignificant people, they chose Pino. He had to be good at what he did because, smiling all the time with teeth like that, it was easy to remember him and people could have testified against him. He had zotzed only four people for the Prizzis, but Charley had confidence in him. Pino was in his mid-thirties and had been a made man for two years.

They sat in silence until the flight was called. Pino made a few attempts to start a conversation but Allan sipped his tea and stared at a mote in the middle distance. When the flight was called Allan John got up as if he were traveling alone and made his way to the long finger which led to the plane. Inside the plane he took the seat assigned to him and, to his relief, Tasca had been given a seat in another part of the plane. When they got to Heathrow, however, one car was waiting for both of them. The driver was standing outside Customs & Immigration holding a sign that said

MR. MELVIN AND MR. TASCA

Pino was careful to address Allan as "Mr. Melvin" because he had been raised to have great respect for lawyers. He also had respect for his supervisor, The Plumber, the lawyer's father, because when Charley got nostalgic he always admired The Plumber's work. "For out-and-out nerve, he was the most, Pino. Once, he actually did try to stuff a guy down a terlet. A big guy."

However, when they were in the car and out of the Heathrow tunnel, and the separator was up between them and the driver, Pino didn't lose any time. "This is how I was told to lay it out to you, Mr. Melvin," he said. "You talk to your sister. Angelo thinks that, at this time, it would only upset her if I talked to her. You tell her we want the seventy-five million, the ransom money for her husband, as forfeit. Then we want the real money—like the eight hundred million Mr. Price has discovered that she transferred from all the Asbury companies—Jesus, your sister must have the nerve of nine Apaches, Mr. Melvin—and the two hundred and fifty million she took out from milking all the companies and shorting the stock. We want that deposited by wire from her banks to a list of banks around the world which I will hand you before you see her. Angelo will handle the shifting of the money from country to country so that nobody can follow it. He wants brokerage printouts of the short transactions your sister has been making with subtotals and a grand total. He wants the transactions validated by a notary, then he wants to know where she put the money and the numbers of those accounts in whichever banks who are now holding the money. Then he wants her to tell those banks to wire the money to the number accounts on the list of the banks I'm gonna hand to you. *Capeesh?*"

Allan looked at him stonily and nodded. The car crossed the Hammersmith flyover.

THE CAR took Allan to Claridge's. He didn't ask where Pino was going. He hadn't spoken to Pino since they had met in the departure area at Kennedy.

Allan checked into Claridge's because he knew it was expensive and he wanted to sting the Prizzis by running up a big bill even if they would never be aware of it. He asked for their best suite, signed the registration card, asked that his luggage be sent up, then took a taxi to the hospital.

"Jesus, you look awful," he said to his sister, who was supine on a bed with her left foot in traction and in a cast and her right arm in plaster and a sling.

Julia nodded sadly.

"And you lost the baby."

Julia nodded sadly.

"I'm very sorry, Jule. I can't really know what it must have meant to you, but I know it was bad."

"Gizza kiss, Al." He leaned over and kissed her cheek softly.

"I have even worse news."

"Charley Partanna."

"No. His assistant, Pino Tasca. They want practically everything you own."

"What does Poppa say?"

"He's out of town."

"But in the meantime, what about Henry? What are they doing with Henry? Where are they holding him? When do I get him back?"

"The way I get it," Allan said lamely, "is that they are waiting on money arrangements."

"What money? The ransom is our money?"

"The pension plans for all Henry's companies. They probably want to milk them first, then you get Henry."

He didn't have the heart to tell her that she'd never see Henry again, that the don had decided that Henry had to go.

"What's Tasca like?"

"Well—he's a *shtarker* like Poppa."

"How old?"

"Maybe middle thirties."

"What does he look like?"

"What can I tell you—he's a wop. But like a Hollywood wop."

"What do they want?"

"Listen, what I tell you they told me to tell you. They want the money."

"The money?"

"They want the seventy-five-million ransom. Then they want the entire layout of the money you made from transferring it out of the companies and they want all your brokerage houses to certify the amount of money you made during the short-selling and they want every dime you made from that. Then there will be the razzle of moving the money from bank to bank around the world and where it comes out no one knows. So far they're going to let you keep the houses and the cars and the boats. But when you understand that you can't afford the upkeep, they'll buy them from you at such a bargain basement price you will hardly get cab fare out of it."

"But that's our money! My money and Henry's!"

"No. They say you double-crossed them when you did all the short-selling, so you have to pay."

"Suppose I won't pay?"

"That's why Tasca is here. Like Pop, he's one of Charley Partanna's boys."

"That's not fair."

"Maybe you didn't hear me. Tasca is an enforcer. You have to get on the phone right here in the hospital and start calling your brokers to cash in."

"You really think—?"

"Tasca looks easygoing because he's smiling all the time—he's tooth proud, I think—but Julia, listen to me—if you don't cooperate, he'll do the job on you right here in the hospital."

"No offense, Al, but I think I have to talk to Tasca."

There was a light knock on the door. Julia made a face at Allan but she called out, "Come in."

A short, pretty woman with gorgeous legs opened the door. "Hello," she said, "I'm Nuala Counihan of the *New York Tribune.*"

Allan held up a restraining hand. "Just a minute. My sister is in no condition to receive the press."

Julia broke in smoothly. "May I introduce my brother, Allan Melvin."

"Oh, yeah," Nuala said. "We talked onna phone in New York."

Allan had protecting his sister on his mind but he couldn't suppress the estimate that this was one fine-looking woman. "I was just leaving," he said, "perhaps I could drop you at your hotel."

"It's all right, Al. I want to talk. But—will you excuse us? I can only say what I have to say to Miss Counihan." She winked at her brother from the off-side of her face.

"Well—I—"

"It's all right, Al."

"I'll be waiting out in the visitor's lounge," he said stiffly and left the room.

❶❺

IN ONE FLASH, as if the sky had been painted with gaudy, colored fluorescent letters, Julia had seen what she had to do the moment this woman had said who she was. It was some kind of miracle because it was going to put a high wall between her and the Prizzis. She wanted to sing out loud because she knew she was saved.

"Please sit down, Miss Counihan."

Nuala sat on a love seat facing the bed in the large hospital bed-sitting-room. "Will you have a glass of champagne, perhaps an *amusé gueulé*?"

"What's that?"

"A little snack. Caviar, paté?"

"I gotta watch my weight."

"Did you come all the way from New York to talk to me, Miss Counihan?"

"Yes. I've been following Mr. Asbury's case since the kidnapping."

"I know."

"The market has been slipping badly in the past three days. And there has been a lot of negative action with the pension funds."

"We'll talk about that later, Miss Counihan, if you still want to. I have something else, something more important on my mind."

Nuala had her notebook in her lap and a pen at ready for appearances' sake. She was also wired.

Julia took a deep breath and exhaled slowly. "My husband was kidnapped by a New York crime family."

"*Whaaaat?* Henry Asbury? Adviser to presidents? Three times Man of the Year by the Federation of American Churches? The tenth Dan and a red, white, and blue belt in karate? Jesus, what a news story!"

Julia nodded emphatically, if sadly, with a certain overlay of hopeless fear for her own safety for having said such a thing.

"How do you know that? My God! I mean, this is terrific!"

"I do not dare to tell you more than this—by very circuitous means, they gained some kind of hold over my husband. They wanted the earth and the moon. My husband fought them. They threatened him, then they took him. They contacted me in Rome and told me what they wanted. They said they would kill me if I didn't go to London and carry out this elaborate plan they had to raise millions of dollars from my husband's companies and by the sale of my husband's companys' stock."

"Which family?"

"It would be worth my life if I told you that."

"Jesus, Mrs. Asbury—I mean, this is sen*sa*tional."

"I came to London so I could talk to my brother—you just met him—he's my husband's lawyer." She brought the faithful handkerchief to her face but this time Counihan was too absorbed to figure that it could be a prop. "I—I tried to do what they had told me to do but it was too much for me. I couldn't do it. I couldn't destroy what my husband had spent his life building. I couldn't." Two large tears rolled down her cheeks.

"Your poor thing!"

"So this is what they did to me." She gestured with her free hand at her broken arm then at her plaster-bound ankle. "And they murdered my baby."

"You can *prove* all this?"

"Prove? How can I prove anything except that I'm in the hospital? Except that my husband's companies have been criminally shattered and ruined—gone. Except that I know in my heart that they have been looting the pension plans of my husband's companies since the day they took him. Except that my baby is dead, my husband is gone and that he may be dead, too."

"When this story breaks in New York tomorrow, they'll be stopped, Mrs. Asbury. This story is going to start a rumble like you've never seen. Just tell me the name of the crime family and we'll take care of the rest."

"I can't do that. I'm afraid. They'll kill me and kill my husband."

"When this breaks you're gonna have more protection than Bush gave Saudi Arabia."

"I can't. I just can't."

"Then I gotta go with this. It's half past one in the morning in New York. Maybe they can make the last edition. I'll be back. Everything's gonna be okay." She rushed out of the room.

Five minutes later Allan John knocked on the door and came in.

"Is she gone?"

Julia nodded.

"What did you tell her?"

"I saw—in a sudden flash—that she was my insurance. I had to use her or lose everything."

"What? How do you mean?"

"I told her a New York crime family had grabbed Henry."

"Holy shit, Julia!"

"I told her they had laid out a plan for me to milk Henry's companies but that I couldn't do it so they did all this to me."

"How can I protect you? This means they will send that *shtarker* Tasca in here to work you over!"

"No."

"Whadda you mean—no?"

"If they lay a hand on me the *New York Herald* is gonna tell the world tomorrow morning that they hit me. They'll be indicted—Corrado Prizzi, Angelo Partanna—alla them, because they know I not only fingered them in a general way but they know I'm a Sicilian, too, and that maybe I am gonna leave a secret note behind—maybe with you for the safe at your office. You'd do that to save my life, wouldn't you, Al?—which names the family, Don Corrado, names Pino Tasca, names Edward S. Price—they ain't gonna lay a finger on me, Al. It was the only way I had to go."

"Jesus, Sis—you gotta have the balls of Richard Nixon." He leaned over to kiss her forehead.

❶❻

CORRADO PRIZZI, his two sons, and Angelo Partanna sat at lunch in the don's quarters at the top floor of the house. It was a vast room; living room, a bedroom, a dining room all in one, while in a small kitchen that was separated from the rest of the space, the don's daughter, Amalia Sestero, worked steadily, stirring, tasting, stuffing, mixing, and preparing miracles of the Sicilian food around which Corrado Prizzi had built a part of his life.

While they waited at table for the food to be served, Corrado Prizzi asked Angelo how Charley was doing.

"He's weak. He's sick and he's covered with spots but he thanks you for the cookies."

"All boys like cookies. He must get well. We need him."

As Amalia staggered in with bowls, platters, plates, and pans of hot, redolent food, the others ate normal amounts, then silently watched Corrado Prizzi eat—he believed mealtimes should be devoted to eating not to talking. Lunch was the main meal and the outstanding event of Corrado Prizzi's day, if not his life. For forty years, nothing had been allowed to interfere with the great moment when Corrado met his lunch.

Even though they had witnessed the ritual many times before, the three men marveled at what they were seeing. It was as though they were observers in the stokehole of one of the great coal-burning ocean liners in that part of the century which was Corrado Prizzi's time. In awe, they watched the frail, small, very old man, his eyes gleaming, his jaws moving to the endless rhythm of his dentures as he did away with fruits of the sea and slabs of meat, interspersed among soups, pasta, risottos; *zuppa di pesce,* a stewlike fish soup made with four kinds of fresh fish, flavored with fennel, thyme, and spices and served with fried toast; *lasagne riccie,* a great monument of wide noodles paved with chopped meat and sprinkled with sugar and cinnamon; *sarde de Beccaficu,* a kind of herring stuffed with bread crumbs and pine nuts cooked in oil and salami with some lemon juice; then *farsumagru,* meat turnovers filled with cheese, hard-boiled egg, onions and parsley, cooked in oil with tomato sauce; hot rolls stuffed with meat; baked tomatoes filled with anchovies, minced salami, capers, and bread crumbs; eggplant and artichokes; almond cakes filled with cream then *gelu i muluni,* an ice made from strained watermelon, flavored with vanilla, jasmine water, chocolate, and candied pumpkin then sprinkled with cinnamon; some figs, two oranges, and half a melon.

Carefully, as he destroyed course after course, the don sipped, gulped, and quaffed golden Mamertino, a strong wine with a walloping aroma, some jewel-red Etna grown on the volcanic slopes of the mountain and just as high in alcohol, and Frappato di Vittoria, a sweet, cherry-red dessert wine from Ragusa.

The three men, having finished their own lunches some forty minutes before, waited for Don Corrado to finish eating so the meeting could begin. Vincent sat back with a newspaper over his face, napping softly, humming "My Way" in his sleep. Edward S. Price worked out some equities on a pocket computer. Angelo smoked a cigar and clipped his nails with the small scissors of a Swiss army knife into a wastebasket held between his knees.

Amalia brought in a cake plate with *cannoli* but Corrado waved her away. "I mustn't overeat."

"I'll leave them on the table anyway." As she left the room, Corrado picked up a *cannoli* and wolfed it down like a sword swallower.

Vincent took the paper away from his face and sat up. Edward S. Price put away the computer. Angelo moved the wastebasket from between his legs, looking expectantly at Corrado Prizzi.

"I been thinking about this crazy woman in London," Corrado said. "The brother is right. It would be an *infamità* to lay hands on her. Besides, we have to keep her alive so she can tell us how to get the money."

He did not yet know that the following morning's edition of the *New York Herald* would seem to him to be an even greater *infamità*.

"But there are other ways to persuade her," he said. "Vincent, tell The Plumber to see that Asbury floats up on the beach of his island out there. Did he have insurance, Eduardo?"

"Two three-million-dollar policies."

"In our favor?"

"Indirectly."

"Just make sure we get it. And have The Plumber make it look like he got thrown off his motorboat and was drowned. The wife, that pain-in-the-ass, will inherit everything he had and suddenly she will see that she, herself, is facing bankruptcy because we are gonna take all the money and because she shorted all the companies; she will also know we are wise to her, that she doesn't need to pretend to have to raise ransom money and she will stop the short-selling. That will tell the wife that there are many ways to take stones out of my shoes. Give her two nights to think about it, then send The Plumber in to talk the business with her—his own daughter, how can she refuse him?"

"That sounds good," Angelo said. "But when The Plumber puts Asbury away, he should first drown him in a barrel of salt water after he conks him. That he should keep Asbury in the barrel of salt water until the ship gets back from wherever it is."

"Why?" Price asked.

"It will bloat out the body, from the water. Make it look like he's been in the water since he disappeared. Where's the ship?"

"It's about a hundred miles off the northeast coast of Scotland," Edward S. Price said. The *Benito Juárez Bennett* was a Barkers Hill container ship. "It will take about six or seven days to get back to Long Island."

"Good," Angelo said. "The lungs will be filled with water to prove he died from drowning."

The Plumber received the coded, unsigned radio message, written in a dialect of western Sicily, aboard the container ship. After he had read and considered the message, he made his plan. He went on deck, ordered a large barrel, sawed the top off the barrel, saw that it was filled with sea-water, then went below to find Henry Asbury.

He and Asbury went on deck. It was a moonlit night. The

small crew of the automated container ship were in their bunks below. As he pointed to the outline of Flannan Island beyond the Outer Hebrides with his left hand, he struck the back of Henry George Asbury's head with an iron pipe in his right hand. Asbury went down heavily. He was wearing the same clothes he had on the day he disappeared. The Plumber picked up the unconscious body and dumped it, head first, into the barrel of seawater, replaced the head of the barrel, wired it shut securely, then climbed up to the bridge of the vessel to instruct the captain to return to Long Island Sound.

❶❼

CORRADO PRIZZI sat, eating his breakfast comfortably on the top floor of the large, old Victorian house that he had deeded years before to the Little Sisters of Pain and Pity (a spin-off of the Blessed Decima Manovale Foundation). The holy order rented the house to Don Corrado for ninety-six dollars a month. There were gold fringes on almost everything because his late wife had been slightly house-proud. There were hundreds of colored prints of pictures in gilded frames and a fine operatic phonograph record collection. The don was a tiny man with the complexion of a great Swiss glacier. The most terrifying thing about him was his smile.

It was his favorite time of day, excepting lunchtime. His breakfast was a small glass of olive oil, as he listened to *La Battaglia di Legnano* (suggested to Verdi by the poet Cammarano), a recording by the Welsh National Opera, and read the morning newspaper.

As he tasted the olive oil, his only breakfast except for a *panzerotti* of boiled tuna and a tart called *pita ripiena*, which was made of layers of ricotta cheese, layers of fried pork, layers of caciocavallo, layers of sausage, and layers of hard-boiled egg, he snapped open the morning newspaper and read the banner headline. He had to read it a second time, then a third. He pondered it as if it were written in an alien language. Not an alien earthly language such as Bessarabian or Twi but a language from an alien planet such as Venus or Pluto. It said

WIFE ALLEGES ASBURY
KIDNAPPED BY N.Y. CRIME
FAMILY, BEATING HER

Julia Asbury Hospitalized by Mafia in London
Loses Baby

As he was staring glassily at the headline, the door to the room burst open and Angelo Partanna rushed in, waving a copy of the newspaper.

"Did you read this shit?" he demanded loudly, speaking in a Sicilian dialect.

"How did it happen?"

"The same fucking newspaperwoman who has been attacking the Asbury companies went to see Julia Asbury and this is what she told her."

"I can see that! But what I wanna know is how Pino Tasca and the brother let the newspaperwoman in?"

"Who could figure she could say such a thing?"

"She said it! She said it! How could they *let* her say it?"

"Whatta you wanna do?"

"Send The Plumber to the hospital to tell the daughter to deny it and to sue the paper for ten million dollars."

"How? The Plumber just did the job on Asbury somewhere near Scotland so he's gotta stay with him until the ship gets to Long Island and he can dump him."

"When?"

"Maybe eight days."

"Then you gotta get Charley on his feet and get him to London to put the fear on the wife and Tasca."

"Why Tasca?"

"So Tasca will do what he's told instead of letting the wife dump all this shit on newspaperwomen!"

"What can he do? Now that the newspapers and the television have this story, he can't zap the wife or the brother because that would bring on an investigation that not even Eduardo can fix. She fingered a New York family. We can't take the chance."

"We can't take the chance that she's gonna tell the name of the family! Better we should knock her off and shut her up." He paused to consider. "We could plant in the papers that it was the Bocca family," he said slyly.

"When the husband's body is found on that island, there's gonna be a lotta noise," Angelo said, ignoring the comment as a frivolity.

"The only way is for Charley to put the fear on her and the brother," Corrado Prizzi said. "Then, when she gets out of the hospital, for Tasca to blow her away. We're talking about our whole business here, Angelo."

"If Charley goes to see the wife someone could make him. And if somebody makes him, they automatically know the name of the crime family that the newspaper is talking about."

"So let Tasca put the fear on her."

"He can't do it like Charley." He wiped his bald head with a white silk handkerchief. "The wife tells the newspaper that a New York crime family lifted her husband. Then the husband's body is found. Then the wife is snuffed. How long you think it's gonna take the cops, the Federal Prosecutor, the U.S. Senate—alla them—to figure out who is the New York crime family if we do that?"

"Angelo, fahcrissake—I'm eighty-six years old. I'm entitled to a little peace. I know I'm right on this. Nobody can prove nothing on us. The wife is a snitch so she's gotta be put in the ground. It's too late not to dump the husband. The Plumber has already iced him. They wronged us so they gotta go."

"But what about the *infamità* on The Plumber on accounta we zotzed his daughter?" Angelo asked plaintively. "What will the American people think of *omertà* if we zotz the daughter of a made man?"

"All right! Go through the motions. Take it to the Commission. But when The Plumber gets back from dumping the husband, Charley has to make the hit. But the main thing now is to keep the daughter alive—at least until she tells us how to get that money."

AT THE MOMENT Corrado Prizzi was staring with horror at the front page of the *New York Herald*, before it was possible for the London newspapers and television to get the story, Pino Tasca waited down the street from the hospital until he saw Allan John Melvin leave. It was 3:19 P.M. London time.

After he watched Melvin enter a taxi, Tasca went into the hospital through the service entrance, took a back elevator to Julia's floor, found her room and knocked on the door.

Julia's eyebrows went up when she saw the stranger in the mail-order suit. Pino smiled his brilliant store-bought smile. Julia was weak, she was feeling sorry for herself and she was feeling horny from being out of action for so long. The unexpected beauty of the smile exhilarated her. It was like the time she had been working at the Executives' League and was walking on Madison Avenue near the Roosevelt

Hotel, long before she had met Asbury, and had heard a voice she knew she remembered coming from directly behind her. She had turned around and had almost fainted from the sensation of looking into the actual, flesh-and-blood face of Cary Grant.

"Mrs. Asbury?" Pino said.

"Yes?"

"My name is Pino Tasca. I work with your father."

"What do you want?"

"I came to see if you were feeling better. They sent me from New York."

"The Prizzis wanted to know if I was feeling better?"

"No. To talk. But that can wait."

He had never seen such a classically exquisite Sicilian woman, the kind that his Uncle Dom used to rave about, but had never seen, while they shot pool at the old Nonpareil on Bushwick Avenue years ago. She was fragile, and not just because of the plaster casts, yet he could see she was strong. Her eyes told him everything about her the way he hoped his teeth told everything about him. They were bold eyes—she was a married woman, after all—yet they were truer than even her astrological chart could be. She had a passionate Sicilian nose and—God!—what a mouth—an army could feed on that mouth and be able to march for ten days.

He saw what his approach to her must be. None of that fear shit. She was a sensitive, intelligent woman, so he would talk to her directly, as if he were on the up-and-up, like he had only her best interests at heart. He would explain that the Prizzis wanted him to put her in the ground but that they were far away and couldn't possibly understand the way things were with her. He wouldn't even make a chop at her. He would play it distant but interested. He would make her see that he was on her side, then, after she signed over the money, then it would be the time to work on getting into her drawers. Ai! If his Uncle Dom was alive and could see what his little nephew was going to creep into, he would cream.

Julia couldn't shake the illusion that she was talking to some

Greek god in a polyester suit. She had never had the luck to find a tall, slender man. From her first date they had been either little hulks with olive-oil breaths or overweight hunks like Henry. This one was built like a buggy whip. She didn't feel even a little bit romantic but she was feeling a very large amount of horny. The grabber was that smile. It made her think of happy pianos. So he took contracts. Big deal! Her father was a contractor second only in scores to Charley Partanna.

She made the mistake of translating the signals from his constant smiling into a conviction that this meant that he was unsure of himself, then he wanted to be liked more than anything. That kind of a man was a pushover, she could play him like a violin.

It was too bad for Julia that she made that evaluation of Pino. He smiled a lot because his teeth had cost him so much money (in airfares, dental fees, and materials) that he wanted to get as much use out of them as he possibly could. There was nothing unsure about Pino. His wardrobe proved that.

Julia knew she would need protection to get her away from the Prizzis on the long skip and jump from where she was to Buenos Aires, so she decided then and there that she could let this grin merchant take her into the sack—not too quickly, not too slow—then she would appeal to his innate Sicilian sense of money. She would lay out her proposition: two hundred and fifty thousand cash right into his pocket at the end of the line with maybe fifty thou down. How could he refuse? She would tell him about the fake passports for his peace of mind, but no mention of Dr. Mitgang and Buenos Aires. After she dumped him, and after Dr. Mitgang had worked his surgeon's magic on her face, the most shining pupil of the great Dr. Abraham Weiler, the flesh sculptor who had given Edward S. Price the face with which he had dominated his world, she would be on her way to vanishing forever. She would fill Pino with a lot of romance about how big and how wonderful the world was and how they would be together until she could pay somebody to do the job on him.

"Please sit down," she said.

He pulled a chair up to the bed, sat down, leaned forward and held her good hand. She could hear him breathe. "I just didn't know you were so beautiful," he said.

"Thank you. Did you go to school in Brooklyn?"

"P.S. 34."

"Me, too!"

"No kidding?" He couldn't believe it; it didn't seem possible.

"Did you have Miss Heckle?" Julia asked eagerly.

"The one with the big boobs? Pardon the expression."

"That's the one!" Julia said triumphantly. "Who was in your graduating class?"

"I didn't graduate, actually. I had this offer to work on an ice truck."

"You didn't graduate from *grammar* school?"

"Not actually." He smiled brilliantly. It cheered her up.

"When do you get outta here?" he asked.

"Today. This afternoon."

"Can I take you home?"

"Thanks, but my brother is going to take me home on his way to the airport."

"He's leaving town?"

"Pressure of business."

"Maybe we could have dinner tonight?"

"That would be very nice. We could go downstairs in my building to the Caprice." She inhaled deeply, causing him to stare at her chest. He became light-headed; almost dizzy. If his Uncle Dom could have seen this chest, he would have postponed dying.

THE *Benito Juárez Bennett* made its way out of the open sea into Long Island Sound, reducing its forward speed to minimum when it was approximately two hundred yards off Bent Island. It was night. No one was on deck except The Plumber, who was removing the last of the wire closure from the large barrel. When he had wrenched the top of the barrel away, he pushed the barrel over on its side. Seawater and a foul stench covered the deck. The Plumber stepped to the opening of the barrel, drew on a pair of heavy rubber gloves, and pulled Henry George Asbury's corpse out of the opening of the barrel. He lifted the body over his shoulder, carried it down a companionway that had been rigged to the ship's side, and lowered it into a waiting lifeboat. He sat in the stern of the boat with one foot on the body while two men rowed toward Bent Island. They beached the lifeboat on the shore and The Plumber, assisted by one of the rowers, lifted the body out and carried it up on the beach.

The lifeboat was rowed back to the *Benito Juárez Bennett*. The Plumber climbed the companionway and went to the bridge to order the navigator to come about and to head the vessel around Montauk Point and into New York Harbor, to drop him at the container ship docks at Red Hook on the Brooklyn side of the East River.

The next day, at 9:27 A.M., the regular beach security patrol of a man and a dog found Asbury's nearly unrecognizable body. Security called the police, the police called the FBI, the telephone operator tipped off her sister on the Montauk paper, and within hours the compound and its beach area were aswarm with news media people. The story went on television tape. The tape was transmitted to the satellite, piped into the networks' newsrooms, edited depending on the viewpoints of the owners of the networks, and the story went out in the lead position on the evening news.

The pictures showed, in succession, a medium long-shot of Asbury's corpse, cutting to the main compound, inserting pictures of Asbury at his best and of Julia Asbury in plaster on a hospital bed. The voice-over of the reporter said: *"The body washed up on the sand, the sand of Bent Island which he owned, is the remains of Henry George Asbury, the adviser to presidents who had been kidnapped, his wife alleged in a London hospital last week, where she was recovering from multiple fractures which were caused, she said, by the same unnamed New York crime family who had kidnapped her husband. Mrs. Asbury charged that the kidnapping was a result of an extortion plot forced upon her husband by this unnamed crime family. If anyone had doubted those charges before today, those doubts would seem to be erased forever by the presence of the body as it was recovered here."*

Despite the hue and cry, a coroner's jury found that Asbury had somehow fallen overboard from his speedboat in Long Island Sound, resulting in "death from misadventure." This took the focus off what had been exploited as a kidnapping but raised endless questions about the ransom note that Mrs. Asbury had received in Rome and which had been examined by the world media. It also tightened the attention on the plight of Asbury's widow, who had been assaulted in London to the extent that she had lost her unborn child. Public outrage, wildly out of focus, was at a white heat. Letters, faxes, telephone calls poured in upon news organizations, executive and legislative desks, and to all law enforcement agencies.

Responding with one great hoarse raucous voice, the news media demanded that Mrs. Asbury be given the total protection of the British police and the American FBI and that she be returned to U.S. jurisdiction aboard the safety of an armed U.S. Air Force bomber or a naval battleship. She had not yet named the crime family because she feared for her life. That family would do anything in its almost total power to silence her forever. She must have maximum protection against maximum evil.

How could it be possible that the widow of such a distinguished American could be beaten and maimed and threatened with death while her husband—the man who had advised four presidents, a man who advised other presidential advisers— had been kidnapped and, despite the coroner's verdict, had been ripped from life and family and tossed overboard at sea to float up on the remote beach that was his island home. What kind of monsters were these *mafiosi*?

There were five principal New York crime families. The television networks thundered and the press inveighed that a Senate investigation of the business affairs of every one of them must be called and all the facts sifted until the murderers of a great man were brought to the bar of justice.

The uproar was so bad that business fell off for whores and pimps in the smaller cities, to say nothing of the service organizations' enormous losses in larger ones. The gambling action from coast to coast was diminished by 27 percent and bookies were wailing. Only loan sharking and narcotics held to industrial norms because legitimate banks had not been lending as a matter of policy and narcotics were beginning to seem to be habit forming. A great sense of public outrage was building across the land, and this ridiculous pressure was costing all the crime families in the country 48 to 50 million dollars a day, so something had to be done. A meeting of the National Commission was called.

The meeting was held in Yuma, in the southwestern corner of Arizona, twenty miles north of the Mexican border, in the ballroom of the holiday home of a chief executive of one of the Barkers Hill companies. The isolated area had a private airfield. The Commission meeting was attended by a single representative of each of the five New York families, and by spokesmen from the principal crime families of Buffalo, Boston, Chicago, Philadelphia, Miami, New Orleans, Phoenix, L.A., Kansas City, Detroit, and Cleveland; only sixteen people, the smallest but the most empowered national meeting ever held.

In practice, there were two Commissions. There was the Big Six, which comprised the five New York families and Chicago, but in the thirties, Charles Luciano and Meyer Lansky created a National Commission, made up of the Big Six and the twenty-odd crime families that provided services to the entire United States and had been invited to join. The Commission became the central legislature body of the confederation of national crime families.

The Prizzi family was represented by Angelo Partanna. Vincent Prizzi had made a big *scompiglio* about how he was the boss of the family so he should be the one to attend the meeting. "This is important, Vincent," his father said. "It takes brains, not muscle. Angelo will go."

The chairman, Morris "The Nudge" Finkle of the Cleveland combination, came directly to the point at issue. "Who ever saw such a *geshrei*?" he said. "You could think the whole world was slipping into the Atlantic Ocean. I know one thing. In my forty years in this business I have never seen such a fuck-up. And there is something else I know. My outfit didn't have nothing to do with this Asbury schlepper who is making all this trouble for us. This is those fucking Prizzis again. They think they shit candy."

Angelo Partanna stood up, this slight, stooped old man with his toucan nose, coffee-colored complexion, and bald head. "You guys gonna let Morris get away with that?" he asked. "I want a vote. I want somebody who can control his mouth to run this meeting. Vote with your hands." Over forty hands went up.

"You're out, Morris," Angelo said.

Finkle stepped down, figuratively. Gennaro Fustino, boss of the New Orleans family whose territory covered most of the southern rim of the United States, was elected chairman by a voice vote that was called by Partanna. He was the husband of Corrado Prizzi's sister, Birdie, and stood five feet two inches tall.

"The wife talking to the newspapers all bandaged up in a hospital," Fustino said. "The husband shows up onna beach which it has cost our industry—so far—maybe fifty million dollars. Morris happens to be right. The only connection these people had was with the Prizzis. So we better ask Angelo how come the whole country is dumping on us and what is he gonna do to stop it." He stared at Angelo, the normal Mafia stare that its young men had cultivated from puberty onward. He sat down when Angelo got to his feet.

"I am gonna level witchew," Angelo said, "and when I tell you that those two people had it set to screw us out of a billion one twenty-five of our money, from our companies which we controlled, and that the woman was hitting the stock markets from New York to Tokyo to short the stocks in our companies and that she was salting all that money—our money—into number accounts in banks all over the world—and I can prove this because we got three world-class computer hackers from Eastern District High School on our payroll who have already gotten into the records of two of the banks—when you unnastan that these people were tryna steal our money—plus putting us onna line with the Feds—the U.S. Senate, the FBI, the Federal Prosecutor, you name it—by queering our moves to loot almost a billion and a half in pension funds, you are gonna vote and you are gonna say that we done the absolutely right thing by zotzing Asbury."

"So whenna you gonna ice the wife?" The question came from directly across the table.

"I need a ruling from here on that—today," Angelo said. "The wife happens to be the daughter of one of our soldiers—maybe summa you know him, The Plumber. So Corrado Prizzi says his hands are tied by *omertà*, that it would be an *infamità* to ice the daughter."

"But—fahcrissake, Angelo," Gennaro Fustino said with puzzlement and exasperation, "you said a loada money is involved here. So do the work on her."

"We think we have solved the problem." Angelo said. "We are gonna have one of our people do the job on The Plumber so that when we zotz the daughter it won't be no *infamità*."

There was an outbreak of approving, admiring applause.

20

THE PLUMBER left the *Benito Juárez Bennett* at its Brooklyn pier and got a taxi for the short ride to his row house on President Street in Red Hook where he had lived since coming to America forty-three years before. When he had moved in, it had been a totally Italian neighborhood; Al Capone had lived on President Street in the early twenties when he was bartending at the Harvard Inn on Coney Island. But later, when Red Hook was cut off from the rest of Brooklyn by the Belt Parkway and the entrance to the Battery Tunnel, things began to change. The Italian bakeries, the stores with the forty-seven shapes of loose pasta and places where you could get ready-to-go *arancine* or little balls of *cicerata* were gone forever. The neighborhood was taken over by Jews, blacks, and Puerto Ricans.

He missed the old days now that he had reached the time of his life when he enjoyed thinking about them. He was nostalgic for Don Corrado's storefront bank which, although it had charged an-arm-and-a-leg in interest, had readily put up the money to let a lot of people send for a lot of relatives and sweethearts in the old country. He looked back fondly on the banquets and dances the don had thrown at the old Palermo Gardens, the most Italian place in the world outside of the Vatican. The don had given them famous orchestras, brigades of Bolognese and Venetian cooks who really knew how to make Sicilian dishes. Everybody in the entire environment preferred Sicilian food, especially when it was made by Bolognese and Venetian cooks. Great tenors had sung there. Jesus, he had met his wife there. Even Irish cops had had a good time there, and now it was gone, burned down, and he was almost an old man—not compared to Don Corrado but certainly old compared to Elvis.

The Plumber was a lumpy, seamed, and leathery Sicilian in

his middle sixties who resembled a male Sumatran orangutan
and who had spent most of his life beating people up or taking
them out when Charley Partanna wasn't available or if they   ·
were having a particularly busy season. He was as uncompli-
cated as a game of solitaire and nearly as simple. Corrado
Prizzi was his paragon. As he unlocked the door to his house
he thought of Julia and he sincerely hoped that she wouldn't
be too upset by the loss of her husband but, on the other hand,
the husband must have left her a nice little nest egg.

By the time Pino took Julia Asbury from the hospital, after he
had packed her tenderly into a taxi and had driven with her
to Arlington House, after he had lifted her up out of the wheelchair and carried her over the threshhold, the way brides are
carried in, and took her right up the stairs to the bedroom,
with Julia's deft assistance, it just worked out that way.

It was a complicated business because of the tapes around
her ribs and the casts on her right arm and left ankle, but she
helped him in every way. After the first kiss, after they had
made it to the bedroom door just off the top of the stairs, they
just went on fire. They were bleating, gasping for air. Then
she began to fumble around his trousers, which he took as
permission to help her do it, while he stretched her out on the
emperor-sized bed.

He took plenty of time. He did it right for both of them. She
helped. It was a tremendous experience which they repeated
again immediately. They were both classic ectomorphs, slender, long people without much meat on them to tire them out,
and they achieved tremendous effects before they moved out
of their third orgasm, all without causing Julia the slightest
discomfort to her ribs, her ankle, or her healing forearm. Pino's
elbows and knees took a beating but he had no idea that had
happened until at least twenty minutes after it was all over
and he had lifted her up into his arms again to carry her up
toward the bidet.

They were sitting in the bedroom, facing each other. Julia
had just confirmed why she had longed for a tall, skinny guy

like this one. Now she knew why. It was partly his manners. No other man she could think of, except perhaps Cary Grant, would have been thoughtful enough to carry her, in her condition, to the nearest bidet. Her mother had always said that courtesy paid but this was a living example of it.

"You have beautiful teeth," she said.

"You have beautiful everything," he answered. He wasn't just thinking of her face, her chest, and her legs. He had had a chance to look at the paintings and the size of her television set. She must really be loaded, he thought, and that warmed him.

"I never seen a television screen that big," he said.

"Let's put something on it. It's time for the six o'clock news."

She blipped a channel selector and the BBC news reader came on. Looking straight at Julia he said, "The body of Henry George Asbury, adviser to American presidents from Richard Nixon to Osgood Noon, was washed ashore on the beach of his privately owned island off the coast of Long Island in New York."

"My God, Pino," she cried out. "They did the job on Henry."

"Yeah."

"You knew about it?"

"Well, Jesus, Julia, it figured."

"Now the goddam media is gonna pressure me to go back to New York for the funeral. What am I gonna wear with all these plaster casts on?" She was trying to be flippant, to sound brave, but Henry had been her husband, he had been a good man and she was sad.

Charley Partanna was still not on his feet after five days in Santa Richenda's. He had developed bronchial problems and had been running a fever. His father came to see him every morning on the way to work. He and Charley would play Parcheesi for ten minutes or so until Charley became too tired to do anything but lay back on the pillows. Twice a week Maerose Prizzi, his longtime fiancée, defied her father's stricture that she be banished from Brooklyn and visited Charley at the hospital, bringing him homemade *cuccidata*, Charley's favorite, which were rolls of sweet pastry filled with cream made with raisins, dried figs, nuts, candied pumpkin, and pieces of chocolate.

Angelo's visit on the morning of the sixth day was concerned with business. He explained to Charley about Corrado Prizzi's problem of the *infamità* if he had the number done on The Plumber's daughter but that no matter how you looked at it, the daughter had to be zotzed because she was stealing Prizzi money. There was only one way: The Plumber had to go first so there would be no *infamità* when they gave it to the daughter.

Charley nodded groggily, half understanding the problem. "That makes sense," he said. "Gimme a couple of days, and I'll handle The Plumber."

"No dice, Charley. The doctor says when the time comes for you to get outta here, you gotta have a long rest inna sunshine with no hassles."

"Then who's gonna handle The Plumber?"

"We're gonna bring Pino back from London for the weekend."

THE WORLD PRESS and television anticipated Julia's attendance at Henry Asbury's funeral by massing in the cul-de-sac at the foot of Arlington Street while police kept them from invading the privacy of the grieving widow. The two days of media clamor had brought the problem to the attention of both the FBI and Scotland Yard. The FBI requested British police protection for Julia, not alone from possible bodily harm but from the media. They knew all about Julia's connection with the Prizzi family through her father, who bore the colorful name of "The Plumber"; furthermore there was pressure from the White House to settle the Asbury case. "We have reason to believe that one of the families has given a contract on her," the FBI fax to Scotland Yard read in part. "Please put under surveillance Pino Tasca, a member of the Prizzi crime family, who is in your city, registered at the Hilton Hotel."

The Yard faxed back: "Will comply with your request and provide protection for Mrs. Asbury. However, Tasca not at Hilton here. He has been staying with Mrs. Asbury as a houseguest for the past two nights. Do you want us to detain him?"

The fax came back from Washington. "Do not detain Tasca but please surveil."

Walter Sidyen, Assistant Director, FBI, telephoned Mrs. Asbury at her Arlington House apartment. He asked her to notify Assistant Commissioner Ferdinand Fairfax at Scotland Yard when she was ready to leave to attend her husband's funeral. "He will have Special Branch men take you to the airport and accompany you on the Concorde to New York."

"That is very kind of you, Mr. Sidyen."

"It is my duty to warn you, Mrs. Asbury, that your houseguest, Mr. Tasca, is a known member of the principal New York crime family and that his presence could be a danger to you."

"You have to be mistaken about that, Mr. Sidyen. Mr. Tasca is an old friend of my father's who, when he heard I was in hospital, rushed to see if he could be of any help. But thank you nonetheless."

Julia left in a wheelchair the following morning accompanied by two burly Special Branch men. It took six uniformed policemen to make a path through the press of shouting newsmen and television cameras, shoving through in a phalanx of flesh to the large Rolls-Royce limousine that was waiting in Arlington Street beyond the door. They got Julia into the car and the two Special Branch men followed her in. As the car moved slowly away toward Piccadilly through the mob of reporters and photogaphers, Julia said, "I always thought that the Special Branch were mainly political police."

"You *are* political, madam," the senior officer said. "What with the outcry over the looting of British pension plans after your husband's death, Downing Street and the entire Cabinet are in an uproar."

When Julia left the apartment with the two cops, Pino came out of the locked second bathroom and put in a call to Vincent Prizzi in New York.

Vincent's base was in the St. Gabbione Laundry, a large, low, triangular building on a pie-cut block in central Flatbush. He had a two-window office that was almost exhilaratingly freshened by the smell of the industrial soap in the turning vats of wet wash outside his door. A table against the wall had a collection of nine-inch-high religious statues grouped below a picture of the Sacred Heart of Jesus, framed in bronze. On the wall facing Vincent's desk there was an orange-framed IBM slogan that said

CREDERE

in large black letters on silver. There were three chairs, a blond leather sofa, and a blond carpet.

He picked up the phone. "What?"

"This is Pino Tasca, boss. In London. Julia Asbury just left for the airport."

"Whadda you want me to do? Did you lay it out for her?"

"I never had a chance."

"Fahcrissake, Pino!"

"The brother laid it all out for her."

"How come?"

"She trusts him. I woulda scared her and she coulda lied to me."

"So what did she tell the brother?"

"I didn't have time to find out. The husband died and it hit the fan."

"So come back here. We got a job for you."

"Now? Today?"

"Of course today. What are you—drunk?"

"Okay. I'll get right out to the airport." He disconnected.

*   *   *

Julia and Pino were on the same Concorde flight but because the Special Branch men were with her Pino stayed in his seat at the back of the plane while she, the last passenger aboard, sat in the front. When the meal was served, Julia gave her caviar to one Special Branch man and her Scotch salmon to the other. She sat silently, sipping champagne and plotting how she would protect her new money.

She would attend the funeral, grieve emphatically for the television cameras, then find Pino wherever he was and arrange to meet him in Lisbon because it could work out that she would need a strong arm with maybe a gun to hold off any accidental, surprise identification. She knew from a lifetime of observing that, when their money was in danger, the Prizzis could seem to be everywhere, so she would need Pino as a bodyguard. At Lisbon she would give Pino one of Henry's forged passports and they would fly to Athens, then double back to Dakar using the second set of fake passports, then take off for Buenos Aires, where before she got into the crucial part, she would hire somebody to knock Pino off or, if necessary, do it herself. Then, at last, the crucial part: she would put herself in the hands of Dr. Mitgang, the Argentinian face sculptor, the most gifted pupil Dr. Abraham Weiler had ever had. He would change her face into something so special that she would never have a problem in making friends with men, and provide her with Latex fingercaps that would give new identity to her fingerprints. No one would ever be able to recognize her as anyone but the widow of the late John C. Tylk, a name on one of her fake passports and, after a couple of years, she would return to gracious living in Rome and Paris. Fuck the Prizzis!

PINO waited in the hallway of The Plumber's house for almost twenty minutes. He had never been so conflicted. He couldn't put out of his mind that he was doing the number on Julia's dad so that Don Corrado wouldn't be committing an *infamità* when he told Vincent to tell Charley, who would then tell him to zotz Julia. Jesus! What a spot to be in. If he didn't do the work on The Plumber he would be in bad trouble with the family. He had taken an oath to obey; it was part of *omertà*, the oath of manliness. So if he did the work on The Plumber he would be sending the only woman he had ever really loved to a boneyard. He had to have time to think!

The Plumber climbed the front steps. His neighbor Mrs. Diamentez, in the next house, propped up on a soft pillow for better street viewing, greeted him loudly. "You're lookin' great, Mr. Melvini," she said. He smiled and waved at her.

When Pino heard the key in the front door beyond the vestibule he made a temporary decision. He would not zotz The Plumber now, as he had originally planned, because that would give him time to get this whole fucking thing figured out. He poured chloroform over a large gauze pad (as he had known in his heart he was going to do when he bought the chloroform) and waited in the darkness. As The Plumber walked past him he slammed the gauze pad over his nose and mouth and held it there while The Plumber's struggles grew weaker. When he collapsed, Pino put one of The Plumber's limp arms across his shoulders and, supporting him as if with the difficulty anyone would have handling a drunk, he maneuvered the two of them down the nine stone steps to the sidewalk and put him in the back of the car he had parked there.

Mrs. Diamentez watched the action and carefully wrote down the license plate of the car into which The Plumber had been dumped. The guy who had dragged him out was making like The Plumber was drunk when he was, as always, perfectly sober. She happened to know after she had done some checking around that The Plumber was a mobbie. They could be trying to take him for a ride.

She telephoned 911, reported what she had seen, and gave the dispatcher the number of the license plate on the car Pino had used to drive away with Mr. Melvini.

It was dark when Pino, with The Plumber slumped in the back seat, drove away from the Battery Tunnel out toward Sunset Park and Bay Ridge. But he consoled himself with the fact that The Plumber must have a real fortune stashed away after thirty years in the rackets, so Julia would inherit a nice buck out of it even if she did have to split it with the brother. That is, he remembered, if the Family wasn't gonna knock her off after I do the job on The Plumber, or even make me do it!

An NYPD patrol car with all lights off was parked behind a billboard so the driver's partner could relieve himself when Pino pulled his car off the highway onto the shoulder. The cop waiting in the car automatically noted the license plates on Pino's car, then entered them into the car's computer. The signal came right back that it was a reported car. He got out of the patrol car silently while he watched the driver come around, open the back door, then drag the body of a man out of the back seat. He dumped the body on the ground, took out a gun which had a noise suppressor, screwed on its barrel, and aimed it at the head of the man on the ground. Officer Abshire yelled, "Put that weapon down!" pulled out his gun, and sprinted toward Pino.

Pino didn't wait to explain anything. He turned back to his car, leaped into it, and took off straight down the Parkway. Officer Abshire bent over the limp form of The Plumber and yelled at his partner, who was running out from behind the billboard zipping up his trousers, "It looks like we coulda just innarupted a mob hit!"

"That ain't all we innarupted," his partner said.

Pino was gone. He had taken the first turnoff past the

Verrazano approach and was not only into deepest Benson-hurst but about three blocks from his own house. The car he had was a hot car that Vincent's people had picked up for him, so he parked it and set off on foot at a leisurely pace for his house.

It was the first time in his career that he had goofed on a contract. He had the feeling that it was the first time that any-one in Charley Partanna's unit had messed up on a hit. It had been a straight open-and-shut assignment but he had been so fucked up with all that lovey-dovey shit about whether he was going to hurt Julia's feelings if he zotzed her dad that he had gone soft and had used chloroform instead of giving it to The Plumber as soon as he had stepped into his house. There was going to be a lot of trouble about this. Vincent was going to take it out on Charley, and Charley was going to have him trans-ferred to some shit assignment like handling broads or keeping bookies in line. Shit!

THE FUNERAL services for Henry George Asbury were held in Christ Church at Park Avenue and Sixtieth Street, at the heart of the high-rent district. The purple marble of its inner portico and the gold and blue mosaic covering the entire arched nave combined to make this perfectly harmonized Methodist church the most beautiful in the city. Julia, who had never been there before, was awed by its splendor, thinking that the whole place could have been built for Henry Asbury to be buried from.

What saddened her more than anything about the day was that Henry had never considered that he could die. If only he had given it just a few moments of thought, she grieved, he would have had cannon-bellowing 21-gun salutes out on Park Avenue and have provided reserved pews for his biographers and the historians who would never stop recording his life and achievements. There had never been a man who could look so deeply and so unendingly into himself, never finding the tiniest crack on the great monument, always exhorting the world with the mighty voice of his presence and his selfhood to regard him well, to envy him, and to pay homage to his memory forever.

An organ was playing. The flowers, rather than being measured by their beauty, might have been measured by their hundred-weight. The congregation of mourners held hymn books in their hands, singing out lustily and with joy that it was not themselves up there in the casket on view.

It was the most crowded, distinguished funeral of the year and was being covered, discreetly, by *Vanity Fair*, with special permission from the widow, who knew her husband would have wanted that. Television and press photographers had been restricted to work in the street outside, intercepting from among the mourners as they entered the church the great executives and salient leaders of the arts and philanthropies, for whom Henry Asbury had been a great patron. Film stars, champions of many fields of sport, great chefs and publicans, political leaders, social arbiters, and eminent men of science were gathered to pay their last respects, many of them beholden for their good fortunes to one or another of the Asbury or Barkers Hill enterprises.

Edward S. Price was intercepted by television cameras as he entered the church. He gave them a perfect ten-second byte: "We have lost a great man. (Pause) We will not see his like again."

Nuala Counihan of the *New York Tribune* sat in a pew at the back of the church, her eyes searching the congregation of mourners in vain, hoping to spot a top hoodlum.

Henry Asbury's widow sat in a wheelchair at the end of the front pew next to her brother, Henry Asbury's lawyer, Allan John Melvin. Mrs. Asbury was wearing widow's weeds, black stockings, black gloves, a black handkerchief to dry the occasional tear, and a heavy black veil to conceal her grief. The solid-silver cruciform casket, forming a cross so that the departed's arms might be flung wide to receive his Maker, rested at her left hand, in the center aisle of the church.

A guest clergyman, the great Methodist divine, Dr. Carter Coffey Cambridge, who as a young man had been Henry Asbury's spiritual adviser when Asbury had been a boy at summer camp in Colebrook, Connecticut, conducted the services and read the eulogy to which had been contributed sentiments from "those who had known him best." A choir, backed by the mighty organ, sang like the pleadings of angels calling him to heaven, and backed up Dr. Cambridge's paean of praise for the works of Henry George Asbury upon the earth. When he finished there was hardly a dry eye in the Church.

"Don Corrado wants to see you," Allan whispered to his sister.

"Tell me later," she answered, sobbing softly.

They made their way through banks of cameras on Park Avenue to the long black limousines that stood behind the great, dark hearse. The cortege took up its sad journey to the helicopter pad on the East River where the family helicopter, an enlarged version of the Marine VH-3, flew Julia Asbury, her brother, and twenty-two intimate friends of the deceased to Henry Asbury's final resting place on his own Bent Island. After the sad ceremony at graveside, after Dr. Cambridge had rolled out a series of rituals and comforting psalms with his deep, rich, and resonant voice, there was a short snack-and-wine observance and condolences in the main house, then the helicopter flew the mourners back to New York. The widow and her brother remained on the island.

"Now—what is this shit about Corrado Prizzi?" the widow asked her brother.

"Angelo Partanna was at my place at eight-fifteen this morning to tell me to tell you that the don wanted to see you after the funeral."

"He wants to put me away."

"If he wanted to put you away, he wouldn't invite you to his house."

"Henry's case is settled, where the hell is Poppa?"

"You couldn't be expected to have read the papers this morning, but Poppa was all over them. Somebody tried to give it to him last night but they made the hit with chloroform and Poppa is in Bellevue."

"*Poppa? Chloroform!* But that's wild!"

"I can't figure it out, the chloroform. The papers said it couldn't have been a family hit because it was such an amateur job."

"Why would anyone want to zotz Poppa?"

"I have a theory and if it wasn't for the fact that they tried to do him with chloroform, it would all make sense."

"What?"

"Poppa is your life insurance. As long as he stays alive, any *mafiosi* would know it would be an *infamità* for the Prizzis to zotz his daughter."

"I'm getting outta here."

"What do you mean?"

"Baby, the less you know the better—right? The doctors say I can walk with a cane in two more days. Then I'm going from here to Kennedy. Then I am gonna take a plane and disappear."

"Julia, please, don't fool around with this. They'll find you."

"They'll never find me. Now—one favor—will you call Pino Tasca and tell him to fly to Lisbon as soon as he can? He's on my side and I'm gonna need protection. Tell him check into the Lutetié Hotel and wait for my call? That's all I want you to do. That's all I want you to need to know."

CORRADO PRIZZI was as close to uncontrolled fury as he had ever been in his long life, because he knew anger to be a waste, but even more it brought the possibility of losing control. His seamed, pale face with its eyebrows like ghosts', his mouth which curled and uncurled like rubber bands in a desk drawer, and his javelin of a nose were like a nest of agitated wasps, his nostrils heaving with indignation. His little eyes rotated, looking heavenward, glaring at whoever had dared to dump all this helplessness upon him. In all his long life there had never been such circumstances as these to try a man. He was outraged; professionally, personally, most perplexedly outraged. He was a Sicilian. He had spent his life within conspiracies so complex that a lesser man would have crumpled under them, but this conspiracy was so simple that he could not find threads of logical explanation to unravel the enigma.

The daughter of one of his most faithful people, The Plumber, a blood relative of the Prizzi family through his own daughter Amalia, a man who had come to him from the old country, from a village not fifty miles from his own village, had stolen one billion, one hundred and twenty-five million dollars from him. His own daughter's niece! But nothing had happened to her. She was the daughter of a made man, one of his own men, and custom was forcing him to go through the rigamarole of *omertà*, his oath of manliness which traditionally, if theoretically, made it impossible to lay a hand on her. The Commission had okayed putting her in the ground because, to them, money outweighed sacred oaths. But it was *his* oath, not the Commission's oath. He was bound by it, so before he could make the daughter pay, he had to do the job on her father, one of his most faithful people.

"Who is this idiot Charley sent to do the work on The Plumber?" he asked Angelo, in their hometown dialect. "Chloroform? What? We use chloroform on a hit now? They're both Sicilian people. How come he didn't try to strangle The Plumber with strands of linguine?"

"I don't understand it, Corrado. The man is a reliable, experienced man. You may remember his father, the assistant *intimidatore*, Lucca Tasca? The man who used the chloroform, Pinocchiaro Tasca, worked under Charley. He did the National Produce and the two big loan shark hits for us last year. No complaints. Onna nose."

"The chloroform was onna nose!" Corrado snarled. "What have we come to, we wanna show somebody the door and we use chloroform? We're a barrel of laughs to every family inna country! And where is The Plumber? He's sleeping it off in Bellevue while the daughter, sitting on our money, is on every news show they got, upstaging everybody including her husband at his funeral!"

"Charley is very hot about all this," Angelo said. "As soon as he's on his feet, he wants to take over personally, axe The Plumber, then put the fear on the daughter until she signs over the money, then he pays her off."

"None of this woulda happened if Charley didn't get the measles."

"He is personally embarrassed that his own man tried to zap The Plumber with chloroform. He feels humiliated."

"So what's he gonna do about it?"

"He's gonna take him out."

"Well, at least Charley won't use no fucking chloroform. He's an honorable man and he will zotz both the wife and the bungler in an honorable way."

"There is just one thing."

"What?"

"The brother says the daughter refuses to take a meet with you."

"*Whaaaaat?*"

"She says she's got nothing to say."

"Nothing? Who wants her to say? To understand, that's why she's coming here! Is the whole world crazy? She steals a billion one from me and she's got nothing to say? How does she think she's still walking around? I tell you, Angelo, if I was fifty years younger I'd be throwing furniture around. All this is ruining my appetite. Amalia works like a dog in that kitchen and this whole *pazzo* business is gonna ruin my lunch. Send a couple of the *ragazzi* to bring her to me. No more Mr. Nice Guy."

An hour before Corrado Prizzi gave that order, Julia had Curry pack two bags for her. She gave her a year's pay and a glowing letter of recommendation.

"Oh, Mrs. Asbury. This is terrible. You are breaking my heart."

"Everything must end, Curry. You know that."

"But what are you going to *do*? How are you going to *cope*?"

"I am going away where I can be alone. Where I can think. The funeral put full stop to my life. I am going to try to put it together again. I need to be alone." Julia's long face was such a tragic mask that it made Curry weep, then run out of the room.

Julia knew people had to work hard for money. God knows her father had slaved away all his life. He was what would be considered "well off" by Reagan Republicans. He might have about five million salted away. But she was trying to earn about a billion two, give or take a half billion, all in one year and tax-free, so it figured that she was going to have to sweat for it. It would be hard, giving up the houses, the servants, the planes, and all the other perks she had once thought would be all she would ever want.

But there had been a smooth side and a rough side. Whatever she got, she had had to take Henry along with all the good things. Now Henry was gone and she had to bite the bullet. Pino was a miracle in the sack but he lacked Henry's substance. Maybe there was no complete answer. Let her take the billion two and let the other guy knock himself out.

After she had written the letter to her brother, telling him to close and sell the houses in Gstaad and Fiji, and the apartments, the real property on which they stood, the planes, yachts, boats and automobiles, and to deposit the proceeds from the sales in her numbered Geneva account, after she had issued instructions to Miss MacHanic to pay such staff as herself and Arpad Steiner a year's salary, with four months of wages for the rest of the people on staffs of her other houses, she ordered the small helicopter to take her to Kennedy.

At Kennedy, she boarded a TAP plane for Lisbon and was gone.

MISS BLUE, executive secretary to Edward S. Price, telephoned Miss Silverschein, secretary to Francis A. O'Connell, Jr., legal counsel for Barkers Hill Enterprises and managing partner of the law firm of O'Connell, Heller & Melvin.

"I think you'd better tell him to jump on a subway and get up here," Miss Blue said.

"But you always send a car."

"Those days are over for Mr. O'Connell."

"When did that happen?"

"Like ten minutes ago."

"But he's booked solid all day. How about Tuesday?"

"Next Tuesday, from where I sit, he could be looking for three or four new clients."

"My God!"

"Just get him here." Miss Blue disconnected.

Miss Silverschein neatly typed a message for Mr. O'Connell, then tried not to run into his office with it. Mr. O'Connell was with a committee of clients. He was explaining some of the finer points of extreme looting under real estate law as Miss Silverschein slipped the note under his gaze. The note said, *"Suggest you explain that your mother is dying. Barkers Hill is in crisis. Price demands to see you NOW."*

Mr. O'Connell read the note, acknowledged Miss Silverschein with a nod, and said to the client-committee. "I have had tragic news, gentlemen. You must excuse me. I must leave this office at once." As he came to the last sentence he began to move toward the door. He was out before they could react. Barkers Hill Enterprises and its many companies represented 31 percent of the total billing of O'Connell, Heller & Melvin. If Edward S. Price was upset, Francis O'Connell was *very* upset.

"What happened?" he asked Miss Silverschein, determined not to panic.

"Miss Blue said you'd better jump on a subway and get up there. She was grimmer than death."

"That's all? No indication of what's happening? I mean, confidentially, between the two of you."

Miss Silverschein swallowed. "Her words were, when I said you'd be free next Tuesday: 'He could be looking for three or four new clients by next Tuesday.'"

"My God! Tell Heller and Melvin." He slammed a Panama hat on his head and dashed for the elevator bank. He caught a cab in Broad Street, settled into it, and began to rationalize that it could all be hyperbole. Ed Price could have just gotten up on the wrong side of the bed, although Price had never behaved like this before.

He entered Barkers Hill Enterprises through its front door on the executive ninety-second floor. For almost nine years, whenever Price had wanted to talk to him he had sent a car for him and O'Connell had entered the Price inner office from the private elevator. Today, the receptionist kept him waiting for twenty-seven minutes after his name had been announced. He was sweating.

"A pity that the air-conditioning had to break down," the receptionist said. "In August."

At last Miss Blue came out for him. "You're looking well, Mr. O'Connell," she said.

"Am I? Uh—Miss Blue—what has happened? I mean, what's going on?"

"Going on?" Her blank eyes stared at him and widened.

Dumbly he followed her to Price's office.

It struck him as odd that Miss Blue's room and Price's office were entirely air-conditioned; quite cool and comfortable. Price's office had seemed extraordinarily long when he had entered from the side, when he had arrived by elevator. Now, facing its full length, Price seemed to be a distant figure, far away. A distant, far, forbidding, and entirely hostile figure.

"Hi, Ed," he said bravely.

Price stared at him relentlessly, looking at him as if he were George Bush and O'Connell were a liberal. "Sit down," Price said.

"Ed, I must confess I'm at a bit of a loss—"

"All I want from you are the complete files of all records and correspondence between the four entities at Barkers Hill which your firm represents—the two insurance companies, the Peagrin and Freen interests, and all the fast-food chains."

"Complete files?"

"And a letter of withdrawal signed by all three principal partners of your firm."

"But what is the *reason* for this?"

"In addition, you will be told tomorrow by Wambly Keifetz that the Bahama Beaver Bonnet Company is withdrawing as clients of your firm."

"Bahama Bea—my God, Ed! What is going on here? What went wrong? How have we offended you? Good God, man— with Bahama Beaver Bonnet that represents over 57 percent of our business! You just can't do this!"

"I'm not finished. I'm going to wipe you out."

"But—*why*?"

"You might better ask your partner, Melvin, that question."

"Allan? Allan Melvin?"

"That is all, O'Connell. You may go now. You will never have any idea what your firm has cost me."

O'Connell felt ill. He had to find someplace to lie down. He got up unsteadily and stumbled to the door of the office and let himself out, into Miss Blue's room. They would have to let over a hundred lawyers go.

"You don't look at all well, Mr. O'Connell," Miss Blue said. "Please lie down here for a moment." She led him to a sofa. O'Connell stretched out on his back and closed his eyes. He wasn't a young man and he had just been brutalized. Miss Blue brought him a glass of brandy. He knocked it back, then got to his feet. "I must go," he said. "May I ask you to call Mr. Melvin and Mr. Heller at my office and tell them to wait for me—not, under any circumstances, to leave?"

"I'll do that, Mr. O'Connell."

He jammed his Panama on his head and tottered toward the elevators.

ALLAN had reached Pino after eight o'clock the night Julia had left for Lisbon. He had called him at the house in Bensonhurst where Pino was a paying guest, where Julia had told him to call; a pay phone. He had been trying to reach Pino since six o'clock, calling every half-hour and getting a different voice every time. At last a voice acknowledged that Pino had come in. It took a while to get him downstairs from the second floor.

"This is Julia's brother."

"Oh. Yeah. How are you?"

"It's better not to talk on the phone. Can we meet?"

"When?"

"Tonight."

"Tonight? Where?"

"I think it would be best if you came to my apartment in New York."

"Jesus!"

"It's important."

"Where are you?"

"The Olympic Towers." He gave Pino the address. "Just tell the doorman Mr. Melvin is expecting you."

"I can be there in about an hour." When Pino hung up he called Julia at Bent Island but there was no answer. He tried the New York apartment but there was no answer. She had about ten flunkies wherever she went, someone should have answered the phone. He wondered what the hell was going on.

He shaved and changed his shirt. He removed his teeth and dipped them in a glass of cold water out of personal daintiness. He held the teeth before him at an arm's length, admiring their beauty. They were the talisman of his life. Before the teeth, he had needed his father's influence to get work with the Prizzis as a package thief at Laguardia airport, clouting shipments of pharmaceuticals, jewelry, and securities as they came in from overseas. It was to supplement his income that he had taken the work as a preliminary fighter, boxing at armories around town, the work that had cost him his teeth. When he heard about Dr. Pincus of Beverly Hills, the movie stars' dentist, he had taken his life's savings and gone to California with a recommendation from his father to the boss of the Caccia family and his entire life had been changed. Everyone noticed him all of a sudden. When he smiled broads laid down, men got fatherly, and he got work in Charley Partanna's unit as an apprentice *vindicatore*. He made his bones. In two years he was a made man and he owed it all to these beautiful teeth.

Pino took a bus to Coney Island, then got on the BMT. At Forty-second Street in New York he changed to the Lexington Avenue line. Some black kids were giving the people a hard time at his end of the subway car. He put the fear on them and they got off at the next station.

Julia's brother had the kind of a pad Pino had seen in rich bachelor movies. It wasn't his idea of how to live but he was glad to see it confirmed in real life. He did not hold against the brother his silence at their last meeting. In fact he looked safer than Julia; Pino felt less wary around him than he ever had with Julia. The brother offered him a drink. He said he wouldn't say no to a little wine and the brother came up with a glass of Marsala that was better than any Marsala he had ever had, even at a Prizzi wedding.

"What can I do for you?" he asked the brother after he had admired the wine.

"Julia left the country this morning."

"No kiddin'? She didn't say nothing to me."

"The Prizzis want her."

"I know."

"She called me just before she left for the airport this morning. She said to tell you to meet her at the Hotel Lutetié in Lisbon."

"The Lutetié?"

"Yes."

"That takes bread."

The brother took an envelope out of his inside pocket. "She asked me to give you five thousand dollars to cover expenses."

"It can't cost any five thousand dollars."

"So if you don't like it there, it can get you home. But let me say what Julia said. If you stay here, the Prizzis are going to put you into the ground. The way they're going to see it, you let her get away, you didn't do the job on her when they told you to do it, you screwed up on hitting her father, and that you want some of the money they say my sister stole from them."

"Yeah."

"So—there's still time to get out on the night flight. If you're too late for Lisbon, you can go into Paris and change for Lisbon."

"Then what do I do? If the Prizzis want me, or me and Julia, they have ways to find us."

"Julia has it all taped. Fake passports, everything. They'll never catch up with you and, when the smoke clears and you and Julia settle down someplace, you're going to be a very rich man."

Pino's conception of riches was what he saw rich people do in the movies and television and whereas he thought that would be nice for a couple of weeks there didn't seem to be any action happening with those kinds of people. But the idea of getting on a slow boat to anywhere with Julia was different. That he knew about. He wanted as much of it as there was.

But, fooling around with Julia to one side, he knew the Prizzis didn't have much time for him because she had clipped them for a tremendous amount of what they valued over anything else. If he stayed around they would give it to him, he knew. He liked the reflected glory of being Prizzi button man in Brooklyn. He was really getting to know the business, working with Charley and The Plumber, but he could see it was a question of staying alive, so he made up his mind.

"Okay," he said. "I'll take the deal."

MR. O'CONNELL limped past Miss Silverschein into his private office. "Mr. O'Connell," his anxious secretary called after him, "are you all right?"

"Get Melvin and Heller in here," he said.

He stretched out on the couch and tried to think. He ran rulings, counsel, cases, and meetings with Barkers Hill people through his head. Nothing. Everything had been impeccable. The firm's relations with Barkers Hill and Ed Price, as well, had been smooth and cooperative. Melvin, Price had said. What could Melvin have to do with Barkers Hill or any of their companies? Melvin never went near them and neither did he ever go near the Bahama Beaver Bonnet Company or Wambly Keifetz, that was Frank Heller's concern just as all Barkers Hill was his concern.

Franklin Marx Heller and Allan John Melvin came into O'Connell's office together. Heller was a bulky man with white hair, black, mourning swatches under his eyes, and a testy disposition. "What the hell is happening, Francis?" he demanded.

"Ed Price wants us to resign from all Barkers Hill accounts plus everything at Bahama Beaver Bonnet."

Heller and Melvin stared at each other as if O'Connell had lost control of his rationality. "Bahama Beaver Bonnet," Heller said. "What the hell does Ed Price have to do with Bahama Beaver Bonnet?"

"He says Keifetz concurs. He says Keifetz wants us out."

"Nobody said anything to me! What's going on, fahcrissake?"

Allan found a comfortable chair. He had seen the light. He waited for the boom to be lowered.

O'Connell sat up and faced Melvin as if Heller hadn't spoken, as if Heller weren't in the room.

"Price explained nothing," he said. "He told me you would have the answer."

"It could be that you won't want to know the answer."

"Let me be the judge of that, please. If we lose those accounts we might just as well go out of business."

"You remember the Asbury kidnapping?"

"Please, Allan—answer the question."

"The Prizzi crime family organized the kidnapping. Ed Price's real name is Prizzi."

"Whaaaaat?"

"Jesus, it figures," Heller said. "I know Keifetz is connected. And Price is bigger than Keifetz."

"Ed *Price*? In a *crime* family?" O'Connell said, dazed. "He's on the board of the New York City Ballet!"

"Anyway, Frank, that's how it is," Allan said gently. "The Prizzis and Asbury were in cahoots on the kidnapping. They got the pension fund loot and Asbury was supposed to walk with the ransom money. But the Asburys double-crossed the Prizzis and short-sold the Asbury companies in the market, after milking them, when the Prizzis thought they were going to pick up healthy, profitable Asbury companies for ten cents on the dollar."

"How the hell do you know all this?" Heller roared.

"I thought you knew. Mrs. Asbury is my twin sister."

"Allan, fahcris*sake!*" O'Connell said with exasperation. "All that is just a lot of fussy details. The point is: how did *we* get involved? What is it that you know that has Ed Price so upset?"

"They want my sister. She disappeared. They want her to turn over all the money she made when she milked those companies. It's about money. About one billion, one hundred and twenty-five million dollars."

"So what can you do?" Heller asked.

"They think I can tell them where to find her."

"Can you?"

"Well, up to a point."

"What do you you mean?"

"I know that when she took off she went to Lisbon. But I don't know where she went after that and neither does anyone else because from Lisbon onward, she'll be traveling on forged passports."

"I have no choice, Al. I am going to have to report this to Ed Price."

"I'll tell him, Frank. We'll get the business back. This is just how they negotiate."

Allan went back to his office, dialed Price's number directly and told Miss Blue that Mr. Price had urgent need to see him at once. She asked him to hold but came back to him quickly.

"Can you be ready to be picked up in a half-hour, Mr. Melvin?"

"I'll be in front of the building."

He told Miss Silverschein to tell O'Connell that he would be going uptown to see Mr. Price in a few minutes. She told him Mr. O'Connell had gone home for the day. To calm himself, Allan read from Benét's *John Brown's Body* for ten minutes, then he put on a straw hat and rode down in the elevator to wait for Price's car.

It was a short enough meeting. Price opened it by saying, "Where is she?"

"I'm prepared to tell you where she went when you tell me you have reinstated the relationship with my firm."

"Consider it done."

"All I know is that her first stop was Lisbon."

"That's all I need to know."

"No. I'm afraid not, Mr. Price. Lisbon was a quick stopover and I don't know where she'll go after that."

"We'll find her."

"No you won't. She's a smart woman, traveling under two false passports."

Price smiled disgustingly. "Where do you think she got the two passports?"

"From her husband."

"Our people got them for him. We know the names, numbers, dates of fake issuance, fake entry stamps, and alleged country of origin of both passports. We'll have her, wherever she is, within forty-eight hours."

JULIA was waiting in the suite at the Hotel Lutetié for Pino to arrive from the Lisbon airport. They had a reserved reunion. They shook hands; no kissing. She led him off to the sitting room after the bellman had delivered his bags. They sat facing each other, talking in the Sicilian dialect in low tones.

"Did the Prizzis make any moves on you?" Julia asked.

"Nobody said nothing."

"Nobody called you? Nobody told you to come in?"

"No."

"That's pretty strange, isn't it?"

"Well, maybe."

"Maybe? They send you all the way to England to put the fear on me, to get me to turn over the money, but you don't do it for them. And they didn't even want to know why? What are they suppose to do?"

"I see what you mean. Well—maybe Charley stepped in for me."

"Well, anyhow, we're outta sight now. They can't touch us."

"Well—"

"I got you a new passport in a new name. Tomorrow we start running to where they'll never find us."

"They are very tricky."

"Yeah? So am I. I have this all set up. They'll never find us, Pino. Come on. We're gonna get you some decent clothes."

"Decent clothes? What's wrong with these? These come indirectly from Johnny Carson's manufacturer."

"You look like an overdressed jockey."

They rode into town in a taxi. Julia had him completely outfitted. They had an elegant lunch at the Aviz with a bottle of Portuguese champagne, then they went to the hotel, undressed, climbed into the large bed and went to work.

"That was like it never happened to me before," Pino said. "I always liked to do it but now—well—I never had it so good."

"I was thinking the same thing," Julia said dreamily. "All my life, until I met you, I was pretty sure I had a weak sex drive."

"If it was any stronger I'd be like unconscious."

Julia was thinking that she actually didn't need to have him zotzed before she went to see Dr. Mitgang in Buenos Aires. He was an easy kind of a man. She hadn't thought of it before but she was going to need company. She would have her money but she would have to be in a strange country for two or three years, until the whole thing had blown over, before she could go to Rome and Paris and take up her real life again with a new face and a new name. It would be convenient to have Pino around. She would have his face changed, although she couldn't imagine what an expert like Dr. Mitgang could do about Pino's wonderful teeth. Even if, somehow, you took his whole face away, anyone would be able to make him instantly by those gorgeous teeth. She sighed contentedly.

"Come on," she said. "Let's fool around some more."

29

CORRADO PRIZZI had put the problem of overtaking Julia into Eduardo's capable hands. He had an international organization and the best information, so Eduardo took charge. He knew Julia had gone to Lisbon using, probably, her true passport but, just to be sure, Eduardo made a note to check outgoing flights to Lisbon that might be carrying a passenger using one of the two names on the false passports. His people in Lisbon were lawyers who hired private investigators who had close business friends within the Portuguese police and the Immigration Service. They were able to check passport documentation from all Lisbon hotels for the three previous days. They had no trouble tracing Julia to the Lutetié Hotel. She had checked out so they went to emigration files with the names and numbers of French and Italian passports that had been issued to the names of Denise Grellou and Eugenia Tylt. The passenger, Grellou, had left for Athens aboard Olympia Airlines Flight #271 the previous day.

The lawyers notified Edward S. Price, who telephoned Vincent Prizzi, who left his office, went to a phone booth on Bedford Avenue, and called a number in New Jersey. The New Jersey respondent called a number in Palermo, gave the Grellou name and passport number, and issued instructions.

Five hours later two men knocked on Miss Grellou's door at a big hotel on Constitution Square in Athens. When Julia opened the door they pushed her back into the room and shut the door behind them. Pino, totally surprised, wearing only shorts, made a move for his gun which was in a shoulder harness hanging on a chair beside the bed. The shorter visitor shot him through the head with a silenced automatic weapon, popping his beautiful teeth out of his mouth. They rolled across the floor, looking like a bodiless predator seeking food but, in truth, it was as if they were Pino's soul leaving his body;

his essence, his everything, but instead of rising to heaven or falling into hell they were, as Pino's meaning was, entirely average, so they stayed on the middle ground. They were the last thing Pino saw in his life.

"Jesus, he had fake teeth," Julia said, staring at the pink and super-white upper and lower chompers smiling up from the carpet. The most memorable part of Pino was smiling up at her, Pino's wonderful smile but without Pino.

She turned with a glazed look to the man who had killed him. For the first time in her memory, fear became a factor to be considered. It chewed up her stomach. It chilled her heart. The Prizzis had set up Henry's kidnapping so they could make a big score. They had allowed seventy-five million dollars, the ransom money, to go to Henry and to her. Instead, she had taken out about a billion two, the difference between the two figures being, to the Prizzis, their money. After they got it back, they would be obliged to punish her just the way they had punished Pino for doing absolutely nothing to them.

"He's dead," she said dully, staring down at Pino's teeth.

"Get dressed," the big man said in a western Sicilian dialect, with a voice that was as cold as chains falling down stone steps. "You're goin' home."

"Home?"

"You know what I mean, whatever I mean."

As they left the hotel room, the smaller man hung the

DO NOT DISTURB

sign on the outside of the door.

The two men flew with Julia as far as Rome where they turned her over to two *shtarkers* from Vincent's outfit. One was Mort Violente, a friend of her father's. His second man was Joey Cloacacino. Violente, who was the chief *intimidatore* of the Prizzi family, would have frightened Siegfried, El Cid, Perseus, Winkelreid, Winston Churchill, or Arnold Schwarzenegger so he nearly turned Julia to stone. With his ferocious moustache and his tiny, close-set agate eyes he looked like a warthog on the

attack. His work had been mainly in the American labor movement, persuading all those who resisted organization by the
Prizzis, and with Prizzi loan sharks to ensure against defaults
or shortages of repayment. He was there to frighten the people.
Joey did the wet work.

As Julia walked between the two men across the Rome airport toward the departure gate, she thought of her *palazzo,* her
classic Rolls which were just sitting idly in Rome. She thought
of Arpad Steiner and Laszlo Lowenstein and of her masseuse.
She sighed heavily.

"Keep your mout' shut, you unnerstan'? You just walk wit' us
into the plane, then you sit between us onna plane, an' you don't
say one fuckin' word. You unnastan'?" Julia nodded vigorously.

As the Alitalia flight left the Rome airport, the chambermaid
in the Athens hotel decided to go into the suite Julia and Pino
had occupied because she had a very promising date that night
and she needed time to get ready. The first thing she saw as
she entered the room was Pino's teeth. The second thing she
saw was Pino's body. She screamed as if the whole thing were
happening on a sound stage in Hollywood and the director had
given her the cue.

The Athens police put out an all-points through Interpol for
Denise Grellou but Julia was back to using her own passport.
French police were alerted. The news media of Europe ran the
story. The American press gave it a few sticks. Pino had passed
away unnoticed because he had been using one of Henry
Asbury's forged passports.

They rode in Tourist. Julia had never been in Tourist but the
novelty soon wore off. They were in the center seats. She was
between the two men. It was going to be a long flight.

After two hours of the flight, Julia had to pee. She cleared her
throat in the direction of Violente. "Shaddap!" he cautioned her.

"I gotta go to the little girls' room."

"So go. Joey goes wit' you, outside the door. Keep your
mout' shut."

*   *   *

She sat staring at the same dumb movie airlines always seemed
to be showing and she thought of how she had schemed and
maneuvered to get away from President Street, Brooklyn, her
father and, most of all, the knowledge of what her father did
for a living. She had never felt any moral objection to his killing or maiming people for a living. That was a part of everything she ever knew about. Her mother would say, "Don't
knock it. Somebody has to do it and it not only got us our
own house and the car but it sent you and the boy through
college, which is something nobody on either side of this family never even thought about doing."

When Julia graduated, when she had her degree, her languages, and she knew which fork to use with what, she was
still a hoodlum's daughter and she knew that wouldn't get her
anywhere she wanted to go. She went home less and less. She
rented an apartment in New York. She got her first job as a
secretary at the Executives' League. She told herself that if she
could only get a safe amount of money she would be protected
from everything her father was, so she married Henry Asbury
which, ignoring the unease that brought her, had widened the
distance between her and her father and President Street and
Brooklyn with buffers of sets of servants on three continents,
houses, grand friends, and everything else she thought she
wanted, yet here she was right back where she started, sitting
between two professional ruffians, two men exactly the same
as her father, *shtarkers*. She had thought she had traveled great
distances, but basically—all the garbage about safe money to
one side—she was right back on President Street. Her problem,
she decided, was that she had never learned how to live or
what was worthy of living for. She had to find out what that
was or she would be doomed to repeating her life over and
over, all because she had convinced herself that the answer to
the whole thing was money. It is possible, she thought, that I
could have been wrong about that. There could be other worth-
while things out there.

She had rolled up the billion two in eleven banks around the
world and she knew that if she were going to stay alive, which

was the first thing she had to do if she were going to find out how to live and what to live for, that she had to keep control of that money somehow because, as soon as the Prizzis had the money or knew how to get it away from her, they would put her in the ground. She had to work out a plan to stall them for thirty or forty years. After that, if they got the money, they would either let her live or they would put her away but she would have gained thirty or forty years in the kind of comfort she had to have. Why couldn't she have been born into the British royal family?

When they had passed through Customs at Kennedy, Violente said, "Yah done good."

"What happens now?"

"Did I tell you to ask questions? We're goin' to Don Corrado's when we find out he wants to see us. Inna meantime we go inta Le Beau Rivage in Canarsie-on-the-Belt."

A car met them at the airport. It was driven by a small man who could hardly see over the top of the steering wheel. Julia sat in the back seat between the two men. They rode into Brooklyn in silence. It was just that she couldn't get used to Violente. She didn't have any idea what he did to people who crossed him but she knew it was something terrible and loathsome.

❸⓪

WHEN the NEW YORK CRIME FAMILY ASSAULTS ASBURY WIDOW story broke in the *New York Tribune* there was a tremendous reaction from the public, the police, the governor, citizens' committees, the FBI, the Senate, and the White House. The First Lady was utterly, shakingly outraged. She ragged the

President night and day to hound every *mafioso* on the East Coast until they gave up the the murderers of Julia Asbury's husband and her baby. At last, desperate to escape her wrath, Goodie Noon turned the entire matter over to the White House Council on Competitiveness, headed by the Vice President. "That will shake them up," he told his wife. "It has put the fear into every other American so why not a bunch of immigrant thugs?"

Public interest reached such a height that when the regular *Tribune* man on the Kennedy Airport beat called in to report that he had spotted Julia Asbury coming off the Alitalia flight from Rome that morning with two men, one of whom was a Prizzi bone-breaker, Mort Violente, but that they had driven away before he could talk to them, Markel called Counihan into his office.

"Maybe we're gonna stay lucky," he said. "The Asbury story is starting up all over again. The wife just flew in from Rome."

"Rome? How did she get to Rome? I thought she was still on her island. Why Rome?"

"Look what we've got right under our nose. Our man, McCarry, makes Violente as a *shtarker* for the Prizzis. Mrs. Asbury was a Melvini before she got married. Al Melvini is an undercapo with the Prizzi family. Somebody just tried to ace him with a bottle of chloroform. Therefore, the Prizzis have to be the New York crime family who beat up Julia Asbury and cost her the baby."

"Jesus, you're right. It figures."

"You never made contact with the brother," Markel said. "So go get him."

This time Nuala didn't call Melvin at his office. She went to his apartment building at six in the evening, forty-five minutes after she left Markel. By pushing her chest at the doorman and flashing an extremely lewd conspirational smile she got herself admitted to the Melvin apartment by saying that she was a surprise birthday present for Mr. Melvin. Wondering where he had taken the wrong turning, the doorman permitted her to go up.

Austerlitz, Allan's man, answered the door. "Mr. Melvin expects me," she said. She looked so sensational that Austerlitz didn't doubt for a minute that Mr. Melvin expected her. He settled her in the library, then went to find the master of the house.

"A woman?" Allan said blankly.

"A very handsome woman, sir, if I may say so. She said you were expecting her."

Allan still remembered the "very handsome woman" from his sister's hospital room in London. More than that he remembered the headlines that "very handsome woman" had caused.

"I'll see her, Fred," he said glumly.

When he entered the library he saw it was the same woman he had hoped it would be and he had the sensation of several Carpathian athletes performing on a trampoline in his stomach. Why had she hit him like this? He had been impressed in a kindly way when he had seen her for that brief moment in London. That was the first impression so, by all rating systems of romantic/sexual jolting, that *first* meeting should have produced the tumultuous sensation he was now feeling. It made no sense. He was a lawyer. He needed things to seem logical. Maybe it had been because he had been so overprotective of his sister that he hadn't really been seeing this magnificent female thing clearly. That must be it.

"Ah, Miss Counihan."

Miss Counihan was having second thoughts on a dual track. On the inside track, running hard and panting with exhaustion, was Lieutenant Harvey Zendt, NYPD Homicide, her constant companion of more than five years. She imagined she could smell the wild-making Truefitt and Hill aftershave lotion. But as she looked across the room at Melvin, the effect of the scent began to fade. It came on her like a clap of thunder that the extraordinary effect this man was having on her hadn't existed at all when she had met him with his sister in London because she had been so absorbed at the chance of a big story from the Asbury widow that she had hardly noticed him. That must be it. That was the only explanation.

"I had to talk to you, Mr. Melvin," she said. "If everything your sister told me should come true, then she could be in bad trouble."

"Like what?"

"Like some New York crime family thinks she walked with a lot of their money."

"No danger. She's removed herself effectively from the scene."

"She's back, Mr. Melvin. Our man at the airport spotted her going through with two men."

"Back? How can that be? When?"

"This morning on the Alitalia flight from Rome. They were out and gone before he could talk to them."

"Rome?"

"And the two men were very rough-looking characters."

"I know nothing about this."

"One of the men with Mrs. Asbury was known to our man at the airport. His name is Violente. He is heavy muscle for the Prizzi family."

"This is very disturbing, Miss Counihan." He couldn't keep his mind on Julia's peril. He kept staring at Counihan's magnificent legs. What was going on here in both his trousers and his head?

"Mrs. Asbury's maiden name was Melvini according to our files. Also, according to the NYPD, a Prizzi muscler is called Al Melvini, which was Mrs. Asbury's maiden name."

"Well—as a matter of fact—he is our father."

"So—putting together Violente with your father and with Mrs. Asbury we come to the very distinct possibility that the crime family who threatened, then savaged Mrs. Asbury, costing her her baby, might well have been the Prizzi family."

"This is terrible. Julia didn't intend to come back. Not so soon, anyway," he added hurriedly. "Will you have a drink?"

"Why not?"

He rang a small bell. Austerlitz appeared as if he had been concealed in a puff of smoke a stage magician had flung at the doorway. "You rang, sir."

"A bottle of that Pommery '61, Fred."

"At once, sir."

The wine arrived, was opened, and was poured.

"I don't drink champagne a lot," Nuala said, "but this is the best stuff I ever tasted."

"Can we talk off the record?"

"Yes. But not indefinitely."

"If my sister is in New York I have to help her. How can I find her?"

"Your father."

"What?"

"Your father knows how to find out where she is. He's on the inside and—he's well connected."

"Maybe you're right." He reached for a telephone. "Off the record?"

"Well, at least until after the call."

While Allan dialed, she studied his face, his build, his mouth, his earlobes, and the long, well-arranged fly of his trousers. She had never seen anything like any of it. There had to be a limit on this or she would go out of control and begin to tear at his clothing.

"Pop? Al. Are you feeling any better?" He spoke in the Sicilian of Sciacca. Why take chances?

"My health is okay," The Plumber said into the phone, which was in the kitchen of the house on President Street because that was where he spent most of his time, cooking, throwing playing cards into a hat, watching television, or making wine.

"Health is what counts, Pop."

"Dignity counts for something, too, Al. Believe me, it cost me something when I found out that one of our own people had gone to a drugstore to move a contract on me."

"It was probably some amateur trying to make his bones."

"Lissen, it's not something I wanna talk about. What can I do for you?"

"Pop, I need you to find out something. Not only for me but for both of us and for Julia."

"What happened?"

"Mort Violente brought Julia in from Rome this morning."

"No!"

"Yes. The Prizzis have her somewhere and I don't know what they are going to do to her."

"Infamità!"

"I know, Pop, but as you know better than anybody, *omertà* is a pack of bullshit to keep outsiders from getting wrong ideas. The Prizzis, your own family, tried to knock you off. Now they snatch your daughter in someplace like Rome and bring her back here to do what only God knows with her."

The Plumber poured a large glass of elderberry wine and gulped half of it down. "Julia is my daughter. Nobody is gonna lay a glove on my daughter."

"Jesus, Pop, I hope so."

"I'll call you back at the office tumorra." He slammed the phone on the hook, finished the rest of the wine, then telephoned Angelo Partanna.

Allan looked across at Nuala with soft lights coming out of his eyes. Lights like distant fireflies in an Ingmar Bergman movie or like the beginnings of the aurora borealis. He pulled himself together. He wasn't going to rush this thing. If he showed her how hooked he was, she could go off him.

"He is shocked and outraged," he told Counihan. "He's going to call me at the office tomorrow."

"And?"

"As soon as they let my sister go, you can have the story."

"Terrific."

"How—how about we finish this bottle of wine, then go out to an elegant dinner."

"Hey! That would be very nice. I just have to make a call."

She called Lieutenant Zendt at the apartment they shared. She told him she wouldn't be home for dinner. She knew it was a major decision.

THE PLUMBER knew all about *omertà*. He knew that the solemn rules of The Honored Society applied only to underlings, outsiders, victims, and witnesses. It was a public relations thing that helped the news media. Respect had to be paid to the police beyond mere money payoffs. They had to be made to look good so the bosses fed them spectacular collars of their own people so everything would come out right in the newspapers and the cops would look efficient. As far as making war on the women in the families, when had they been safe? If they stood in the way, most important if they were costing money, they were hit or beaten up. Look at Maerose Prizzi, Vincent's daughter, who her father thought had embarrassed him when she went off with another guy while she was engaged to Charley Partanna. Vincent had *exiled* her! He had forbidden anyone to *talk* to her for the rest of her life! Corrado Prizzi kept up a front about how much he believed in *omertà*, but over the years, he had been its worst offender.

What The Plumber had to do, he realized, was to gain the sympathy of Angelo Partanna, a cunning man and himself a proud father, then to have Angelo and himself explain the whole thing to Charley because Charley not only respected his father but he wasn't very bright, which was to say, The Plumber thought, not very much brighter than himself.

He got into his battered 1978 Buick and drove out to Angelo's house in Bensonhurst. Angelo lived on a nice street, Eighty-first Street, with lots of shade trees in front and with a backyard full of fig trees. The house was near enough to the Italian bakeries, the street vendors, and the Jewish delis to sustain the good life. It was almost half past seven when he got there.

Angelo was surprised to see him, but he was glad to see him. They sat in the living room, which was still just the way she left it when his wife died fourteen years before.

"You look great, Al," was all he would say about the disgrace of the chloroform.

"I'm okay, Angelo. Except that somebody sent Mort Violente all the way to Rome to bring back my only daughter, the child of my heart."

"I heard about it. She robbed us of over a billion dollars."

"Who wouldn't if they had a clear shot at it?"

"You're right."

"Now—I'm a made man for almost thirty-five years but I'm not gonna pull no shit about *omertà* or nothing like that. Also, I know the family has ways of getting back the billion. But I'm a father and you're a father. You know what is going on in my heart when I think of what they could be doing to my little girl. So I am asking you to talk for me with Don Corrado because it wouldn't look right if I went to him directly."

"Well—"

"Or, if you don't think that's the way to go, then talk to Charley about this being his department—I mean, I been workin' for Charley for a lotta years—and him and me can then go to the don as a problem inside the organization and then the don can let Julia go, with us being the ones who have to get her to give back the money."

"Well, the don would naturally turn her over to Charley anyways and because I'm a father and I feel for you, I'm gonna talk to Charley about setting this up."

"That's all I want, Angelo."

"If you're so sure that *omertà* is a buncha bullshit with the don, how come he put out the contract on you? You hadda go before they could do the work on your daughter or it would be an *infamità*."

"He put out the contract because it had to be seen that he had done something. It was all a smoke screen because Julia had him stopped cold. He never could lay a finger on Julia until she told him how he could get at the money she robbed from him. *Omertà* had nothing to do with it—as usual."

"I'm gonna have dinner at Charley's tonight. I'll call you later."

CHARLEY PARTANNA lived in an apartment with a terrace in Brighton Beach, a neighborhood on Coney Island away from the amusement parks but near the shopping on the Manhattan Beach side. The neighborhood had suddenly become so Russian that he had been shocked into patronizing a take-out blini joint.

He was feeling pretty good. The fever, the chills, the conjunctivitis, the cough, and the headaches of the measles were gone. Better yet, he hadn't infected anybody because he hadn't seen anybody except Pop and Maerose and they were all right. Better still, his appetite had returned, so he had invited his father over for a completely blini-free dinner.

Charley was a good cook, maybe not as good as he rated himself but he tried to understand flavors and textures while he blended them and he was critical of other people's cooking if it seemed to take flavors and textures for granted. Charley didn't strive for artistically arranged presentations of food. He believed instinctively that if emphasis was placed on appealing to the eye something had to be missing in the flavor and texture department. As it happened, he was also a demanding housekeeper because he had loved his mother and he had admired all the things she did around the house so he tried his best to do as well in his own life. He washed his own window curtains twice a year, made his bed neatly as soon as he got up each morning, mothproofed closets, vacuumed, scrubbed floors vigorously, was horrified and outraged when he found a cockroach, did his own shopping, read many magazines, particularly women's service magazines for the tips they contained, and only brought new women to the apartment when he was in love with them, which was most of the time.

Charley was the most woman-susceptible man since Henry VIII or John F. Kennedy. He had fallen in love 1,434 times in his life, each time violently, passionately, and, at the time, forever. He believed in the ideal of womanhood and all the mating practices that went with it. Officially, he was still engaged to marry Maerose Prizzi, but since her banishment from Brooklyn Charley saw her only under unusual circumstances such as when he had fallen out of love or was in between falling in and out of love with many more than several women. Charley was not a womanizer. He did not merely collect scalps the way many other young men of his experience had attempted to do. Charley had to be in love if he as much as invited a woman to dinner or to the movies for the second time. His behavior was impeccably considerate to all women, even to those women with whom there was no possibility of his falling in love.

He was in a wistful stage. A passionate affair with a young, pretty manicurist named Gertrude Ganz, whom he had met in a chance encounter in a Brownsville barbershop five weeks before, was on the rocks. Dining out ten days before, he had discovered that despite her calling, she had dirty fingernails, so any feelings he had had for her vanished with the speed of a fleeing cavalryman.

Being womanless was a condition that left him purposeless and vulnerable. Something had to give. He devoured women's magazine fiction in search of a substitute, for some romantic escape that would fill the void. Sometimes that worked. Most of the times it did not. So he cooked. When his heart was alone he found it a mate among his pots and pans and in his larder. When he was especially distraught, footless and bereft because he was loveless, he invited his father to dinner because his father, more than anyone else, appreciated his cooking.

It was summer so he had set up an awning out on the terrace and had placed a big, standing fan to blow on them but not on the food. Because his father liked Piedmontese wines, he had chilled a bottle of slightly sparkling freisa to drink before they sat down to eat.

When they did decide to eat, after Pop had established what a good son he thought Charley was, after gossip about out-of-town hits and scams, they settled at the table and Pop went into ecstasies as he always did when he ate Charley's food because he said it was, flavor for flavor, the same food his late, lamented wife had cooked for him for over thirty years.

They started with a couple of bowls of *le fette* (because his father liked Tuscan food better than any other food, even Sicilian) which was a pretty amazing thing to Charley but, he figured, his father was an old man so he liked simple, honest food, but in fact it was because his wife had been a Tuscan woman originally who had been moved to Agrigento when her father had had an opportunity arise with the local Mafia there. She cooked both Tuscan and Sicilian and so did Charley.

Le fette was red cabbage soup with slabs of toasted black bread that was flavored with garlic. Then his father's favorite pasta, *strozapreti*, dumplings made with ricotta and Parmesan cheese, beets, spinach, and egg and served with gravy covered with grated Parmesan cheese. Up to that point in the meal he had poured Pop some Bianca Vergine della Val d'Arbia. It was light and delicate and hard to get but he had had the family's food courier bring him in a few bottles in his personal baggage because his father liked it. His father didn't like fish, a funny kind of a lapse for a Sicilian born so near the ocean, so Charley had made *polpettone alla Florentia,* a massive pile of meatballs from lean veal, some lean and some fat cured ham, mixed and rolled in flour, then cooked in butter and served in a puree made from cooked onions, carrots, and celery, herbs and spices.

With the meatballs he switched the wine to Brunello di Montalcino, a wine that was so big that it had been aged in the cask for six years before bottling, which gave it staying power, then it stayed in the bottle for two years before being shipped and, because a restaurant owner Charley knew had said it shouldn't be drunk for at least ten years after that, Charley had had him put some aside and hold it for him. It cost, but it was for Pop.

His father was a light eater, so Charley decided on some hearts of artichokes, cooked with mushrooms and cauliflower in a cheese cream sauce that punctuated the meatballs. When

Charley had chosen the menu he couldn't resist adding some of Pop's favorite, a specialty of Mama's from Agrigento, *fungi Ncartati*, mushroom caps grilled with bread crumbs, grated pecorino, minced anchovies, garlic, oil, lemon juice and parsley, so he canceled the baked eggplant. After dinner they had some raisin cookies made from chestnut flour with the coffee. An elaborate dessert would be too heavy for Pop. A glass of Occhio della Pernice, from the Val di Pesa for his sweet tooth, rounded out the meal.

Pop really enjoyed it. That gave Charley great pleasure.

"You sure watched your mama cook, Charley. If I woulda closed my eyes, I would think she was back, makin' those wonderful things from her heart."

"You gotta have a good meal once in a while, Pop."

"It must feel good, after almost two weeks inna hospital to know you're goin' back to work on Monday."

"Yeah? Work? What came up?"

"Not that kinda work. Not yet anyhow. It's the Asbury woman. She stole about a billion two from us."

"So? What am I here for?"

"It's no use doin' the job on her until she says where she stashed the money."

"Ah."

"So first you put the fear on her. Then you find out where the money is. Then you do the number on her."

"Whatever you say, Pop."

"There is one problem. She is the daughter of The Plumber—in your *regime*. He came to me. He appealed to me as a father. He said he was only askin' for no rough stuff on his daughter. Like he wanted to know if he could go with you when you talked to the daughter to help you talk her into saying where the money is. What can we lose? She is the daughter so, when the father asks her, she will feel it is her duty to tell him."

"But when she tells where the money is, then I blow her away?"

"Of course. She stole from us."

"Pop, excuse me, but how can I do that to the daughter with the father right there? It wouldn't be right."

"You got a point. Okay. Don't take The Plumber witchew."

THE FIRST edition of the *New York Herald* blew the lid off everything. The headline said

**MAFIA MUSCLE MEN BRING
JULIA ASBURY BACK FROM ROME**

Prizzi Crime Family Behind Threats and Beatings

The story on the front page, carrying over to pages four and five, was worse. It said that Julia Asbury was being held against her will somewhere in New York City. It demanded that the police and the FBI force the hoodlums to release her.

All other newspapers, the television, the radio, and the wire services picked up the *Herald* story instantly. The effect of the media assault almost put Corrado Prizzi in bed. He couldn't believe that they would dare to print what he was reading.

Vincent called at ten o'clock in the morning when the don should have been listening to his phonograph collection.

"Pop? Vincent. Captain Hanley, head of the Borough Squad, just called me."

"Yeah?"

"He said they were processing a warrant for my arrest and would be coming out here to pick me up as soon as it was ready. He figures it can only be postponed for, at the most, forty-eight hours."

"What kinda police protection is that?"

"He says the only way out is to have the Asbury woman show up in some public place like do a shot on *Good Morning America* or something so that everybody would know she was okay because she would say she was okay and say that the newspaper stories were a lotta crap because she came back on her own free will."

"I'll handle it," his father said.

The don canceled lunch and had a substantial second breakfast instead. He called a noon meeting at the sealed top floor of his house overlooking the giant's teeth of the Manhattan skyline. Angelo Partanna, Edward S. Price, Vincent, and Charley attended. Angelo and Eduardo were wearing suits and neckties. Charley wore a blue-and-white-striped shirt without a tie but with the sleeves rolled up. Vincent wore a leather jacket but his socks didn't match. Corrado Prizzi wore an old brown bathrobe over a striped flannel nightgown and long gray woolen stockings.

It was a baleful, harrowing, outraged meeting. Vincent's psoriasis, which he had had under fairly good control for ten days, went into plague proportions. He couldn't sit still. He itched everywhere, so he scratched everywhere until his father sent him from the room. "Go inna closet and scratch yourself," the don shouted. "When the whole house falls down on us maybe that will help your itch!" Edward S. Price smirked.

"I'll try some ointment," Vincent said, leaving the room.

The don passed around a box of Havana cigars that were imported for him by a friend in the CIA. He poured them coffee from a tall vacuum bottle and offered his guests cookies. Everyone remained grimly silent until Vincent returned to the table.

"It's much better," Vincent said, taking his seat.

"Angelo, take over 'til I can calm down," the don said.

"First things first," Angelo said smoothly. "Vincent has to tell Violente to give the Asbury woman to her brother, the lawyer, because she trusts the brother and he knows that he better go along. Then Charley puts the fear on her until she agrees to go on *Good Morning America*—like Captain Hanley said and like Vincent's lawyer absolutely urges—or *Donahue* or on *Oprah Winfrey*—and say the right things. Then Eduardo tells his people to set up the interview. They'll go for it because she's hot news."

"You can say that again," Corrado Prizzi said.

"How about *Geraldo*?" Vincent suggested, scratching himself violently between the shoulder blades. "His show really gets to the meat."

"*BASTA!*" the don said. "All right. That gets us off the hook with the cops and the FBI about how we are supposed to be holding her against her will, but after the television, what happens?"

"She comes here to talk."

"So what do we talk about?"

"We ask her where's the money?"

"And if she won't say?"

"Put a blowtorch on her feet," Vincent suggested.

"We burn her feet off and we'll all be thrown inna can!"

"Well, we can't zotz her," Angelo said, "at least not until we get the money."

"Even then it's gotta look like an accident," Vincent said. "And no car crash or a fall outta a window. I mean we'll have to give her a fatal infectious disease."

"That is for later!" the don said testily. "How do we get the money?"

"First we bring her in and talk to her. Charley puts the fear on her. Then we tell her that the original deal where she keeps the ransom money still stands. At least we can tell her that she can keep ten million of the seventy-five million ransom money." Angelo spread his hands wide. "I mean, that's reasonable."

"And if she don't take the deal?" the don asked.

"Then we offer her a chance to stay alive a little longer by paying us the interest on the billion two. How much would that come to, Eduardo?"

"I could average it off at about seven and a half percent. Say seventy million a year."

"So like in about eight or nine years we'd have our money," Charley said.

"No!" the don said. "Take *interest* on our own money she stole from us and she keeps all the rest? Never! She must pay all the money now and we get the money *and* the interest!"

"That's the whole point, Corrado. How do we get the money?" Angelo asked. "The computer hackers have only been able to track down two number accounts. First, we should raid those so at least we'll get something."

"Of course raid the accounts! It's our money! How much?"

"About twelve million in each account."

"Get it!"

"But how do we get the rest of the money?"

"We could threaten to report her to the IRS," Charley said.

"They would only try to confiscate the money if they could prove she had it," Eduardo said. "But you're right. We should show the woman that we can harass her until her life isn't worth living. For instance, I could get a Senate investigation going and a federal prosecution on charges that she had plotted and organized her husband's kidnapping and murder just so she could get that money."

"No Senate investigation, Eduardo," Angelo said. "They could get into like what happened to the pension funds of the Asbury companies and we don't want that."

"But the kidnapping of her own husband and the fact that he was offed—that's very good," Don Corrado said, nodding approvingly. "Whatta you think, Angelo?"

"We would have to give them some of our own people to take a fall with her if the charges are gonna hold up in court."

"So give them The Plumber!" the don said shrilly. "He snatched the husband. And Pino Tasca. He was with her in London when she robbed us. And Violente and Joey Cloacacino, who were with her in Rome and came back with her. She's The Plumber's daughter so we make it like she schemed with him and he got some of our soldiers to do the work! At the very least she'll know she's gonna face like ninety-nine years without the possibility of parole. At the most after we build an airtight case she'll know she's gonna face the chair. She'll crack. She'll give us the money then Charley can put her inna ground."

JULIA spent the night at Le Beau Rivage in Canarsie with Violente and Cloacacino in the adjoining room with the connecting door open and the telephone line ripped out of the wall. She slept well because she knew she was safe. The money was the only thing that interested the Prizzis and she knew she would be safe if she refused to tell them how to get at it. While she was having breakfast, brought in on a tray by Joey, there was a large commotion in the next room when Violente read the *New York Herald* story that carried a mug shot of him on the carryover page. "Look at this picture!" he yelled. "They made me look like some kinda *shtarker!*"

At eleven-thirty Violente went into Julia's room. "Charley Partanna is here," he said.

"Par*tanna?*"

"Listen to him and keep your mout' shut."

Violente left the room. Seconds later Charley came in through the open door. Julia was seated on the edge of the bed. He pulled up a chair, placed it directly opposite her, and sat down.

Jesus, he thought, how come nobody warned me? This is a classically beautiful wop broad, this is like she stepped out of a painting by some old-time Italian master. He had never seen such perfection: the hair was like Dolores Del Rio only more so, her nose was a ringer for Sophia Loren's, of which he had never seen equal, but the eyes! What mystery, what haunting unknown memories they hid! They glistened. They burned like anthracite. They made him think of the La Brea Tar Pits in L.A. which he had never seen but had read about. And what a chest! He estimated a B cup, but with nipples like thumbs. He tried to concentrate on the work he had been sent to do. He fixed her with an iron, terrorizing glance which grew into a stare, which grew into such a threat of a promise of pain and wracking grief that, for a moment, he was glad he could not see what he was beaming upon her.

"What's the matter?" she said.

"Whatta you mean?"

"Why are you making those faces at me?"

"Faces?" This had never happened to Charley in his life since he had developed the science of putting the fear on people.

"Aaaaah! *Now* I remember," Julia said, giggling. "You are putting the fear on me. My father used to tell me how your father made you practice blanking out your eyes and hardening all of the muscles in your face. Did you *really* do that in front of a mirror for hours every day when you were a kid?"

"Listen, this ain't no laughing matter. You're in bad trouble. Like whatta you think they sent me here for?"

"To put the fear on me."

"You got it wrong. They sent me to tell you that you are going on *Good Morning America*. They are gonna tape you this afternoon."

"What for?"

"To tell the whole world that you came back from Rome because you wanted to and that nobody is holding you against your will."

"My God, you people are the end."

"Please, understand me. Either you do the interview our way or I am gonna have to break both your legs in two places."

Julia liked this man. He had her father's no-nonsense get-to-the-point directness. And whereas he didn't have Pino Tasca's build, he had a baffled look about him that won her heart. Why make him unhappy? She would much rather make him happy.

"Okay," she said, "I'll do it." It was like the old ad, she thought, promise them anything but give them Arpège.

"Your brother is coming here in a little while to take you to the television," Charley said. "We already talked to him. He's gonna do right."

"Do right?"

"Lemme ask you something."

"What?"

"Would it be okay if I kissed you?" He couldn't believe he was saying it. Jesus, had he lost his mind? This woman had been the wife of an adviser to presidents.

"Kiss me?"

"Yeah. You know, just a little one."

She was mystified to discover that she liked the idea. "Okay," she said.

Charley got up slowly and sat down next to her on the bed. He didn't put his arms around her because he thought she might think he was planning to pull her over, down on the bed. He kissed her softly on the lips, then drew away. It was a sweet and tender kiss but it jolted both of them as if they were two elementary particles who had been racing toward each other from opposite directions until they had arrived at the speed of light inside the interaction halls of an accelerator/supercollider, propelled by rings of superconducting magnets, thousands of them, achieving energy hundreds of times greater than any that had ever been achieved, deepening human understanding of the nature of matter. Every boson, graviton, photon, and gluon of their mutual being reached out to the other's. Fresions containing every quark and every lepton of their shared meaning gave them insights into their major uncertainties.

"My God!" Julia said involuntarily.

"Yeah," Charley answered. "It was a beautiful moment."

He got up, turned his back on her, rearranged his clothing, and left the room. His quest had ended. He had found the perfect woman. He was in love.

Julia sat on the bed, dazed. What had happened? she asked her memory. She must have been hornier than she had thought. Everything had changed as suddenly as if she had been hit by a 9.5 on the Richter scale. She had to watch out. This could get serious. She wasn't about to fool around with a Prizzi *vindicatore*.

Twenty minutes passed before Violente brought the brother into the room.

"Are you all right, Julia?" Allan asked.

"I—I think so."

"You look so odd."

"It's been a rough three days, Al. What are you doing here?"

"You're going on *Good Morning America*. They will tape the interview this afternoon in New York."

"What kind of an idea is that?"

"I'll tell you in the cab. We've got to go."

When Julia got into the waiting taxi, Nuala Counihan was seated there, surprising Julia. "Miss Counihan!"

"Nuala is very much a part of all this," Allan said. "She gets an exclusive on what's going to happen today." Allan told the driver where to go. As the taxi left Le Beau Rivage, Violente and Joey Cloacacino were in a cab right behind them.

"Did Partanna talk to you?"

"Yes."

"Then you understand what you have to say in this television interview."

"I understand what they want me to say."

"And?"

"I'm not going to say it."

"Jesus, Julia."

"She's right, Al," Nuala said. "She has two locks on them. One the money and two, she's gotta keeping battering them to hold on to her edge. This is no different than war."

"I don't get it." He looked at Julia.

"Al, look. If I do what they want, that means I caved in and I give them more power over me. But if I blow their hair off they stay off-balance. If I shake them up they'll have respect for me. I'm only doing what Poppa taught us."

"What do you mean—shake them up?"

"I'm going on the show and tell the truth. Every detail. How two Sicilian *shtarkers* came into my hotel room in Athens and shot poor Pino. How they flew me to Rome and handed me over to the two Prizzi thugs and how they flew me to New York and locked me into Le Beau Rivage."

"Holy shit, Julia. This is a risky business!"

"It's the only way to go," Nuala Counihan said. "Drop me at Forty-third Street, then, as soon as the show is over, call me at the paper and tell me she said it the way she's gonna say it and we'll confirm the whole thing on the front page tomorrow morning, on the street before the show can go on the air. Now," she said to Julia, "who's Pino? And what happened?"

❸❺

CORRADO PRIZZI was enjoying his light breakfast: mainly a glass of olive oil to wash down a *cuddiruni* pizza and a baked *focaccia di fiori di sambuco*, layers of pastry dough filled with salami, lard, and fresh elder blossoms, while he watched the eight to eight-thirty segment of *Good Morning America*. The prerecorded interview with the Asbury woman was scheduled to go on the air at 8:20. He was dabbing at his thin lips with a damask napkin when the interview began. When it was over, four minutes, twenty seconds later, he had to call out for Amalia to help him to make it back to his bed.

Was it some trick? Had the Bocca family, his enemies, made a mocking videocassette and somehow slipped it into his television set so that when he turned it on, this impossibility came on the screen? he asked Amalia pathetically. He told her to pull all the window curtains to darken the room so that he could try to think what had been done to him, who could have done it, and why they had done it.

Vincent! His own son had claimed that some cop and some lawyer had urged that the only way to save Vincent from arrest and conviction and to nullify all those rotten newspaper stories was to put the Asbury woman on the television. And he had allowed it to happen! She had told thirty or forty million Americans, people who relied on his organization for their daily needs, that his soldiers had not only lifted her from a hotel room in Athens but had done the job on one of his own men, the boy with the expensive smile, Pino what's-his-name.

She had told everybody in the country that she had not only been held against her will but that, as soon as the program was over, on which she was intended by the Prizzi family to lie and say that everything was fine, that she had neither been kidnapped nor was her life threatened, she would be taken back to Le Beau Rivage in Brooklyn and locked in a room until she signed away all of her husband's estate.

What was the world coming to? Don Corrado moaned into his pillow. A thief who steals from a family, then tries to run away and hide? Of course she was brought back to face justice. What did anyone expect?

He called out weakly to Amalia to pour some Seidlitz powders into a glass of water. It would settle his stomach. As he was drinking the cure, Angelo Partanna burst into the room.

"INFAMITÀ!!!" he shouted.

"You agreed," the don said feebly. "You signed us on for the whole thing."

"It looked like the only way to go! Who could expect such a betrayal? What kind of a woman are we dealing with here?"

"Bring her to me. This morning. As soon as they bring her back from that television."

"Whatta you gonna do?"

"I gotta make a deal with her while I still got something left."

"There have to be other ways."

"Do you know one, for instance?"

"We should find out the weak link in the people who are closest to her. She has a lotta servants. Some of them been with her for years."

"So?"

"One might have a record. We could lean on them."

"Aaaah."

"Depending on what comes up, people like that could come in handy."

"Find out. Put good people on it."

*   *   *

Allan John Melvin watched helplessly as the two *scellerati* rode off with his sister in a taxicab, then decided he didn't have the spunk to go to the office. He found a telephone booth to complete his contract with Nuala Counihan at the *Herald*.

"Nuala? Al Melvin. She did it."

"Terrific! Did she change anything?"

"No, God help her."

"She's doing the right thing, Al."

"I wish I knew what you people have in mind."

"Don't worry about it. It makes good sense."

"How about lunch?"

"Swell."

"How about Lespinasse at one-fifteen?"

"What's that?"

"The restaurant at the St. Regis."

"Oh. Okay."

"See you."

All at once he did feel like hitting the office. He also felt like passing out quarters to bag ladies, or maybe taking tap-dancing lessons, because he realized that the air in New York had turned into champagne. He flagged down a taxi and went downtown.

Nuala was not only waiting when he got to the St. Regis but he had the distinct impression that she had changed her clothes.

"You look wonderful," he said, leading her into the restaurant. They had some nice, chilled white wine. He recommended that she start with a fricassee of wild mushrooms and artichoke hearts. "They spoon it out on chervil-flavored rice with a few squirts of truffled oil."

"I never ate stuff like that," Nuala said. "With my family it was meat and potatoes all the way."

"That comes next. A venison stew with brandy and pepper sauce."

"I'm game."

"Very funny." Allan ordered the food and a different colored wine, then he blurted, "Are you married?"

"Well—"

"Separated? Divorced?"

"I live with a guy."

"How long?"

"Five years."

"It's like being married."

"I know."

"Can we do anything about it?"

"Let's give it time."

"I could be hit by a cab. Anything could happen. What then?"

"I can't just roll a bomb into a room."

"As you said—we'll give it time."

"I could tell him tonight."

"Let me lay it out. I love you. I'm sure about that. I'm a mature lawyer who's been around the block a few times and I've been alone—by my own choice—for a year or so. I'm not running up a dark alley when I tell you a thing like that. We could build a life on it."

Her eyes filled with tears as she kept nodding. She wasn't sure whether she was weeping for Harvey, Al, or for herself.

JULIA ASBURY sat facing Corrado Prizzi on the top floor of the Victorian house in Brooklyn Heights. Angelo Partanna sat away from them, away from their unbroken line of vision directly at each other. Don Corrado was dressed in a black suit with a black tie. Julia wore a black and white pants suit and her diamond and sapphire choker.

There was no food in sight other than a plate of cookies. They sipped black coffee while Julia wondered how a man such as her husband, a man who had more *amour-propre* than the late Charles de Gaulle, could have gone to this little old man, hat in hand, sweating bullets, to sell him his soul in return for a few winning tickets. It must've been that Henry, as smart as he was, never had enough of anything; he was on the make for at least twice as much of life as anyone else could ever have, and this little old man had given him what Henry thought he wanted, at an interest rate that made compounded usury seem like philanthropy.

"How have you been?" the don asked.

"It's been a hard three weeks," Julia said.

"Everything is settling down now."

"More or less."

"Have you talked to your father?"

"I haven't had the chance."

"I met your brother. A nice man."

"He's a lovely man."

"You like the cookies?"

"Very much."

"They're homemade. My daughter makes them."

"She's my aunt."

"I know. What are we going to do about the money?"

"I'm going to keep it."

"We have two young boys on a retainer. They're computer hackers. They were able to break into the numbers for two of your banks. We transferred the money."

"Two isn't so bad. And it looks like they were stopped cold at two."

"That's right."

"So that's all you're gonna get."

"It looks like a standoff. If we hit you because you took our money we can't get our money because you won't be able to tell us if we hit you."

Julia shrugged.

"And if we like cut off your fingers and toes one at a time until you talked, it would get back to that newspaper snitch and she would lay it all out onna front page."

Julia shrugged again.

"My son Eduardo feels that if two big banks have the kind of secrecy that can be broken, then it figures that some of the others will."

"But it takes time."

"You musta thought about this. I know that you know it can't go on like this forever. How did you figure it?"

"First, I get the original seventy-five million ransom free and clear. The rest of the money goes into government bonds in my name and I keep the interest."

The old man nodded, not agreeing but not disagreeing.

"Then you put me in charge of building up Henry's companies again. While I was selling them in London, you were buying them so, if they can be put in the black, you'll make a hefty profit."

"In charge?"

"As Chairman and CEO of Asbury Industries, the control company. I know about the companies. Henry and I were pretty tight on that and my brother was Henry's lawyer on the inside, so I can't miss. However, if I do go wrong and I don't bring the profits up to par in eighteen months, you get the difference between the ransom money, the big money I transferred, and the money I made on the short-sales—less the money you tapped out of my two bank accounts—but if I do put the companies back on their feet, you give me twenty percent of the profits on everything the companies make after I get them back to where they were before the collapse started to happen eight or nine months ago."

"That can be done."

"And my accountants have the right to audit the books at any time."

"Well—"

"And tell your son, Eduardo—Edward S. Price, that is—that he is to give me his full cooperation and the resources of his advisers."

"I will do that."

"But no interference."

"You drive a hard deal."

"But you already took down about a billion three from the pension funds. I'll never see a dime of that."

"There is one other point. How are you going to explain the charges you made to the newspapers and on the television this morning?"

"I will testify that when I saw those two American faces at the Rome airport, in hysteria, I went to them for help, then the whole thing turned into an extortion plot that had nothing to do with any organized crime families."

"But how about the charges you made in London that we beat you and cost you your baby?"

"I will say that, in the excitement and joy in the possibility of actually seeing my husband again, I tripped at the top of the staircase, fell down its full length, struck my head badly and, when I came around—after those people came in to find me—that, under concussion, I hallucinated and fantasized that I had been attacked by the only credible force I could think of—the Mafia."

"Well, I suppose it could all work out. Whatta you think, Angelo?"

"Since 1981, the politicians have proved that the people can be made to believe absolutely anything. Eduardo has a very big public relations department. They could put the right spin on this."

"Have another cookie, my dear," the don said, lifting the plate and extending it to her.

When Julia left them Corrado Prizzi sighed heavily and stared sadly at Angelo. "The time has come for the *repulitura*."

"Mopping up? Mopping up what?"

"Send Charley to talk to Violente and Cloacacino. Let him put the fear on them, then tell them they gotta take the fall for the scam they tried to work on Mrs. Asbury. He can tell them that we'll take care of their families while they're in the can and pay for the lawyers. Then, when they think everything's been straightened out and they're in the clear, have

Charley whack them. That will take out the last stone the Asbury woman put in my shoe."

Edward S. Price had to agree, however reluctantly, that his
father had made the correct decision in bringing an end to the
constant irritation by Mrs. Asbury. "Her brother is a competent-
enough executive," he told his father. "He'll be a help. It remains to
be seen whether she will be able to grasp the complexities of
running a business the size of Henry Asbury's spread, but we'll
give her all the help we can."

"Do better than that, Eduardo. Make sure she either makes
good or figure out how to make her think she is making good."

"I'm going to dinner at her place on Friday night. That will
break the ice."

"Be very nice to her, Eduardo. She owes us a lot of money."

VINCENT PRIZZI summoned Violente and Joey Cloacacino to a meet in his office at the St. Gabbione Laundry.
After they had been there for about five minutes Charley
Partanna came into the room. He looked at them coldly with
the basic *fratellanza* stare of hostility and contempt. Violente
returned the stare with an advanced stare of chief *intimidatore*
of the family. Charley immediately raised the ante by two
grades, to a degree of threat that was beyond Violente's skills.
Joey Cloacacino whimpered. Violente paled. Charley moved up
the intensity of the fear he was projecting and Violente crum-
bled as Joey began to weep. Vincent looked on with total awe
at Charley's silent coercion, thinking, better them than me.

"Jesus, Charley, give us a break," Violente said.

"I got two kids, Charley. Just tell me what you want."

"You gotta take the fall for what you done to Mrs. Asbury."

"Whad we do? We handled her with kid gloves. Ask her. She likes us."

"You let her go on the television," Vincent said.

"You told us! We could make up a thing like that up?"

"You grabbed Mrs. Asbury in Rome," Charley said, getting back to the point, "because you thought you could shake her down when you got her back to Brooklyn. *Shaddap!* It was in alla papers! She named you by your names on that television show!"

"But what the hell, Charley—"

"The family is gonna stand by you. The best lawyers. And if you have to go inside, your families are gonna be taken care of plus we'll get you the shit concession for whatever joint they put you in."

Violente perked up. There was a big opportunity here.

"But what about Pino?" he asked.

"That happened in a foreign country."

"Mrs. Asbury told the television that after the Palermo guys hit Pino they took her to Rome and gave her to us. That makes us accessories."

"Was she under oath on television? What she's gonna say in court is that she ran away from those *shtarkers* in Athens then when she got to Rome, you were the first Americans she saw so she went to you for protection. You saw who she was and you decided on the scam."

"The Feds could hang a kidnapping charge on us."

"The charge is gonna be extortion. You'll get five to seven and you'll be out in fourteen months with a big bankroll."

"Do we get our old jobs back?" Joey asked.

"Of course. Plus a nice bonus and a welcome-home party."

"How about that?" Vincent said with awed approval.

"Terrific. Absolutely terrific," Violente said.

The men all shook hands, smiling broadly.

"And the Republicans think they have a lock on family values," Joey said. "They could learn plenty."

Charley relaxed his expression and became his old, approachable self. He put an arm around each of their shoulders and took them out to the Calabrese delicatessen for a big slice of mushroom pizza. The heat was off them. Their worst fears had been imaginary. The future looked rosy.

THE FIRST thing Julia did when she got back to the apartment on Sixty-first and Park was to dig out Miss MacHanic's telephone number and call her.

"I'm back," she said. "Everything's fine and I want you to come to work."

"That's wonderful, Mrs. Asbury. And you were terrific on *Good Morning America*."

"Thank you. I really enjoyed doing the show. Can you reach Arpad Steiner?"

"Yes, Mrs. Asbury."

"Please call him and rehire him and tell him to reestablish the staffs at all the houses just the way they were."

"Yes, Mrs. Asbury."

"Particularly, Rose Curry."

"Will do, Mrs. Asbury."

"You and Steiner and Cook might just move in here at Sixty-first Street tonight so that I'll be covered. Then gradually, say by next Wednesday while the weather is still nice, Steiner can staff Bent Island. Then, perhaps you can go over the A list for a dinner party here—about twelve people—on Friday. Make it a point to invite Edward S. Price. Then, Donald Trump and his friend, the Kissingers if they're free, and the papal Nuncio. With his chamberlain that will just make eight. Be sure we have sea bass. The Nuncio adores it."

"Yes, Mrs. Asbury."

"Make a note to send a nice flower arrangement for Mr. Asbury's grave along with me when I fly out to Bent Island Saturday morning. And get some new croquet mallets. The ones we have are looking rather shabby."

As Julia finished that sentence Chief Inspector Mulshine, NYPD, and two detectives from the Commissioner's office arrived at the apartment. Julia asked that they be shown into the library. After ten minutes she joined them.

They were respectful but implacable; they wanted to know all the circumstances of her kidnapping in Rome, her incarceration in New York, and how it had happened that she had appeared on *Good Morning America*. Julia gave them a vague, dreamlike account of what had happened.

"Who are these men?" Mulshine asked.

"I don't know. Clearly they were some sort of gangsters. Their language was terrible."

"But you named them on the show."

"Oh, I heard their names. At least the names they called each other, but I don't know who the men were."

"Did they harm you in any way?"

"No."

"Tell us again how it all happened, Mrs. Asbury."

Julia went through the fantasy she had proposed to Corrado Prizzi: how she had been nearly hysterical when she had escaped from Athens and how, after she got off the plane at the Rome airport she saw these two American faces and how instinctively she had turned to them for help only to have them take advantage of her state.

"Who were the men who attacked you in Athens?"

"Some kind of awful foreigners. They spoke some weird language or broken English, then a quarrel broke out—about what I will never know—and they shot one of their own men."

"Is there anything else you would like to tell us?"

"That is all there is to tell you. Since that first awful day when they murdered that man, I have been in shock from the constant threats and duress. I was so frightened I couldn't think."

"How did it happen that you went on the television show this morning?"

"They told me how they would torture me, then finally kill me if I didn't agree to go on national television and say that I had not been kidnapped, that the whole thing was just newspaper sensationalism."

"This is a pretty weird story you're giving us," the older detective said.

"Weird? Weird? The whole thing is about as logical as any nightmare."

"We'll be in touch, Mrs. Asbury," Chief Inspector Mulshine said. They all shook hands solemnly and the men left.

HOMICIDE LIEUTENANT ZENDT was singing "O Solo Mio," in the shower, repeating the title over and over again to fill in for the words. He used the Luciano Pavarotti arrangement, if deviating from it considerably.

Little does he know how alone he's gonna be, Nuala thought sadly. In my whole life, she thought, I couldn't imagine ever having to do a thing like this to Harvey.

"Hey, what's for dinner?" he yelled across the open threshold to the bathroom.

"Something special."

She had brought in a dinner from the delicatessen: boiled ham, potato salad, Joosh rye, a six-pack of Heineken, and a gang of coleslaw. She had the table set with the horseradish mustard and the romantic lighted candles. When Harvey came out dressed in a very short pink terrycloth bathrobe and a pair of clogs, the food was on the table.

"Jesus, am I hungry," Harvey said. "I hadda witness an autopsy this afternoon."

"That should set anyone up."

"You have a good day?"

"Yeah."

"Whadda you hear from the Mob?"

"She really creamed them today. It'll be on television tomorrow morning—*Good Morning America*—about four hours after our first edition hits the street."

"We wrapped up the movie producer case. It was a straight homo thing. Schmalowitz picked a kid up in a gay bar, took him home, and the kid brained him."

"Please! Harve! Not while I'm eating."

"Bert Mayers on my team said it couldn't be a homo thing because Schmalowitz was Jewish and it's against their religion."

"Harve, I have something I gotta tell you. I don't think you're gonna like it."

"So tell me."

"I fell in love with a guy."

He grinned shyly. "Me?"

"No."

"Whadda you mean—no?" His face went blank, then slowly like smoke filling a jar it became horrified as the shape of possible truth became clearer.

"He's the Asbury woman's brother."

"The *law*yer?"

"Yeah."

"What is this? I can't believe this. Why are you telling me this?"

"I gotta move out."

"Why should you move out? I'll move out."

"I did it, so I gotta take the responsibility."

"Listen, Nuala. These things happen. I did it myself once."

"Did what?"

"I banged a broad."

"Whaaaat?"

"Well—yeah. Those things happen. I never saw her again. She was selling Irish Sweepstakes tickets."

"Get one thing straight, Harvey. Nobody ever banged me since we been together. That includes the Asbury woman's brother."

"I can't believe it. You're walking out on me. I can't believe it."

"I had no control over it. I was perfectly happy like up until maybe a coupla days ago—I mean, I figured that sooner or later we would be married. But it didn't work out that way. So I'll pack and get out and move into a hotel."

"And leave me with the dishes?"

"What dishes? We had ham and potato salad."

"One more night together. Whadda you say? It could change your whole perspective."

"No way, Harve. It would just make us feel empty and cheap."

"Not me! It'll make me feel like I'm all in one piece again. I can't just let you walk out. I gotta do something. I gotta think of something."

"If there was only some friendly way! I love you, Harve. I always will. This thing is just something else."

"I know, babe. What the hell."

"We just sort of drifted along until we became just a couple of old buddies. I mean, I'm young. Where's the romance in this? Dinner in your bathrobe. And some dinner. I mean, we let it happen to us, Harve, and the fact is I don't want it to happen to me. I see a chance to live like a woman should live and I'm gonna take it."

"But what am I gonna do? How am I gonna get by?"

"Come on, Harve—you can always buy another Irish Sweepstakes ticket."

40

AS IT DEVELOPED, neither the Kissingers, the Trumps, nor the papal Nuncio were available to join Julia for dinner Friday night. "How can that be?" Julia asked Miss MacHanic, genuinely offended because Henry Asbury had been a dear friend of all of them.

"I think we'll have to give the recent publicity a chance to be overtaken by other events," Miss MacHanic said. "The World Series, the Paris collections, and the presidential debates are coming up, and any one of those will blot out any memory of the hardships you endured."

"But the trial of those two men will be happening. I will have to testify and be in the headlines all over again."

"You could ask for a postponement."

"Wonderful! A two-year postponement. Ed Price can fix that."

"It's a pity," Miss MacHanic said, "but surely not everyone on the A list will react the way these people did and, besides, we only gave them five days' notice. Chances are they actually *did* have other engagements."

"Of course. They could be sailing. They could be in Saratoga or Montecatini or Mr. Kissinger could be deep in some war room with Goodie Noon."

"Shall I draw from the A list?"

"Has Mr. Price accepted?"

"Yes, Madam."

"Then it shall be dinner for two. Mr. Price was the target for the exercise anyway and he certainly doesn't need to be reminded that I am friendly with Kissinger. However, cancel the sea bass. It's not a must any longer and I'm not all that fond of it. Tell Cook we will start off with a *paté chaud de caneton au Chambertin*, then a *gratin de queues d'écrevisses*, followed by a *perdreau* casserole, *choucroute*, and *purée de pommes*, then some St. Marcellin and some Brie with a few nice pears."

"And the wine?"

"Cramant Blanc de Blanc '61 to start, I think. Then the Romanée-Conti '71. Top it all off with a bottle of Pommery 1966 and a good cigar."

"We have the Monte Cristos and Larranagas Mr. Asbury got from the State Department."

"Either one. No matter. But everything must be perfect. Tell Steiner he must *drill* the people who will be serving."

"No fear, Madam."

Julia lived on the upper floor of an eighteen-room duplex in the apartment building Henry Asbury had bought for her on the corner of Sixty-first Street and Park Avenue. Her own apartment had nine capacious rooms. The staff: Steiner, the butler; Frau Zaug, the housekeeper; the cook, Madame de Caunteton; Curry, Blanton, Tichenor, and Doreen: personal maid/hairdresser, housemaid, tweeney, and kitchen slavery respectively; Laszlo Lowenstein, driver; and Agent Gallagher, chief bodyguard; all lived on the floor below. Both floors had separate elevators that reached a street entrance on Sixty-first Street, rather than the more obvious one on Park Avenue. Agent Gallagher had supervised the hiring of the doormen, liftmen, handymen, and dog handlers of the building. The footmen, laundress, masseuse, Mrs. Asbury's *wha-rang-do* instructor, a Korean monk capable of tossing karate black belts and seventh Dans to all four points of the compass, handymen, and seamstress all lived off the premises as did, of course, the groundsmen, artisans, and the people who ran Julia's boats and planes.

There was a murmured grandeur about the apartment just as there was a shouted grandeur about Henry Asbury. His flat statement to his peers was: "Anything you can do I can do better." In 1986 he had acquired the great English country house, St. Bartholomew's, in Dorset. He bought everything that had been a part of it: works of art, flooring, sheep, furniture, tenants, arras, flower gardens, servants, and pergola/follies, almost everything but the view, and had selectively transferred much of its contents to the apartment in New York. The admirable Steiner had come out of that deal, and Curry, Blanton, and Tichenor as well as a remarkable *écuyer tranchant* who could carve both breasts of an ortolan by throwing it into the air and making two swift strokes with his knife.

The bas-relief wood intaglios in the entrance hall, attributed to Grinling Gibbons, surrounded James Richard Blake's portrait of the Lady Evelyn with her beautiful daughters, as if drinking tea from perfectly executed *trompe l'oeil* china cups in the luxuriantly English St. Bart's gardens. The entrance to the apartment led into the extravagant Marble Hall, occupying three central bays of the east front, reproduced precisely from designs by William III's Huguenot *dessinateur*, Daniel Marot, with its giant acanthus moldings round the doors, its huge bracketed frieze, the great cartouches over each chimneypiece, and the elaborate ceiling inset with reproductions (mixed with imported originals) of roundels by Zucchi, Hamilton, and Morland; a marble chimneypiece by Spang, with caryatid figures of Ceres and Bacchus.

Julia's bedroom was lined with crimson flock wallpaper, done by the eminent Dublin paper stainer David Hanley, surrounding what had been one of the greatest baroque beds ever romped upon, the Dorset original, fully canopied in scarlet and fringed with ingots of gold, installed in the apartment in 1985 against the possibility of a visit by Ronald and Nancy Reagan, the Dalai Lama, or Margaret Thatcher, come to him for his kind counsel.

If Edward Price was surprised that he and Mrs. Asbury would be dining alone he gave no sign of it. Julia looked more than merely ravishing, she was spectacularly put together. A little bit of Cartier here, a little bit of Givenchy there, the haunting and provoking scent that Henry Asbury had had Picasso create for her, one of his last acts on earth, all of it gracing a figure that would have left Messalina crestfallen, supported on legs that would have shamed Mistinguett, and filling Price with gratitude that there would be no other guests at dinner.

Julia wore the wondrously extravagant jewels that Henry Asbury had acquired through the great fences of Europe and Asia.

Price heard himself talking almost gaily, eating like a trencherman and, to his amazement, listening to this woman when she spoke. He never did that as a rule because it spoiled them. He could not believe, purely and simply, that this vision of cultured accomplishment could be related to The Plumber, whom Price had known since his own boyhood; a peasant ruffian.

Julia responded solemnly to the aristocratic lineaments that Dr. Weiler had sculpted into Price's face so many years before because she could not fathom how he could possibly be the brother of Vincent Prizzi. She had never seen and, possibly, had never heard of Lord Curzon, on whose exalted visage Price's acquired face had been based, but she knew caste when she saw it and, since caste was second only to security in her judgment, she felt herself falling in love with the idea of bringing together two great dynasties, the Price empire and the wide-ranging Asbury domain. He was not too old to produce children. Together they could create a family of American princes who would so overshadow the Kennedys as to cast them into total darkness. But that was for the future, just a fleeting thought, really. There were more vital things to consider now.

They dined in Julia's famous Titian Gallery with its massive oak floorboards, whose walls were lined with eleven of the great Friulian painter's tapestry cartoons ranging from life-size to bust-size. Along the center of the room had been placed a long, rather wide Florentine table. Julia and Price sat facing each other at table center, each served by two liveried footmen overseen by the incomparable Steiner.

Price responded with great zest to what others might have regarded as ostentation. Although they conversed in English, occasionally Julia would lapse into flawless Sienese Italian, utterly U and timeless, because she knew that he would know that she knew he was only a Sicilian. The air-conditioning was full-on, permitting a roaring log fire in the fireplace at the far end of the room with its elaborate plasterwork overmantel, an Elizabethan feature for which St. Bart's had been famous. The paneling in the room dated from the time of the sixth Duke.

It was an extraordinarily successful dinner on both a personal and a business level. Price had had his instructions from his father, so he put up no opposition to Julia's proposals and, because he was between mistresses, his loins were yearning. He had known some fine-looking women in his time but surely never one as magnificent as this one, not one who had combined taste with acumen.

The business alliance was forged. Price's cooperation was assured. Julia was to take over the helm of Asbury Industries the following Monday morning. The signal would go out to all Asbury offices throughout the world and the business news media would be alerted.

"I hope this will be a close relationship," Julia said. "I want that more than anything."

"It will be, my dear Julia, if I have anything to say about it."

They had coffee in the library which had been modeled on the library at St. Gallen; three storeys high with each wall, excepting that provided by the floor-to-ceiling windows, lined with thousands of leather-bound books. Edward S. Price drew on a mellow Davidoff cigar and sipped at a thirty-year-old cognac while Julia laid out her plan to resuscitate the maimed Asbury companies: credit plans within credit plans, stock flotations, high-yield bonds, retrenchment, as well as her ideas for new companies. They were absorbed by her visions for more than three hours.

"Mrs. Asbury," Price said, "I am not a betting man but what you have just told me constitutes a sure thing."

"Please call me Julia," she answered shyly.

What Julia had not confided to Edward Price was that she had, weeks before, hired a research organization and had sent her brother Allan to Japan to recruit two native specialists and to use them to conduct research in specific areas of Japanese industrial management.

"Asbury Industries is one hundred and thirty-seven companies, so the best way to look at it is as if it were the tiny industrial complex of a country standing all by itself. Japan, no matter how else anyone looks at it, had to make a superhuman comeback after World War II to get where they are today. They are a small country—I mean compared to us or to the combined European market, just as Asbury Industries is small compared with Barkers Hill, so they had to do something to make the country work the way it works today."

Allan reported from Tokyo that he had signed Gyo Fujikawa, professor of national economic development at the University of Tokyo, a woman with an intimate knowledge of the attitudes and practices of the Ministry of International Trade and Industry, as Julia had requested, and that he had stumbled on a possible new product for the United States and Europe, freeze-dried sushi. "It has the raw fish and the cooked rice, all the consumer has to do is add water. How can it miss?"

"Grab it," Julia said.

When she had worked with Professor Fujikawa through four eleven-hour sessions and found out what she wanted to know, she adapted it freely and modeled the operation of her central headquarters office on that of the Japanese Ministry of International Trade and Industry, the tough, ruthless driving force that executes the Japan Inc. policy and which would transform her own executive home-office force into the capital and brains of all Asbury companies. She set up new research laboratories, held out the carrot-and-stick of capital and new technology, scanned the horizons for new businesses that she could develop while heartlessly eliminating losers. When one of her public utility companies announced a reduction in service during an energy shortage, she jerked the company president into New York, took his hide off for announcing the cut without consulting with her, and saw to it that the word got out to the entire business news media, driving home her point with all the other 136 Asbury companies. She put a stop to Asbury companies paying high dividends and, in effect, brought about instant cartelization, presiding at secret meetings that fixed prices, set production quotas, and maintained a large slush fund for both political parties in power. She made all segments work not merely for themselves but for the overall profit of Asbury Industries.

She indexed the salaries of middle management to the profits of their companies and divisions. She eliminated executive planes and limousines. She instituted a system of rewards through money and promotions for cost-saving innovations and increased profits. She expanded health services and established child-care centers for employees. She made Asbury Industry companies a desirable place in which to work if only because of her new "earned points" bonus systems.

Edward Price's offices were high in a tall building on the Avenue of the Americas. Julia's offices were high in a tall building in Rockefeller Center. They spoke on the telephone two or three times a day. They had lunch once, then twice, a week in Price's private dining room which rotated guest chefs, one a month, from the three-star restaurants of France. Each Friday night it became a tradition that they would dine together at Price's impossibly expensive dining club and Julia made progress toward her goal of forming an American dynasty.

ANGELO asked Charley to ride him around Flatbush in his panel truck because he wanted to talk business.

"Violente and Joey made a lot of trouble," he said. "Pictures in the paper, giving people the idea that we were in back of the whole business about Asbury and his wife."

"I know."

"Corrado has decided that the time has come for us to whack them so they can't make no more trouble."

"Right."

"You oughta get a new car, Charley. This heap is ready to call it quits."

"It only looks crappy, Pop. It goes like a watch."

"Better it should go like a car."

Charley decided he would have to whack Violente and Joey Cloacacino on the same night because if one found out that the other one had been hit he would start running and that would complicate the work. They were both easy. Violente was a family man who always had dinner at home with his wife and kids. They lived in Brownsville. Charley remembered the wife from the LePore wedding, she was a skinny little woman whose family had been city people from Catania. Violente had three kids.

At five forty-five Charley parked his battered Dodge panel truck two doors down from the entrance to Violente's apartment house and waited. Violente got off a bus in front of his house at five minutes after six. Charley slid out of his car on the sidewalk side, taking an Ithaca Mag 10 Roadblocker with a 22-inch barrel with him. "Hey, Mort," he called out. Violente turned toward the voice and Charley blew him away with a projectile that shredded him into pieces which were all over the street. Charley got back into the panel truck and drove away to handle Joey.

Joey would either be coming home to his mother's house in East New York after seeing a movie, or he would be running a matinee with his girl friend at her apartment in Flatbush. The Plumber had said that because it was a Friday, Joey would probably be with the girl. Charley regretted this. It meant he was going to have to give it to the girl because it wouldn't make any sense to leave a witness hanging around to hang it on him. The Plumber had given him the girl's address, so he drove to her place from Violente's apartment house, parked the car, and went into the building.

He carried a silenced, plastic Glock 17 lightweight pistol, with an seventeen-round magazine that chambered 7.62mm bottleneck cartridges. When he rang the doorbell, the girl opened the door. Charley shot her through the right eye, stepped over her body, closed the door while Joey's voice called out, "Who is it, honey?" Charley went into the kitchen where Joey was sitting at a table holding a glass of red wine. Charley knocked him out of the chair with two shots, then bent over his body to drop a round into the side of Joey's head. He left as quickly and as quietly as he had come in.

When he got back to his place at the beach he called his father and told him everything had been taken care of. Then he put a dreamy Jackie Gleason medley record on the machine and sat on the terrace, thinking about Julia Asbury again.

Charley couldn't get Julia Asbury out of his mind or his trousers. He would awaken in the early hours of the morning and, by force of the memory of her lips, have to get out of bed and take a cold shower. He took to seeing Maerose Prizzi for the comfort it brought him, arriving at her apartment at odd hours in the night.

They had been engaged now for nine years. Charley had been aware of her, as Vincent Prizzi's daughter, by the time she was five years old and he was in his teens but they hadn't met each other until seventeen years later, at the old Palermo Gardens. After that, one thing had led to another.

Mae had decorated Charley's apartment, leading to their formal engagement, but Mae had become confused at their engagement party, attended by Corrado Prizzi, the family priest, Father Passanante, and the elite of the national crime community, and she had run off with some guy to Mexico. Her father had sent two of the *intimadatori* to bring her back and that's when he had her exiled from Brooklyn. However, because Corrado Prizzi had originally announced it and because his daughter Amalia, Maerose's friend, had forbidden him to retract the announcement, Maerose and Charley were still engaged. After a respectful amount of time had passed they began to see each other again, mostly at family christenings, weddings, and funerals which Amalia had persuaded her father to persuade Vincent Prizzi to allow her to attend, and at the occasional tryst at Charley's or at Mae's apartment.

The basic cause of the present fleshy alliance was that Charley had no idea of how he could get together with Julia Asbury and now that the don had made her head of that enormous combination, she was even further away. She sat at the head of 137 companies and what was he? A mere *vindicatore*, a contractor. The gulf would become so vast in his fevered imagination that he would get dressed, grab a cab, and ride all the way in to New York, to Maerose's place below Murray Hill, and battle his sense of loss on top of her, around her, and among her.

Although Charley was more motivated toward the sex act when he was in love, that was simply a measure of his feeling. He read Barbara Cartland novels, women's magazine fiction during the day, while he waited for assignments and, avoiding movies that advertised crime and violence, he steadfastly believed in happy endings and the realization of one's secret heart. He was a man in love and, since he was denied any chance of being with his beloved, there was no way he could discover flaws in her and fall out of love.

Julia's dad worked for him so, as a kind of transference, Charley told The Plumber to come into his office at the St. Gabbione Laundry. The Plumber said he couldn't because *The Eternal Light* was just about to come on television.

"Television? It's three o'clock in the afternoon."

"That's when it comes on. So come over here."

Charley found him in the kitchen on President Street, drinking dandelion wine and cutting his toenails. The kitchen was not the sort advertised as a gourmet kitchen. It had a stove, a refrigerator, a table, two chairs, and a 1976 Dr Pepper calendar hanging on one wall.

"You missed it," The Plumber said. "It's just over."

"What?"

"The television show. What's on your mind, Charley?"

"I was wondering if you heard anything from Julia."

"Julia? My Julia?"

"Yeah."

"Not lately. Why?"

"She's a fine-looking woman."

"She's a pain in the ass."

Charley stopped beating the bushes. The Plumber worked for him. "I wanna get her home phone number."

"Which home? She's got a lotta homes."

"The New York one."

"No."

"No what?"

"I don't have it."

"Then get it."

"Where?"

"From her brother fahcrissake."

"He calls me sometimes. The next time he calls I'll ask him."

"Call him now and ask him."

"Hey, what's got into you? Why would anyone wanna talk to Julia? She's the original Cold-Ass Mary."

"Listen, Al. I got my reasons and I don't needa explain them to you."

"Okay, okay." The Plumber pulled open the table drawer and took out a copy book that had COMPOSITIONS printed on its cover. He leafed through a few of the lined pages until he found what he wanted. He dialed the telephone, asked for Mr. Melvin, said his father was calling, and waited.

"Al? Pop. What's Julia's home phone?" He listened, writing down the response on the corner of a page. He hung up the phone, tore off the corner, and handed it to Charley.

As soon as The Plumber called him, Allan John Melvin telephoned his sister.

"I don't know why, but Pop just called and asked for your phone number."

"*Whaaat?*"

"Yeah."

"He hasn't called me since he was made a Knight of Columbus and that was before I was married."

"I just thought you'd like to know."

"Thanks, Al. I appreciate it."

HOMICIDE LIEUTENANT ZENDT called Nuala
Counihan at the Lombardy on East Fifty-sixth Street at
7:45 P.M. just as she was about to leave her room to join Allan
John Melvin, who was waiting for her in the lobby.

"Harvey! What happened?" She had a terrible vision that he
was calling from a hospital after some kind of accident.

"The two guys? Violente and Cloacacino?"

"Yeah."

"They got whacked about an hour ago."

"Whacked?"

"What's left of Violente looks like a jigsaw puzzle, but with
the other guy they also took out his girl."

"Three people?"

"Two different weapons. The hits were in different parts of
Brooklyn. It could have been two different contractors."

"Gimme the details."

"You gotta pencil? And be sure to say that Lieutenant Zendt
of the NYPD is confident that he will break the case."

"You are?"

"Are you kidding? Go prove anything."

As soon as Nuala hung up, she called the front desk of the
hotel and had Allan paged.

"Al? Jesus, they just blew away the two guys who grabbed
your sister."

"Yeah?"

"About an hour ago."

"How do you know that?"

"A friend of mine—a cop—is on the case. Anyway, I gotta
call the story in, so I'll be a little late getting downstairs."

"No problem."

As they hung up, she called the paper and dictated the story.
Allan called his sister from a lobby phone. "A friend of mine,

a cop, just called me and told me that the Prizzis—who else could it be—hit Violente and Cloacacino about an hour ago."

"Who did it? Partanna?"

"Who knows?"

"I bet it was Partanna."

"Anyway, I thought you'd want to know."

"It had to be Partanna."

After she had filed the story, Nuala did some makeup repair and a body check, then went down to find Allan. She apologized for the delay.

"You are so beautiful, Nuala."

"Nobody has said that to me for a long time." She thought of what a klutz Harvey was compared to this one who understood that we do not live by bread alone.

"Let's walk a little. I'd like to show you off."

"Where'll we have dinner?"

"I was thinking, maybe Indian food."

"Apache or Iroquois?"

"More like Gary Cooper and the Bengal Lancers."

"Where?"

"Down the street and around the corner. Maybe shrimps to start, with mustard seeds and sour curry leaves. *Basmati* rice in saffron *biriyani*, with chicken paved with nuts and raisins. Sitar music. Maybe a lamb vindaloo if you like it hot or maybe Mogul lamb with yoghurt and turnips."

"God, I'm glad I found you, Al."

At eleven o'clock the paper was on the street with the headline

GANGLAND SLAYINGS OF ASBURY
KIDNAPPERS SHOCK CITY

Father of three murdered. Double killing in love nest.

TWENTY MINUTES after Allan called her to tell her
the news about the two *shtarkers*, Miss MacHanic came in to
say that a Mr. Charles Partanna was on the telephone. Julia
couldn't understand the feeling that overcame her. This man
had just killed three people and now he was calling her as if
they were in the same dancing class and his mother had told
him to escort her there.

She tried to modulate by telling herself that her own father
was this man's assistant who did the lesser jobs when the boss
whacker was too busy. Even though the call and the caller had
shocked her, she still held on to the memory of the unexpected
sweetness of his only kiss; how, when he had her in his power
while they were sitting on a bed, he had been so careful not
to frighten her by pulling her down. He had only leaned into
her and had brushed her lips with his. It had been so unexpected, so out of character with all of the boys in the environment with whom she had grown up, but in its way so much
more manly and intoxicating, that she had thought about it
again and again, sometimes yearningly. She took the call.

"Mr. Partanna?"

"Who?"

"Is this Mr. Partanna?"

"Oh. For a minute I though you were saying you were Mr.
Partanna."

He had a voice like a lion, she thought. That is, if she were
a lioness and they were conversing; a very rumbly, scratchy,
deep, Kissingeresque kind of a voice, in fact, exactly what a
lion's voice might sound like. It reminded her of heavy city
traffic, Klaxon horns, stripped gears, transmission problems.
Until Charley called she had been deep in plans to bring
Edward S. Price to his knees, but this unexpected summons,
the memory of a rare, perfect moment in that hotel room in
Canarsie had erased dreams of glory.

To Charley, Julia's voice sounded like distant flutes; liquid music coming from an ancient Attic forest.

"A lot has happened since we met." She could have bit her tongue. Christ! What a thing to say to a man who had just iced three people. She hoped he wasn't sensitive about his work.

"I been thinking about you and I wondered if we could work it out that I could like take you to dinner or something like that."

"I'd be delighted. When?"

"I was thinking—like tonight?"

She shuddered involuntarily; part ecstasy, part horror. "I can't tonight. I have a standing dinner invitation for tonight."

"You're gonna eat standing?"

"No, no! I meant it is a dinner date I have every Friday night. Business."

"Oh."

"But perhaps some other night."

"Like maybe Monday night?" He wanted to say Saturday but people like Mrs. Asbury probably always hit the town on a Saturday night.

"Monday would be fine. I'll expect you here at seven-thirty for an aperitif."

"Whatta you like to eat?"

"Anything. Anything at all."

"I know where they have real *salsiccia alla Siciliana*—I mean like from Agrigento—*al punto del coltello*. And I mean with wild fennel and hot red pepper flakes and caciocavallo cheese."

"Oh, Charley!"

"Wait! They also do a pasta *ammudicata*."

"With more red peppers?" They had both been raised to believe that hot red peppers excited the sexual organs.

"Listen—you could even have it *di fuoco*."

"Wild!" Lately she had been eating so much bland French and American restaurant food that she hadn't realized that she was yearning for food that would make her entire body zing while she ate it and washed it down with some rough red wine. What was the wine her father used to drink on feast days like St. Joseph's Day?—Primitivo di Manduria from Leporano, which changed color from violet to orange.

"You think they have a wine called Primitivo di Manduria?"

"I'll bring a bottle to be sure."

"Maybe you'd better pick me up at seven so we can be sure to get there on time wherever it is."

EDWARD S. PRICE'S Phantom Six Rolls-Royce with its seemingly deaf-and-dumb chauffeur and postillion (they responded only when spoken to in the dialect of eastern London), its precautionary sawed-off shotguns (by Holland & Holland) tucked into blond leather holsters discreetly on the inside panel of each front door; with its stock ticker and red telephone (which was connected directly to a red phone in his father's apartment); with its pop-up computer holding a worldwide data bank of financial, mineral, and agricultural resources; its electronic map-locator system and television screen; its bulletproof body and windows; and its platinum Saint Stephen's medal embossed on its fully equipped bar, arrived at Mrs. Asbury's apartment building entrance at 7:29:07 P.M. Edward S. Price had called ahead from the automobile to advise Julia that he would be arriving in nine minutes, twelve seconds. Julia was emerging from the building as the enormous limousine, eleven inches longer than the Royal Scotsman locomotive, drew up at the entrance.

An hour before he arrived, Price had sent a card by courier to tell her that he had deeded a small flower farm he owned in West Palm Beach to her name so that she would never want for fresh flowers. As Henry Asbury had already owned a flower farm in Louisiana which he had willed to her, Julia felt she could have had a surfeit of flowers but, flowers were flowers. Mr. Price could hardly be expected to notice the difference between the product of the two farms if she sold off his crop to retailers.

The postillion was holding open the door to the car's tonneau as she came out. She swept into the car. The postillion shut the door, leapt into his place beside the driver, and the significant automobile moved out into traffic.

"We are going to my dining club," Edward Price said.

"How nice."

"It's on the 109th floor, on top of the Consolidated Securities building downtown."

"It's new to me."

"It only has eight members, each chosen by his ranking among the top eight wealthiest men in the Western Hemisphere, as rated annually by *Forbes* magazine."

Julia patted his hand reassuringly. She thought of Henry Asbury because he and Price were two of the most *male* creations she had ever known. They both listened to their utterances before, after, and during the time they were speaking them. They saw their slightest prejudice, particularly their patronage of women, as being the law of the land and they were both mirror-fuckers from birth. Henry at least had an edge on this one because, although he had always marveled that he filled his own shoes, he had had some kind of weird humor about the whole thing.

"How splendid you look, my dear," Price said, really making an effort not to sound patronizing but failing badly. "What a sweet little frock."

She could have brained him. The "little frock" was not only the work of the greatest living couturier but it had been sent back to Paris twice for editorial revisions before she would wear it publicly. If they had been going to any other restaurant than this ego-trough of Price's, the other women guests in the place would rush off to the power room to weep over the challenge that this "sweet little frock" would be flinging down before them.

"I just feel so comfortable when I wear it," she said.

"How sensible you are, Julia, dear."

The security at the dining club was absolute. The identity check took almost twelve minutes to complete to the satisfaction of the grim uniformed security guards. While they waited, they were settled in an anteroom with glasses of Dom Pérignon '28 while the genetic confirmation of their hair follicles was made. "A genetic ID check may seem excessive," Price said, "but only fifteen months ago we had an imposter who not only gained entrance to the club but dined here. It was a close call. As it turned out, the fellow was only in the hundred-and-seventy-thousand-a-year bracket. Can you imagine the humiliation that would mean for the Reagans if they happened to be dining here as guests?"

At last they were escorted into the express elevator whose operator was fully armed. They entered the club to be greeted by each of their names (members were required to provide the names of their guests in advance). They were escorted to their table by the large, muscular maître d'hôtel. As he left, a pale, somewhat frightened-looking young woman who wore a blue-and-white toga appeared at Price's side. "My name is Calpurnia," she said, "I will be your food taster for this evening." As she left, Julia looked at Price with concern. "A *food* taster?"

"The club has twenty-six employees," Price replied. "Any one of them could poison the food."

"The food taster could do it."

"By God, you're right. It's a bit of an adventure dining here, wouldn't you say?"

The food was only fair, Julia thought, but she knew that was of no interest to the eight members. Members dined there because they, above all others from the northernmost rim of Canada to the southern edges of Tierra del Fuego, were entitled to dine there.

Charley Partanna arrived on the dot of seven. He carried the bottle of wine in a brown paper bag. They had a glass of champagne, in Julia's library, chatted about the weather for a burst, then Julia blurted compulsively, "I see where the two men who grabbed me in Rome were killed."

"Yeah. I read about it." That was all they had to say about *that*. *Pace* Violente and Cloacacino, Julia thought.

Charley had had his people lift a new sedan for the night because when he looked at the panel truck he knew it was no car to move Mrs. Asbury around in. They drove to the West Thirties between Ninth and Tenth to a dingy-looking restaurant called La Festa which was down eight steps. There were twelve tables having four places each and nine diners. The waiters were old men who wore tablecloth aprons, white shirts, and black bow ties.

On the way into the restaurant Charley said he should have brought flowers or a box of candy but he figured she would have a lot of flowers.

"One can't have too many flowers," Julia said gaily, thinking of the floral pieces he had probably ordered for the Violente and Cloacacino funerals. As a moviegoer she believed that after hoodlums killed people they always held to the etiquette of sending excessive amounts of flowers to the funerals. She wanted to ask Charley about that but she didn't dare.

She stared at him while they talked. It was very, very hard to understand how he could be a man whose trade was killing people. He was gentle. He was—well—even banal as he talked about astrology and Michael Jackson's nose job and how the Mets were playing nice ball, yet she had known that he was the *vindicatore* of the Prizzi family for many years. Well, *tant pis*, she thought. The complexities of modern society had brought out all sorts of incongruous specialties. In many ways maybe it wasn't all that much different from being a butcher. People had to kill things to ease the way for civilization, at least as this word concerned the development of cities. Where would the National Rifle Association be if we all suddenly came out against the sportsmen of the inner cities?

A man who was obviously the proprietor of the restaurant got up from his dinner, wiping his mouth with a large napkin as he came forward to greet Charley, carefully ignoring her.

"Mr. Partanna! What an honor, signore!" he said. Julia, a linguistics major at the Università per Stranieri at Perugia, placed his accent as being from or around Basilicata. "How good of you to order in advance so that we could do precisely the right thing. Ah! I see that you have brought wine! How original! Please, this way. The lady must not be kept standing."

Julia had not eaten such wonderful food since her childhood. When her mother had been alive she had always been curious about new flavors and new dishes. Her father certainly couldn't know about this restaurant because, even though he hardly ever called her, he would have called her to tell her about food like this.

"How did you find this place?" she asked Charley.

"The company I work for owns it," he said. "They wanted to have a place in New York for when they came over here."

His *company*? Who was he kidding? It was a Prizzi joint! So her father had to have eaten here and the son-of-a-bitch had never said a word. She smiled at Charley. "It really is very good," she said. "It could make a fortune if it were uptown."

"Yeah, but you'd only get a lotta people."

They didn't talk much during the meal. They had both been trained in childhood that food was for eating, in-between was for talking, but while he chewed and savored, Charley marveled silently at how kind fortune had been to him. He was with the perfect woman: a staggering beauty; a society leader, possibly a social arbiter; an intimate of the great and near-great; and a very snappy dresser. It also seemed clear that she liked him, even admired him, he dared to think.

Julia, during those times of ingestive silence, was wondering why she had never been so aware of death before. She had grown up in her father's house and inevitably, after a time, she came to know and later to take for granted that he made the greater part of his living through the sudden deaths of other people. She realized she was now twenty years out of touch with the environment. Anyway, insofar as she and her brother had been concerned, that was what Pop did. Even making it possible for them to go to universities and law school. But this man who was eating so animatedly across from her was the Prizzi *vindicatore* and it dazed her that she was so attracted to him.

The wine was right. The service was deft. Charley asked for and got a second helping. He signed the check and left a fifty-dollar bill for the waiter. They got back into the lifted car and Charley said, "You wanna go to my place?"

"Where is it?"

"Brighton Beach."

"I'd love to see where you live." The hot red peppers seemed to be working, she thought.

They drove all the way from the West Side of Manhattan through the tunnel, out along the Belt Parkway, not talking much. Julia was thinking about Sinatra's song that said how it was when it was real. Now it was happening to her and it was almost as good as being rich.

CORRADO PRIZZI, his son, Eduardo, and his *consigliere*, Angelo Partanna, were meeting on the top floor of the house in Brooklyn Heights for their regular Wednesday morning business conference. In the background, a recording of the German comic opera *Der Widerspenstigen Zähmung* was playing. The three men drank coffee and munched on cookies as they ran through the gross earning tallies of their insurance, banking, oil and gas, fast-food, armaments, real estate, foreign currency speculation, mining, communications, and manufacturing companies to Don Corrado's satisfaction.

As Angelo changed the recording to Dallapiccola's *Il Prigioniero*, Don Corrado held up his hand for silence as the overture entered the clarinet solo by Dame Hilary Jackson. When the solo finished the three men applauded as if the great clarinetist were in the room with them, then the don asked how Mrs. Asbury was doing after six months in her job at the helm of the 137 Asbury companies.

"I can only say that she is a miracle worker," Eduardo said. "With three exceptions—and they were hopeless cases long before Henry Asbury left the company—she has not only made them all viable again, she has put seventy percent of them in the profit column."

"Very nice," Don Corrado said. "How did she do that?"

"She merged some, she set others up with new credit lines, she installed new products or initiated new procedures. She cut overheads, retired a lot of deadwood and—I think I can safely say—this time next year those companies will be returning a greater profit than they ever did in the best days under Asbury."

"How does she know how to do that?" Angelo asked.

"Because she is the most Sicilian woman we'll ever meet," Corrado Prizzi said. "Excepting my late, beloved wife."

"I would have said more Japanese," Eduardo murmured.

"Japanese? The Plumber and her mother came from a village not fifty miles from Agrigento," Angelo said.

"She must have sat up nights with Asbury, going over every operation with him," Eduardo said. "She knew those businesses better than I ever did from the day she moved into their offices."

Don Corrado nodded, gratified to have had confirmed a judgment that had been forced upon him. "I often wondered why it was that Asbury would give her anything she wanted—a Roman *palazzo*, more diamonds than even Elizabeth Taylor could wear, an army of servants waiting to welcome her in all their houses—the cars, the yachts, the planes and helicopters—everything."

"He gave her whatever she wanted," Eduardo said, "because they both knew that if it weren't for her, they wouldn't have had what they had. She is a treasure."

There was a deliberative silence that was broken at last by Don Corrado. "You have been a widower for too long, Eduardo," he said.

"How do you mean, Poppa?"

"You should have a good woman at your side, someone who cares about the things you care about. Someone as beautiful and as talented as Mrs. Asbury."

"Listen to your father, Eduardo," Angelo put in gently. "He is sharing his wisdom with you."

"Well—as a matter of fact—I've been seeing Mrs. Asbury regularly twice a week," Eduardo said. "Once for our regular review meeting on Tuesday mornings and once for dinner at my club every Friday evening. I must say I find her a most attractive woman."

"She already has everything she needs and a few months from now when she puts those companies in the black again she will also have seventy-five million dollars as a dowry plus an enormous share of the profits from all those Asbury companies. With all she has and will have she couldn't cost you a cent."

"I understand. Oh, I understand, Poppa."

"Then can I look forward to welcoming a new daughter into my family?"

"Yes, Poppa."

"Don't rush anything. Perhaps just a little more romance and a little less business at your Friday-night dinners."

"Yes, Poppa."

"Maybe we should do this the old-fashioned way. Maybe I should tell The Plumber to come to me and offer his daughter to become my daughter. The way we used to do it in the old country."

"No, Poppa. It wouldn't work. Mrs. Asbury wouldn't understand. She is that far removed from the environment."

"Just the same, when the time comes you must ask The Plumber for his daughter's hand in marriage. It's only right."

When Julia had agreed to drive out to Brighton Beach on the night of her first dinner with Charley, they had done just that and nothing more. Charley had been courtly but distant. They had driven all the way to Brooklyn with Julia brooding fervently about the possibility that she might be confronted with sex.

She admired his apartment. He brought her a nice glass of wine. They sat out on the terrace. But nothing happened. Absolutely nothing.

She waited tensely for him to make his move, expecting (at first) that he would just lift her up in his arms and carry her into the bedroom, but he didn't even show her the bedroom. She became more and more avid for him to come on to her. Instead, he began to play what looked like a series of six audiocassettes of Sousa marches. He explained his admiration for Sousa marches. "You can't dance to them but you can sing along in your head with them, which is more than you can say for rock. And you know what? I read in a magazine that he sold 'Semper Fidelis' and 'Washington Post March' to some music publisher for thirty-five dollars each. Go figure that."

They were into the second cassette when he said suddenly, "I used to play the tuba in the Holy Name Society band." Then he told her about the tuba. "I played an F tuba," he said. "It normally has three valves but on mine there was a fourth valve. You work it with your left forefinger. It lowers the tuba by a fourth and gives the gap between B—which you get with the three ordinary valves depressed—and F. I mean, I could hit the G-sharps in Sousa's *El Capitan*. I mean, I was playing an F tuba."

"Is that so?" The double portion of hot red peppers she had eaten must be having their effect, she thought, because no matter how much she talked about Sousa and tubas she was getting hornier and hornier.

"Once you play the tuba, you never forget it," Charley said wistfully.

"I'm surprised that you didn't keep it up."

"Well, I hadda go to work before I hadda chance to go to high school and play in the band there, so I pawned the tuba."

Charley had quit school because he had his first big success at what was to be his career when Corrado Prizzi was baffled as to how to whack out a Bronx heroin wholesaler named Little Phil Terrone. Charley had been thirteen when his father had told the don, "My Charley is the only one who can get close enough to that little prick to blow him away."

Every Saturday afternoon, Terrone would throw about twenty dollars' worth of silver into a crowd of kids who were always waiting for him on Gun Hill Road. Charley just mixed with the kids and while Terrone was enjoying the scrambling for the coins, Charley came up behind him and blew the back of his head off.

His father was proud of him. Corrado Prizzi marked him for important things. He was a made man at eighteen with three completed contracts under his belt. Julia knew about his legend the way Spanish kids knew the legend of El Cid. Her father had told her the Terrone story many times, wagging his head with admiration. Charley had been her idol since she had been in her teens.

"But I could pay you something on the ukelele," he said. "I only know two songs but they're pretty good." He shut off the cassette player, went to a closet and brought out a sandalwood and mother-of-pearl ukelele, tuned it, then played and sang "You're the Cream in My Coffee" followed by "In a Little Spanish Town 'Twas on a Night Like This." "My mother liked those songs," he said, as he finished with three tricky chords. "I played them for her every night before I got in the business."

When they had been at the apartment for about forty minutes he looked at his watch, said it was getting late and that they had better be thinking about getting back to New York. Julia had crossed and recrossed her legs more than thirty times and she was embarrassed to discover that she had been staring at his fly. All through the ride back she decided that he planned to make his move inside her apartment, but when she asked him if he would like to come up for a few minutes, he just said that it was getting late, that she had a long day ahead and that she should get her rest.

She wanted to scream.

She wondered with intuitive accuracy if he would go straight to Maerose Prizzi's apartment as soon as he left her. She knew about Maerose, the long engagement, the misunderstanding with Vincent Prizzi. She and Maerose had gone to school together; grammar school, high school, and to college with the nuns. She had automatically admired Maerose because she was a Prizzi but she had also liked her most of the time until she had snared Charley Partanna, the dream man of every girl in the environment. Then Maerose had baffled her by jilting Charley, and Vincent Prizzi had driven her wild with frustration by being able to enforce that Charley and Mae were still engaged.

Julia considered herself beyond all the constraints of her childhood and her teens when her father had ruled her and the Prizzis had ruled her father. She had overtaken Charley Partanna at last and she wasn't going to let him go. Looking back, she saw the inevitability of finding each other because, for as long as she could remember, it had been fated; they had been meant for each other. He *wanted* her, she could feel that with every sense she had cultivated for all of her life. She wanted him. Ed Price was just the bait in the trap to land Charley. Price was only money. She had money. Charley had been her dream since she was a little girl and now he was singing under her window.

It wasn't until the fourth time he took her to dinner (after the third time he stopped using hot sedans, but drove them in a rather battered, Julia thought, panel truck). He was wearing a new suit, very conservative, dark blue.

"A nice suit," Julia said.

"You like it? This tailor comes from Hong Kong once a year with samples. Nothing flashy. You tell him which sample, he measures you then, after you forgot all about it, the suit comes. It even fits."

They had dinner at a roadhouse in Englewood Cliffs, New Jersey, which was patronized by hard-looking types and where the band singer reprised "My Way" four times in one hour, making the patrons misty-eyed. People knew Charley but kept their distance. After dinner and no dancing they drove up along the Palisades for a few miles. Charley parked overlooking the river. There was a huge moon.

"I gotta say this to you, Julia," he said. "I'm in love witchew.

I mean I love you. I can't help myself. You are like the sun, the moon, and the stars to me."

Julia was exalted in the way a freshman coed would be if the biggest man on the campus had laid his heart at her feet. "Charley! What a wonderful thing to say."

"I read in a magazine that, at the annual meeting this year of the American Anthropological Association, they worked out the difference between real love and plain lust and they decided that it is quote an intense attraction and longing to be with a loved one unquote. That's what I feel for you, Julia. I love you."

He put his arms around her and, if possible, kissed her even more tenderly than on that day on the bed in Le Beau Rivage so long before. Then he took her into the back of the panel truck where he had installed a large air mattress, whisked her pantyhose down to her ankles then off and, with deftness and devotion, he got out of his trousers as quick as a fireman and pleasured her beyond her imagining, beyond the virtuosity of the late Pino Tasca, and so far beyond her experiences with Henry George Asbury that the comparison was a mockery.

She was transported in large measure because Charley had sent away to a company in Racine, Wisconsin, for an unguent preparation called LateComer that was guaranteed to delay male ejaculation for twenty-three minutes while in no way inhibiting the female's orgasm(s). Charley had followed the directions carefully, if overabundantly, in the men's room at the roadhouse before they had driven into the solitude.

Julia could not believe that she would ever have been able to repeat and repeat such coarse outcries and soar to such apogean heights of enduring sensation which recurred and recurred and recurred as she lay, sunfishing for an eternity.

When their frictions at last eroded the inhibiting salve of postponed deliverance, Charley burst then crashed and they lay still for many minutes.

They were in love. As Charley panted, "Not *in* love. I love you, Julia. 'In love' is just something that it comes and goes, but 'I love you' is forever. This moment is to me like forever, as maybe somebody like Shakespeare already said."

"I love you, Charley," Julia whispered and the entire emotion was so arousing that they went at it on the air mattress all over again.

46

NUALA COUNIHAN still lived at the Lombardy. Allan had pleaded with her to move in with him at the Olympic Towers but she told him she had tried that once before with a man and it had all ended sadly. He offered to set her up in her own apartment anywhere in the city but she said that would make her a kept woman and that her mother had strongly disapproved of kept women. "Once a week she would say to me, 'If there's any bigger parasite than a kept woman, it would take a Nobelist in biology to discover it.' "

That left only one solution: marriage. Allan was for it, she was on the fence. "It's just too early to talk about that, Al," she said. "We have to approach that gradually. I'll live at your place like from Thursday night until Mondays and we'll get to know what we're like."

"For how long?"

"I only know that with Harvey we let it go on too long and we became like roommates or fraternity brothers."

"So let's set a time. Six months?"

"Six months should do it."

"Okay. I'm going to write it in my agenda. Six months from now—that's like the middle of August—I ask you to marry me again and if the answer is no, then you move in with me."

"And we become like fraternity brothers."

"Never! We extend the options six months at a time."

"It will never work."

"Make me an offer," Allan said.

"That's fair. If we don't decide to get married in six months—that first six months—we split."

"I couldn't take that."

"Neither could I. Then, okay, after six months—too bad about my mother—I'll be a kept woman."

"Should I draw a contract?"

"Well—it wouldn't mean anything but it would make a nice memento to reread when I'm old and gray. Just a letter of agreement. No witnesses."

"Something's in the air, like romance. I think my sister is fooling around with somebody."

"Like who?"

"I don't know. I sense it. We're twins and we could always tell what the other one was thinking. I am getting strong vibes from her."

Edward S. Price started off modestly. He gave Julia the flower farm in West Palm Beach, then he sent her a pale, off-white lap robe for her car, made of shahtoosh, woven from the neck hairs of the ibex goat, an animal that roams the upper levels of the Himalayan Mountains. The ibex lives at about seventeen thousand feet but in April it descends to the timberline to forage on the leaves of low-growing trees. As it feeds, it scratches its neck on the tree's limbs, leaving clumps of neck hairs on the branches. These are gathered by children from the valleys and taken to the villages. The collection of hairs is sent to weavers in Srinagar.

The natural yarn is a taupish shade that rejects dyes, but the pale, off-white natural color that comes from one small spot on the goat's neck is worth a king's ransom because perhaps a hundredreth of one percent of the total hair gathered is of that shade. The diameter of the neck hairs is so fine that it requires 150 hairs to produce one inch of fabric but the thermal value of the cloth is ten times its weight. The sweet little coverlet cost Price $39,200—and he had bought it from a man who dealt in "hot" merchandise. Shahtoosh is so sheer and weightless that when Price sent Julia the lap robe, the gift was enhanced by being passed through a three-carat emerald ring, a present that was the more banal of the two perhaps but nonetheless appreciated by Julia.

When she admired the shoes of a company whose wares were displayed in the windows of a Fifth Avenue shoe store, he bought the shoe company and gave it to her as a Columbus Day present. It was that sort of courtship.

He took to kissing her hand in greeting, then her hand, her forearm, and her elbow when they parted after the Friday night dinner. Then he kissed the small hollow between her collarbone and her neck until, on a succeeding Friday night, after he had suggested that he go up to her apartment for a nightcap, he embraced her passionately and kissed her full on the lips.

"I adore you," he whispered into her left ear.

"Edward!"

"I have fought with this, Julia my dearest. You are widowed for less than a year, I for only seventeen months, but it is too big for me. Your beauty, your mind, your style, have overwhelmed me."

In his sixty-six years, in which he had appeared to be a devoted servant to his work at Barkers Hill Enterprises, despite the aloofness that his erect, spare form, his cold, drawling speech, and his aristocratic visage seemed to stamp upon his ego, id, and aims, Edward S. Price had devoted a lifetime to being continually sexually aroused.

Beginning at nine years of age with a middle-aged French governess into whose care the boy had been placed so that he could be at ease with the principal European languages, away from the roughening influences of his family environment, little Edward had gone on to be seduced by various small girls, traffic wardens, lady wrestlers, passing strangers, tutors, vaudeville artistes, and burlesque strippers whom he encountered at stage doors in theaters in New York and in Scully Square in Boston.

As a boy he had listened raptly to his father speak about livestock. "If the boy lifts a calf once a day from the time it is born," his father had said, "as the calf grows by tiny degrees, day after day, the boy should be able to lift the full-grown bull by the time he is a man."

It is possible that Corrado Prizzi was introducing the importance of gradualism in his son's life, but Edward S. Price had translated his father's wisdom in sexual terms. He had never let a day go by without undergoing sexual expression and, as a result, he was indeed able "to lift the bull" throughout his youth, middle age, and into the autumn of his life. Perhaps some of the ardor had gone, but that had been replaced by dazzling technique and extraordinary male-member disciplines.

As he had matured, he had married. As he married, he accumulated mistresses. Price had married three times, had enjoyed forty-six mistresses, and had managed to be surprised in his bed at 119 weekend house parties in eleven countries as the rumors of the size of his fortune grew greater and greater.

The marriages had been sources of much joy, the first two at any rate, joy that crashed into despair because his first wife, Hester, child of a great Boston family, had died of pneumonia after breaking through thin ice while skating on the pond on her father's estate. The second, Georgiana (Gigi), had run off with a Hungarian contortionist of a small traveling circus in central Europe whom she had met in the tearoom of the Adlon Hotel in Berlin while traveling with her husband. Gigi Price had tired of circus life after three years, had attempted to return greatly chastened to the Price marriage bed, but her husband had long since divorced her and married Nina, an adventuress he had met when her hat blew off and landed in his lap while she was riding two rows ahead of him on the upper deck of a Fifth Avenue bus.

Many people had warned Price against Nina. She had been everybody's darling around New York. She was supposed to have worked the great transatlantic liners playing cards "professionally." After two years of marriage to Price she had made the mistake of giving him a severe, if transient, venereal disease which disturbed Price's dignity to the extent that Nina Price had died in a sudden accident. She was struck by a hit-and-run driver while strolling alone on a country road during a summer weekend visit with friends. She had never regained consciousness.

Julia was pleased by the expression of Price's passion. She took it as the final endorsement of her leadership at Asbury Industries. Price might fake his feelings for everything else but not his feelings for money and status.

Her business accomplishments *were* a sexual thing to Edward Price, she knew. They stirred him much as aphrodisiacs had stirred ancient biblical kings. Julia wanted these responses to become habitual with him until he had convinced himself that he couldn't live without her. Not only would it be good tactics, but it stirred her own cup to see this cold, grasping, distant man transformed into a heavy breather because he had been aroused by his belief that she could make money for him. Besides, there was Charley. She wasn't sure, but she could be in love with Charley.

All that was true up to a point. The difference between Julia's analysis and the facts was simple: Edward S. Price was not aroused. He had been waiting for what only he would see as an opening, then he would dive through it believing, in his maleness, that Julia would be grateful, then eager, then abject, about submitting to him. After it was clear that she was in his power, he could gradually pave the way toward her ultimate delight when she realized that he would be proposing to marry her. It was the model male-female plight by which the human race has been upheld.

If she looked good to him now, she reasoned, she would look like Marilyn Monroe crossed with Cleopatra after she held out on him for six months or so. He had become shiny-eyed. His hands weren't steady. She knew she could score heavily if she held out, so she said breathily, "Oh, Edward. It just wouldn't be right if we—if we did what I can see in your eyes."

"Not right? Why?"

"It's an ancient rule. People have been careful to observe it for thousands of years. One must never—never, never, never—make love where one works."

"Nonsense!" But she could see that he was off-balance and she was off the hook.

"We've got to give it time, Edward. If we rush into something like this we could be spoiling something very, very beautiful."

She had talked him down. The tenuous hold he had on erection had lost its grip. It would be down, down, down all the way.

The encounter with Julia was an almost entirely unmanning experience for Price. Since he had made his fourth million dollars, his sexual advances had never been turned down by a woman, and he had made his fourth million when he was twenty-eight years old. He had planned the moment of his entry into Julia, living as though it had already happened; a benignly satisfactory joint performance. He had been thrilled to possess such a sexually inspiring woman if only in his imagination but in a manner which he knew would soon be a reality. He was confident that she would be sexually exalted by her appreciation of the amount of money he controlled and the extremes of power that he possessed. And he prided himself on being rather a phenomenon for a man who was sixty-six years old.

CHARLEY was sure somebody was tailing him wherever he went, so he talked to his father about it. "They change cars and they change people when I'm onna street," Charley said, "but somebody is making all my moves."

"So we'll double up on them," Angelo said. "I'll have The Plumber follow whoever is following you in a car and get a coupla people from Vincent to walk behind whoever is walking when you walk."

"Thanks, Pop."

The Plumber parked behind a new BMW 525 two days later, as it parked down the street near Charley's apartment. Charley got out of his car and went into the apartment building. The man in the BMW was on the car telephone when The Plumber opened the car door behind him, slid into the back seat, and pressed a cold gun barrel into the back of the man's neck.

"What is this?" the man squeaked. "A stickup?"

"Out!" The Plumber said.

They got out of the car together. The Plumber held the weapon in his jacket pocket, prodding the man with it in the small of his back.

The three men sat in Charley's living room (done in apricot and green by Maerose Prizzi).

"You been following me four days," Charley said pleasantly.

"Not me," the man said.

Gradually, Charley put the fear on him. They sat there, three men staring at each other, as Charley slowly increased the power of the fear. The man broke.

"I only work for a company. They assigned me to you. Today's my first day. Believe me. That's the facts."

"What company?"

"Potomac Security of Washington, D.C."

"Who hired them?"

"I don't know. How should I know? They're the company."

Charley turned to The Plumber. "Tie him up in a cellar someplace until we can check him out."

"A cellar? I *hate* cellars," the man said.

"You're gonna hate this one worse than you ever hated any cellar," Charley said. "Is that your car or the company's car," he asked the man.

"Mine. And brand new."

"Have somebody pick up the car and sell it," Charley said to The Plumber.

"*Sell* it?" the man said. "I got nineteen thousand arreddy in that car."

"Get him odda here," Charley said.

Charley went back to Pop that evening, about an hour after The Plumber had taken the tail away. "It's some private eye company in Washington name of Potomac Security."

"I'll talk to them," Angelo said.

The following morning Angelo called Potomac Security and asked for the name of the head of the company. His name was Ben Teazle. Angelo asked to speak to him.

"Teazle here."

"Mr. Teazle, who hired your company to follow Charles Partanna in New York?"

"I don't know what you're talking about and if I did it would be privileged information."

"One more warning. Who hired you?"

Teazle hung up on him.

Two nights later Teazle's house in Alexandria, Virginia, burned to the ground.

Angelo called him again the day after the fire. "Who hired you to tail Charles Partanna?" he asked quietly.

"Who is this?"

"It's the fella who had your house burned down. Now—are you going to give me this simple piece of information or do we have to go to work on your kids?"

"My *kids*?"

"You wanna get a call in a coupla days saying they been, like, drowned? One at a time. We aren't unreasonable. We just want a name, an address, and a telephone from you."

"The client is a very powerful man."

"Would he drown your kids?"

Teazle cooperated. "Barkers Hill Enterprises," he said. "For the personal attention of Mr. Edward S. Price. But, Jesus, don't touch my kids."

"What did he want you to find out?"

"He wanted to know which women Partanna was seeing and what he was doing with them—with tapes and photographs."

"Probably some kinda pervert."

"Yeah. I suppose you could say that."

"Thank you, Mr. Teazle. We are sorry for the inconvenience about your house. We will check out your facts and if necessary get back to you."

Angelo decided that since blood was thicker than water and money was thicker than blood, and since Eduardo was Corrado Prizzi's son who also controlled a few billion dollars in assets, that he should talk the matter over with the don before sharing his information with Charley.

He called on the don between breakfast and lunchtime.

"A funny thing came up," he said. "Somebody put a tail on Charley."

"Who?"

"We traced it down to a private eye company in Washington. Name of Potomac Security."

"Who put them on Charley?"

"That is the tricky part."

"Who, fahcrissake!"

"Eduardo."

"*Eduardo?* My Eduardo?"

"Yeah."

"What for? Why would he do that?"

"He wanted to find out who Charley was going with."

"Going with? Why should Eduardo care who Charley goes with?"

"Charley is going with Mrs. Asbury and so is Eduardo."

"Mrs. Asbury? Mrs. Asbury? She talks to the *Pope.* She had dinner *upstairs* with the President. She knows *Sinatra*! Why should she go with Charley?"

"Maybe she likes him."

"Then the world has gone crazy, that's all I can say."

"But you'll talk to Eduardo?"

"About what?"

"He's got to stop hiring people to tail Charley. I mean, it

could be very bad for us, considering Charley's work, to have a gang of private eyes watching everything he does."

"You're right, Angelo. I'll talk to Eduardo. You skip the weekly meeting next Tuesday and I'll talk to him."

Having resolved the central problem, by having Corrado admit that Eduardo was into a very dangerous thing, Angelo felt he could now talk to Charley. They sent out to a *pasticceria* for a light lunch of soup, pastry, and rolls and had lunch in Charley's office at the St. Gabbione Laundry.

"Well, I found out who had them following you."

"Who?"

"Eduardo."

"Ed*uardo*?" Charley was puzzled. "What does he need to know that he doesn't already know?"

"Like who you are going with."

"I don't get it."

"So who are you going with?"

"Well—like once a week I see Maerose."

"And?"

"Maybe twice a week I take Mrs. Asbury out."

"Eduardo also takes Mrs. Asbury out."

"*Whaaaaat?*"

"The don has decided that Eduardo should marry Mrs. Asbury. I mean, it's a very heavy business thing."

Charley just stared at his father. He turned white, red, white again, and his jaw fell heavily to his chest. "I don't believe it," he said. "Eduardo must be like sixty-five years old."

"Eduardo is also loaded with money."

"So is Mrs. Asbury. How much money can she use in a twenty-four-hour day?"

"Be sensible, Charley. You gotta back off."

"I can't back off, Pop. She's the woman of my dreams and that has nothing to do with money. I love her. I think she loves me. This is the most serious thing of my life."

"That changes things."

"It's the name of the game."

"If that's the way it is, then let Eduardo take his chances. Let the best man win, like the old saying goes. Even Corrado ain't so old that he can't understand that."

On Tuesday morning Edward S. Price arrived at his father's house driving a nondescript Chevrolet coupe because he didn't want his driver or anyone else to connect him with the Prizzi family. He was admitted at the front door by Calorino Barbaccia, who guarded the entrance to the house with a sawed-off shotgun in his lap.

Price climbed the stairs to his father's top-floor apartment wishing, for the 527th time, that his father would install an elevator, but since his father rarely left the top floor, that was unlikely.

The two men settled down to go over the weekly figures. "Aren't we going to wait for Angelo?" Eduardo said.

"He got tied up."

Eduardo opened the first file folder and began his recitation of the numbers. Corrado Prizzi listened intently for about fifty-five minutes until Eduardo had finished.

"Very nice," he said. "Eduardo, tell me something."

"Yes, Poppa?"

"Why are you paying people to keep a tail on Charley Partanna?"

Edward S. Price stared dumbly at his father.

"You hired the Potomac Security people outta Washington to throw a twenty-four-hour stakeout on Charley. That was a very dangerous thing to do. Dangerous for Charley, dangerous for the family. Why did you do it, Eduardo?"

"Poppa—look. I have made my plan to marry Mrs. Asbury but on at least two nights of the week when she isn't going out with me, she is going out with Partanna."

"Of her own free will?"

"Yes."

"She likes Charley?"

"I suppose one would have to say that."

"I can't understand it, a woman like that."

"Yes. It shocked me."

"Then we got two conditions here. One, you gotta take the tails off because that's bad for our business and two, you gotta play by the rules."

"Rules?"

"Whatta you want me to tell you? You can always hire people to find out more than you ever wanted to know but with women you gotta let nature take its course. You gotta try harder than Charley. You gotta win her heart. I mean, she decides, not you or the Potomac Security people, If you push her too hard in the wrong way you could push her right to Charley. This is basic stuff, Eduardo. Get that through your head."

VINCENT shut himself into his office at the St. Gabbione Laundry. He was preparing to work out his income tax return. He was humming "I Found a Million Dollar Baby (In a Five and Ten Cent Store)." He had an IRS pamphlet of instructions on how to cope with the new tax law but he kept reading the same lines over and over again, unable to understand where to start. The instructions said: *"The first number needed is on Line 31 of Form 1040, adjusted gross income. Next is Line 34, itemized deductions. Taxpayers with an adjusted gross income above $100,000 should multiply the difference by .03 to get their deduction limitation."* Vincent had never reported an income, as manager of the laundry, of more than $18,200. *"Subtract that number from the itemized deductions. Next subtract that number and the amount for personal exemptions from the adjusted gross income minus $150,000, divided by $122,500, times $636, times the number of exemptions. The result should be*

added to the tax calculation while calculating the additional Medicare tax of 1.45 percent for each dollar earned between $1300 and $125,000 and consumers must figure the effects of an additional tax of a nickel a gallon on gasoline, 16 cents on a six-pack of beer, and 4 cents on a pack of cigarettes."

Vincent slammed his meaty fist and forearm down upon the desktop in a fury of frustration causing a sudden recurrence of his idiopathic thrombocytopenia purpura which generated almost instant black-and-blue marks to appear even at a touch as light as a feather. He picked up his telephone and did what, each year, he was determined not to do: he called an accountant.

Breathing hard, he shouted at the closed door, "Send Charley in here."

After eight minutes the door opened and Charley came in.

"Siddown," Vincent said.

Charley sat on the blond leather chair furthest from Vincent's desk. Vincent had advanced acidity of the stomach which made his breath somewhat unpleasant.

"The Sputacchiera family in Cleveland needs a guest hitter to work out an organizational problem they got," Vincent said. "When can you leave?"

Charley didn't want to go anywhere. He had Mrs. Asbury on his mind and Eduardo breathing down his neck. "I'll send The Plumber," he said.

"No dice," Vincent said. "This is a request. They want the best. They asked for you."

"How long should it take?"

"You fly out in the morning. You do the work. You get outta town and come back."

Charley was deeply, irrevocably, passionately in love. Twenty-four hours away from Mrs. Asbury could give Eduardo a tremendous edge. Eduardo could buy her away from him, possibly, although he certainly didn't think Mrs. Asbury was that kind of a woman, but it could happen. He couldn't take a risk like that. Eduardo had all that money. All he had, essentially, were the special restaurants and the tube of LateComer.

"They could send the guy to New York. I could meet him at the airport, do him, then dump him."

"What would that prove in Cleveland? That's where their problem is and that's where they gotta make the impression. Whatsa matta witchew, anyways? They're gonna pay twenny-five grand for the work."

Charley couldn't come clean, man to man with Vincent, about being so in love, because he was engaged to Vincent's daughter. "Okay," he said. "But it would help if they sent a picture. Last time we did a guest appearance, The Plumber blew away the wrong guy."

"Don't worry," Vincent said, "I'll get you a picture, his name, where he lives and where he eats. It's just a courtesy hit, but when they come to us, they expect quality."

"When?"

"You could figure to leave on Monday."

Ah, shit! Charley thought.

"Monday night is my steady date night," he said.

Vincent glared at him.

"With Maerose," Charley added hastily. He knew she would cover for him.

When he got back to his office he called Julia. "Mrs. Asbury? Charley. It's like gonna break my heart but I gotta go outta town Monday night."

"No La Festa?" She had come to look forward all week long to the food in that restaurant. "Oh, Charley, what a disappointment." She would miss the cooking but she would also miss the tremendous experience in the sack at Charley's apartment while they were digesting.

"I thought maybe Wednesday night."

"Let me look. Oh, dear. I have a New York Public Library fund-raising dinner Wednesday."

"How about lunch? Wednesday."

"Lunch would be fine."

"I know a nice place in Staten Island. It's right across the Verrazano Bridge from my place. They do a nice *caciu all' argentiere*. They spread it on homemade bread then put tuna and clams on top. And they have a sensational *lacrima Cristi del Vesuvio*."

"How do you *find* this food?"

"Actually, my company owns the place in case we ever have to go to Staten Island."

Julia decided she could shoot her father.

Charley handled the hit in Cleveland without any problems. The guy was a barber who had ruined Sal Sputacchiera's hair when Sal had fallen asleep in the chair. Hair-wise, Sal used George Raft as his role model but this barber, Gus Grenig, cut the hair so short that it stood up on the sides like he was some hick. People *smiled* at him when he came into a room.

Charley had the barber's picture so he sat in a car the Sputacchieras had picked up for the job, in front of the building where the barber had his shop. Sputacchiera's people had left an Israeli Desert Eagle in the glove compartment. When the little old man came out, locking his barbershop behind him, it was 7:10 P.M. Charley rolled down the window and called out, "Hey, Gus!" The barber turned, it was the right guy, so Charley put him away with four rounds from the nine-round magazine.

Charley drove the hot car to the Loew's theater downtown where a Sputacchiera driver took over and drove Charley to the airport. He made his flight in plenty of time. But he got back to New York too late to call Mrs. Asbury in case she might still be available for dinner. He tried to shrug it off, telling himself, hey, that's the business you're in.

④⑨

ALLAN AND NUALA were in the fourth month of their proposed six-month trial period when something happened that altered things. Nuala told Allan she was pregnant. "How about that," she wailed, "just when that goddam Osgood Noon has vetoed the Family Leave Bill for the third time."

"*Preg*nant?" Allan said. "But I thought—"

"Allan, I'm Catholic."

"So am I. What does that have to do with it?"

"Well, I mean—we use the rhythm system, not the Pill."

"That's why there are so many Catholics."

"Well, now there's gonna be at least one more."

"It's terrific."

"What?"

"Now you have to marry me. God, this is wonderful. A husband and a father almost at the same time. I can't believe it. My sister will be beside herself with envy and admiration."

"What am I gonna tell my aunt in Ireland? She lives in a very small town, Kilmoganny, and everybody will know about it."

"Tell her you got married, what else?"

"When I was a little girl I used to imagine what my future husband would say when he proposed but nothing like this ever entered my mind."

"But you will marry me?"

"Oh, Allan! With all my heart."

"Big wedding? Small, just family? Or elope?"

"Nobody on my side, my aunt is too old to travel and the nuns at St. Scholastica of Umbria are all retired by now."

"What's that?"

"An orphanage. But very upmarket."

"If I had known you were an orphan I would have been nicer to you."

*   *   *

190

Julia was ecstatic when they took her to dinner and told her the news.

"Where are you going to live?"

"At Allan's place."

"That's very nice but it's not very big and it's far from the Park, really. I mean, you'll be pushing a baby carriage uptown on Fifth Avenue through all that traffic. And, I mean, you'll need help, after all you'll probably want to keep working, Nuala, so you'll need a nanny and a cook at least, and they take up room."

"Come on, Julia!" Allan said, reproving.

"There is very nice twelve-room apartment in my building," Julia said. "Only two blocks from the Park. I own the building, as Allan knows, so you could take the apartment over for maintenance and taxes whatever they are. And the security in the building is the best in the city."

"Julia, how generous! How sweet you are!"

"My wedding present. And you're welcome to use the houses in Rome, Aspen, Gstaad, Acapulco, or Bali for your honeymoon. After all, you could only be married once."

EDWARD S. PRICE did not give up easily. When three weeks had passed after his father had refused to interfere in matters of the heart, at a regular meeting with his father he spoke up before Angelo Partanna arrived.

"Poppa, I realize that it is your firm belief that when two men seek the same woman that each man must take his own chances."

"That's right."

"I can see where that would apply if the conditions existing between the two men were approximately equal."

"So?"

"Charley Partanna has one very big advantage over me. I mean, money is only relative. I may have more money than Charley but so has Mrs. Asbury. The one enormous factor of inequality between us is that Charley is about thirty-six and I'm sixty-six. I mean to say, Mrs. Asbury certainly doesn't need my money—or Charley's—but it is only natural for a relatively young, handsome woman to be drawn more to a man closer to her age than to a man who is almost twice her age."

"So?"

"You and I both see the consolidating advantages of my marrying Mrs. Asbury but, under the circumstances, Partanna is cluttering up a quite unlevel playing field."

"And?"

"Although it seems impossible to me, suppose Mrs. Asbury were to become smitten with Partanna? If that happened it would seriously damage our intentions toward Mrs. Asbury, I mean, it could knock me out of the running entirely."

"And—?"

"Partanna is already seriously engaged to Vincent's daughter, Maerose. If Vincent knew that Partanna was seriously courting a woman other than his daughter, his honor would be grievously violated. He might arrange that harm come to Partanna, one of your most valuable men. And the honor of your granddaughter is involved. Allow me to say that you would need to see your obligation to her, to your son, and to your faithful *vindicatore*, Partanna."

"So?"

"It is clear that someone with all the authority of the *fratellanza* must speak to Mrs. Asbury's father so that he may see it as his duty to speak to Mrs. Asbury about the unseemliness of her association with Partanna. To forbid, as it were, any further connection between Partanna and the daughter."

"The *Plumber*?"

"Yes."

Angelo Partanna entered at that moment. Corrado Prizzi wanted deeply to discuss the entire matter with his old friend but Angelo was Charley's father so it would be very hard for him to get the point. Similarly, he thought, Mrs. Asbury's father, The Plumber, worked for Charley Partanna, the other principal suitor, and could feel that he owed loyalty to Charley. He would have to handle this carefully so that Angelo wouldn't be offended, so that Charley wouldn't know what was happening, and so that The Plumber could get it through his head what he had to do. Also, there was something very shaky about the proposition. The Asbury woman hadn't lived under her father's authority for at least twenty years. If she threw her father out when he made his demands, then told Charley what was going on, Charley would naturally come to him for an explanation and how could he tell him that he and Eduardo were rigging Mrs. Asbury so that the family could get all its money back, considering the fact that Charley and Mrs. Asbury were having an *idillio*?

The whole thing almost ruined his lunch excepting that Amalia was preparing polenta with baby clams with a marvelous sauce drizzled over it, after a nice dish of sweet-and-sour baby onions and sliced salami and a bottle of Greco di Tufo from Avellino which even snobs who carried on about northern Italian wines gave the highest marks. If he knew his Amalia, and he did, there would be a *contorno* of orange and lemon salad with the polenta, with some of her perfect almond tarts and a few glasses of Marsala Superiore.

After the meeting with Eduardo he told Calo Barbaccia, his doorman, to tell The Plumber to come to see him at four-thirty that afternoon.

When The Plumber was shown into the room Corrado had had his nap, having instantly digested his lunch the way an ostrich can digest a pile of tin cans. He bade The Plumber to be seated, offered him a cookie, and got down to business.

"What am I going to say to you, Alberto, is only for our knowledge and one other—your daughter."

"My daughter, *padrino*?"

"As her father, you are to forbid her to continue to see Charley Partanna."

"My *daughter*? Charley Partanna? Somebody gave you mixed-up information, *padrino*."

"No,! It happened because those two bandits, Violente and Cloacacino, decided to make a business out of her."

"How did Charley get into that?"

"What's the *diffe*rence? Go to your daughter and tell her she must stop seeing Charley!"

"Can I talk to Charley and get this thing straight in my head?"

"NO! Fahcrissake, Alberto! What are you, some kind of a *zuccone*?"

"But Charley is not only my *capo*, but he can be a very violent man."

"I am your *padrino*. Am I some kind of Signorina Pudibonda? Do you think of me as your kindly family priest?" Suddenly, without warning, he put the fear on The Plumber. Eighty years of putting the fear on people had been the prime reason for his ascension to power as the head of the Prizzi crime family which dominated both terror and public service throughout North America, Mexico, and into certain areas of the Common Market. The Plumber, who had considered himself (almost) immune to the affliction of the fear through a glance, almost fainted.

"I will talk to her, *padrino*," he blubbered. "I will go to her directly when I leave here. She shall do as you say. She shall renounce Charley Partanna."

AS THE PLUMBER entered Julia's apartment he stared up at the huge painting of Lady Evelyn Hunt and her daughters, and said, "Who's that?"

"No one we know, Poppa. It was painted about 1760."

"1760? A woman like you can't afford new paintings?"

He was dressed as she had never expected to see him, in a black suit, a white shirt, and black tie. His shoes were polished and, although she knew it wasn't probable, he could have changed his underwear.

She guided him toward the study, purposely avoiding the Marble Hall because its stateliness might have unmanned him. "It's such a lovely surprise to have you come to see me, Poppa. You were always too busy to come here before."

"I know. I have this thing about coming to New York." That was the truth. He had not been on Manhattan Island since the day, three years before, when he and Charley had knocked off Dandy Eddie Abramowitz and two of his people in front of a steak house on the East Side. "Jesus, Julia, this is like a museum," he said.

Settling him in the (relatively) small music room, seating him beside the antique harp that Lady Jemma Jupp had played looking across the green valley toward Wardour Castle while dreaming her beautiful dreams, Julia asked if he would like something to drink.

"Maybe a little glassa wine," The Plumber said. Steiner, having anticipated the needs, entered with a tray containing a bottle of champagne, a glass, and a silver tea service for one. He poured the wine for The Plumber. "Hey, I said wine," he said, "not ginger ale."

"It's champagne, Poppa."

"So *that's* champagne."

When she had settled him comfortably Julia sat across the

room from him and waited for the explanation of why he had decided to visit her for the first time in her life.

"You prolly wonder why I came here," The Plumber said.

"Not really. I'm just so glad to see you. And looking so well."

"This is a new tie."

"Very nice."

"I wanted to tell you I was sorry you lost your husband."

"Poppa, that was almost a year ago."

"Still, it's hard." He cleared his throat, sounding like a boar about to charge. "What I came to tell you, Julia, as your father who therefore has the right to tell you—remember it is an ancient law of our people that the children submit to the wishes of the father," he said, then gulped the champagne to fortify his resolve. "What I gotta tell you is that I forbid you to see Charley Partanna ever again."

"Whaaaaaaaat?"

"That's it. That's the way it's gotta be."

She imagined herself saying, but did not say, "Poppa, are you crazy? I see you here and there at weddings and funerals since I was nineteen years old and got out of the house and you're gonna come in here and tell me who I should have as my friend?"

"Does Charley know about this?" is what she said instead.

"No."

"Whose idea was it?"

"I don't think I'm supposed to talk about that."

"You work for Charley but I know Charley didn't tell you to say that. Was it Vincent, then? Vincent doesn't want Charley to see anybody because he's engaged to Vincent's daughter?"

"Yeah. Well, something like that."

"But how would Vincent know I was seeing Charley?"

"How do I know?"

"It wasn't Vincent, was it, Poppa?"

The Plumber didn't answer.

"That leaves Edward S. Price and the don."

"Jesus, Julia, I don't know people like Price."

"So it was Corrado Prizzi."

"I didn't say that."

"Why would Corrado Prizzi care who I was dating?"

"Who said Corrado Prizzi? What I said was, I order you to stop seeing Charley Partanna."

She fell back into another wholly imaginary statement but just letting it run through her mind made her see things more clearly. "And you can go pack your feet in a cement block," she imagined she was saying to her father, "and take a flying fuck to the moon. **OUT!**"

That is how she wished the entire conversation had happened; but she had cross-examined him enough to find out what the score was even if she hadn't handed him his hat and had him thrown out onto the pavement on Park Avenue.

Instead, she said, "I don't know how anyone got the idea that I was *seeing* Charley Partanna. He was very pleasant to me when I was locked up with those two *shtarkers*, Violente and Cloacacino, so when he asked me out to dinner once, I accepted because he was also your boss."

"Yeah?" The Plumber said incredulously.

"However, if the idea offends you in any way, I will, of course, refuse any future invitations. Now you mustn't get yourself upset about this, dear Poppa. Please, have another glass of champagne."

She saw clearly what was behind the whole rotten attempt at manipulation. It was that bloodless son-of-a-bitch Price who had gone whining to his father to get Charley drop-kicked out of the stadium. Price had put people on them, that was for sure. When he knew Charley was in the competition—what competition?—he had put up his father to call in Pop and lay down the law to him. What could Pop do but read the riot act to her? The *capo di tutti capi* gives him an order and he does it. Kill this one. Break that one's arm. Blow up that one's car with him in it. Tell your daughter to stop seeing Partanna. What was Pop supposed to do? He did what was expected of him. Where everybody but she was concerned, he always had.

She sat alone in the elegant study and considered her options. Should she call Allan in, on the two-heads-are-better-than-one formula? She rejected that. Allan would give good counsel in any other kind of a problem but he was too Americanized to get inside this one. This was Sicilian in a way that started when the Greeks had occupied the island in the fifth century B.C. Archimedes was a Sicilian from Siracusa and in the fourth century B.C. the Greeks-become-Sicilians had taken Italy. Then, when the Saracens moved into Sicily, forcing the Greeks out or absorbing them, things *really* got crafty. What Greeks are to ordinary plotters, so is the Arab character to Greek, she thought. She had to summon up some of that if she hoped to keep the wholly assimilated Greek-Arab-Sicilian Prizzis in line.

If she told Charley about what Corrado Prizzi had ordered The Plumber to do, she would be pulling down the temple on top of all of them. Charley had family obedience ingrained in his soul but she knew instinctively that his *amour-propre* would not permit him to accept such interference. She knew Charley was in love with her. Maybe she was in love with him. No matter what, that wasn't the way to go.

She could go to Don Corrado and make a big scene but that would only put her out in the open and cut her options. She had to keep her eye on the main chance which would be realized by taking over Ed Price. Price had certainly put himself out in the open and had cut his own options when he put a tail on Charley and had gone to the don to persuade him to have The Plumber talk to her. Ed Price was ripe for the picking so she would let him get overripe until he dropped from the bough and fell to the ground. When she had him, she would be able to take over Barkers Hill Enterprises so gradually that both Price and Don Corrado would be grateful for her know-how. The don was an old man. He couldn't last forever. Ed Price had lost himself inside a labyrinth of mirrors. She could control the billions of dollars that Barkers Hill possessed.

CHARLEY had worked himself into such a state of indignation that Eduardo could have the gall to put a tail on him and Mrs. Asbury that, despite his father's urgent advice to the contrary, he had decided that he had no recourse but to lay the whole injustice before the don.

"What can he tell you, Charley?" Angelo said. "Botha his sons are in this up to their hips. Vincent thinks you wronged his daughter because she jilted you, and Eduardo is not only hot about a woman you think is private property, but by getting involved with another woman, you are cheating on the don's own granddaughter."

"Lissen, that ain't the issue here," Charley said hotly. "The issue is that Eduardo is about seventy years old. Three wives. He's had his turn at bat. Now he's trying to rain on my parade. But do I put a tail on him? No. Do I go to the don with a booka rules that says Eduardo is wrong? No. Well, no more Mr. Nice Guy. I'm gonna get this thing straightened out with the don."

Before Charley had a chance to make his move, it hit the fan. Vincent was diagnosed as having an aneurysm of the abdominal aorta. He had gone into the St. Gabbione Laundry that morning feeling a belt of twinges all around his middle, front, and back. He had had so many diseases, disorders, and physical malfunctions in his life that he had become perhaps more sensitive to symptoms than most people. He called Dr. Lesion as soon as he got to the office. Dr. Lesion had made Vincent an exception to his industry's rule against making house calls. He came to Vincent's office at the laundry within the hour, made an examination, urged that Vincent go to Santa Richenda's immediately for X rays. The X rays confirmed the aneurysm.

Vincent was made ready for surgery. "Jesus," he said to his

daughter, Maerose, "and I'm not even old enough for Medicare."

The surgeon, Dr. Hampton, told Maerose Prizzi and Angelo Partanna, as immediate family, that the surgery would be touch-and-go, that the odds were 30–70 against Vincent surviving.

"We're not worried about that," Maerose said. "My father is very strong."

"How long is he gonna be off his feet?" Angelo asked.

"If he makes it," the surgeon said. "He won't be strong enough to move around much for about eight weeks," the doctor told them. "After that he'll need about five months to get all of his strength back. He's going to lose a lot of blood and the whole thing will be an enormous shock to his system."

"So we'll figure eight, ten weeks," Angelo said. "He's very strong."

It was ten o'clock in the morning when the operation began. At six o'clock that evening the surgical team had sewn in a Dacron aorta, eight inches long, and had pumped nine pints of hospital blood into Vincent. At eight o'clock when the procedure was completed, Vincent had an eleven-inch-long incision down the center of his abdomen.

Maerose and Angelo waited for Dr. Hampton to come out of the recovery room. When he did, he was visibly troubled. "You will have to be ready for the worst," he said. "It looks pretty bad. Maybe he'll pull through, but I have to tell you that I don't think he will."

"Don't worry about that, doctor," Angelo said, patting the surgeon comfortingly on the shoulder. "Do you think the operation worked?"

"Everything went by the book. Everything went as we planned it."

"Then he is gonna be okay. You'll see. Vincent is very strong."

Charley Partanna was called to lunch with the don and Angelo the next day at twelve-fifteen. Charley was a young man with a healthy appetite but lunch with the don was too much to contemplate; not because he was in awe of the don but because he had never been able to handle the amount of food that came to the don's table. Amalia was a wonderful cook. Everything was absolutely authentic as if they had never left the old country but Charley couldn't take the nine courses and the three helpings. However, as always, he got through it, accepted a Mexican cigar and a glass of *grappa*, and waited to be told why he had been invited to lunch.

"You heard about Vincent?" the don asked.

"You mean the operation?"

"I talked to botha his doctors and I called a contact I have at the Mayo Clinic. Vincent is gonna be outta action for a coupla months."

"Yeah?"

"You're Vincent's *sotto capo*. So now I want you to be Acting Boss."

"Boss?"

"Acting."

"I am honored, *padrino*."

"I'm gonna give you two extra points on the car dealership shipment overrides for the Eastern Seaboard and one point on the fruit and vegetable markups for the New York area."

"Thank you, *padrino*. That is more than generous."

"While you are Acting, don't do any *vindicatore* work. If it comes up, farm it out to The Plumber. And you can use Vincent's driver or you can pick your own driver."

"I like to drive myself."

"It don't look right. And you gotta have a bodyguard. The Boccas still got a grudge against us."

"Some grudges are right, *padrino*."

"Whatta you mean?"

"There is something I gotta talk about."

"First, have a cookie, more *grappa*. Then you'll talk."

He lifted a plate of cookies with one hand, poured a *grappa* with the other, and smiled terribly.

"What's on your mind, Charley?" He had a pretty good idea what was on Charley's mind. He was trapped between the can opener and the can.

"Eduardo hired some private eyes to put a tail on me."

"Whaaaaat?"

"Suppose they had been tailing me when I did that job a Cleveland last week?"

"Charley—why would Eduardo put people on you?"

"Because we're both taking the same woman out."

"Taking her *out*? Eduardo?"

"No, no. Not like that. Keeping company."

"Who told you this?"

"The woman. Her father is one of my people, The Plumber. He told her, she told me."

WORD got out fast that Charley was the new Boss. Television camera crews began following him around as he ducked out of his car to hurry into places like the Monongahela Social Club where Vincent had always met with his *caporegimes*, or in the Prizzi box at Shea Stadium, or as he entered or as he left his apartment house at Brighton Beach. He had to have Rocco Sestero organize the Television Engineers and Technicians Local 107 hastily, then to threaten the television networks and stations with a prolonged strike if they didn't call off their people, but the newspapers put photographers on him and kept calling the laundry to line up interviews until thirty other things happened in the world that turned them to other quarries. But Charley was a four-day wonder, the youngest Boss of a Mafia family in a proud line of leaders who had given their lives to the service of the American people.

He got enough news media space to make him the face of the week. To his horror, to the outrage of Corrado Prizzi, to the consternation of Edward S. Price, *Time* magazine put him on its cover. The story that went with it had been put together from clips and from anonymous interviews with members of the Bocca family, so there were some surprises there for Charley and Corrado Prizzi.

It was the nationally naked prominence of looking at his head and shoulders in a NYPD mug shot that was three years old and that, due to its flat lighting, made him look like he had just busted out of either jail or his teens. All of the pride he took in the carefulness of his dress was shattered. In the mug shot he had no tie on, he needed a shave, and his eyebrows looked like they hadn't been trimmed for two weeks.

Corrado Prizzi's dismay over the *Time* cover was based on his natural aversion to any publicity that could tend to disturb the onward flow of his business but since the scarifying experience with the Asbury woman he had looked on all public attention as a plague. He was amazed to see, going over the weekly tally sheets with Angelo that, if anything, loan sharking and pornography sales had gone up after the *Time* cover hit the stands and the volume of heroin and cocaine turnover in state prisons increased by as much as 7 percent so, although he watched for threatening manifestations warily, there didn't seem to be any bad effects. He hoped they wouldn't show the cover to Vincent because it would be bad for his recovery, but at no time did the publication affect Corrado enough to make him talk to Charley about it. He knew Charley felt the way he did about landing on a goddam magazine cover.

However, *Time*'s coverage had a deep effect on both Edward S. Price and on Vincent Prizzi. Vincent wanted to fling the entire magazine issue into the wall across the hospital room but could only muster up enough strength to nudge it off his bed onto the floor. He decided that Charley had hired press agents to build himself up so he could take over as permanent Boss of the family. He fantasized that Charley was conspiring with Hollywood agents to have a movie made of his life story when, for the past ten years or more, Vincent had been hoping for a deal like that for himself.

Edward S. Price had the most severe response to the *Time*

cover, its accompanying story, and the buildup of television and newspaper coverage that had preceded it. He could see it only for the effect it would have upon Julia Asbury. She was an American. She had been trained from birth by her culture to worship celebrityhood. His own *Time* cover twelve years before, which had been based upon his philanthrophies and his leadership in the encouragement of the arts, had been long forgotten—if she had ever known that it had happened. She would see Partanna as a modern corsair, a swashbuckling romantic figure of a pirate on whom had been conferred a *Time* cover, the knighthood of celebrity. Price began to devote most of his waking hours to devising ways that might offset Partanna's advantage over his own courtship of the woman he and his father had chosen to become his wife, entirely overlooking that Julia's maiden name had been Melvini; that she was The Plumber's daughter and that she saw everything through the lenses of that environment.

Julia, of all those affected, was devoutly thrilled by Charley's *Time* cover. She bought eleven copies, one for each of her houses, and sent them off with instructions that they were to be placed on coffee tables so that, if she entered a room, she could seem to appear casual as she scooped up the *Time* copy and settled down in a comfortable chair to stare at it. For as long as she could remember—as a child, as a teenager, as a young woman—she had thrilled to shivers of admiration over the achievements of Charley Partanna as the industry's ace *vindicatore*. Then she had matured as a woman to realize what every other woman in the *ambiente* had dreamed of, thrilling to what had happened to her; she had banged Charley Partanna.

CHARLEY grew a moustache and wore a beret so no one could recognize him as the youth who had stared out at them from the covers of *Time*. That shook up the *caporegimes* and those of the *soldati* who came in contact with him daily but Charley refused to be inhibited by the nickname of Frenchie Partanna that some wise-guy columnist had hung on him. He was forced to have Cusumano Viscere break both legs of a joker who had called him Frenchie to his face so that word would get out that he didn't appreciate the name.

He went about his daily work doggedly, fixing prizefights and basketball games to load the outcome of gambling nationally. He had his Washington people lobby once again for an increase of the postal rate, the second in three years, so that the Prizzis could realize the benefits of the increase through their merchandising of recycled postage stamps.

It wasn't that he was trying to outshine Vincent, he was just doing the job. He organized the icing in Miami of two Bolivian drug lords as a favor for the Colombian cartel, sending The Plumber and a soldier in Tarquin Garrone's regime to do the work. He poured money into research on designer drugs that could transport users into moods that were both hideous and benign, and reached out to develop new markets for them. He poured $8 million of the family's money into eleven of its thirty-six Political Action Committees to lobby the Congress to increase its own pay by 32 percent, forcing the lawmakers into action in support of his crusade. He made certain that they all knew who was the patron behind this windfall so that his people could be sure that narcotics remained illegal and that no cramping restrictions would be placed upon firearms.

Somehow through it all, in spite of the many new responsibilities that weighed him down, he found time to see Mrs. Asbury because he had fallen deeply in love with her.

He still called on Maerose at her Murray Hill apartment in the early hours of the morning because, as his fiancée and as a woman who had grown up in Vincent's house, he could talk over the the day-to-day problems of running the Prizzi crime family. Maerose had accused him of having another woman. She was sensitive to his moods and when he seemed absentminded she decided he was thinking about another woman. "Mae, fahcrissake," he would say, "how can we do what we are always doing if I was doing that with some other woman?" But at the same time Charley was courting Mrs. Asbury. He had the family fund a restaurant on Third Avenue much nearer her apartment building so that, when he could tear himself away from his work or from Mae, they wouldn't have to drive all the way across the city or face the journey to Staten Island. To staff it, he imported two cooks from Venice and one from Bologna and the place was packed out until Mrs. Asbury happened to say that there was something wrong with the food.

"Wrong?" Charley said. "What's wrong? These are terrific cooks."

"It doesn't taste Sicilian to me."

The next morning Charley fired the cooks and replaced them with two from Enna and one from Agrigento. Business fell off, but Mrs. Asbury was in seventh heaven. "Jesus, Charley," she said, "I swear to God this food is better even than La Festa or Staten Island."

They never overate because they knew the reason they were meeting. There was no more of that back-of-the-van stuff and Charley didn't have the time anymore to drive her out to his place, then bring her home. He was also stuck with a driver now so, after the driver took them to the joint on Third Avenue, Charley and Mrs. Asbury walked back to her apartment and later—much later—the driver picked Charley up after Charley phoned the car and told the man where to pick him up—always on a street corner, never at Mrs. Asbury's apartment building because that would have compromised her.

Charley went head over heels about Mrs. Asbury. At her insistence he shaved off the moustache and went back to wearing an ordinary felt fedora. No matter how busy he got with his work and, what with subverting the labor movement, going through all the intricate moves of bribing politicians and police officials, assigning contracts for hits, keeping up with the public's relentless demand for cocaine, and adding to the American cost of living by his chains of tributes that took effect as soon as the goods were moved into the cities, tributes that were then added to the cost of almost everything to be passed on to the consumer, Charley was always thinking about Julia Asbury and how, despite his engagement to Maerose Prizzi, he could ask a classy woman like that to marry him.

JULIA disturbed Edward Price, three separate times, by asking him before business meetings or during their weekly dinners whether he had seen Charley's *Time* cover. Julia knew that Price knew that she knew he was a Prizzi, and Price knew that Julia knew that he knew she was The Plumber's daughter but they never acknowledged that to each other except in careful, indirect ways.

"Charley who?" Price asked.

"The current *Time* cover. The Prizzi family boss, Charley Partanna."

"I must have missed it. I was on a *Time* cover myself not so long ago."

"You were? How fascinating."

When she asked him for the third time about Charley's cover, he allowed himself to show his irritation. "I don't under*stand* your overriding interest in this hoodlum," he said. "I may have seen the magazine but it is hardly something I would remember."

"Oh, I think anyone who actually saw it would remember it. It is a very striking picture."

"As I recall, it was the photograph of what seemed to be a mentally arrested young man, taken by the police. He was unkempt, unshaven, and entirely uncouth. Is that the *Time* cover you mean?"

"Then you *did* see it." She patted his hand. "But no matter. It was just something which occurred to me in passing."

Price had overinterpreted her interest in the magazine cover. He had decided, based entirely on the surveillance reports he had read from the Washington detective agency, that she was so preoccupied with Partanna that she couldn't hold it within herself. Grimly, he decided he had to get some lock on her, that presents like diamonds and flower farms weren't enough. He was going to have to take her to bed because, knowing his own incredible appeal to women, he would bond her to him eternally once he had made love to her. He knew that he just happened to have the gift of being able to turn the most frigid of women into volcanos and this was no frigid woman. However, he wouldn't make love to her tonight because he had taken a double dose of hypertension pills before going out to dinner. She had a tendency, probably the perfume she used, to send his blood pressure soaring, and hypertension pills were the enemies of erections.

Julia, on her side, had been using Charley's *Time* cover to pique Price's interest in her because, within the year, she was going to propose that Price move up to Chairman of the Board of Barkers Hill Enterprises while she took over as CEO and Allan was assigned to run Asbury Industries. To do that she had to be sure she had Price on the hook.

After dinner the following Friday night as Price's limousine had reached the entrance to Julia's building, Edward Price suggested that she invite him upstairs for a nightcap. Julia showed no surprise, although she was aware that Price hardly drank anything other than an occasional sherry before dinner. She reasoned that it wasn't any nightcap he would be after but that he was about to make his move.

They sat in the library, dwarfed by the four thousand leather-bound volumes that soared to the twenty-two-foot ceiling.

"I've always admired this room," Price said. "I had no idea that Harry was such a scholar."

"Oh, yes," Julia replied.

Steiner brought in a silver tray holding a bottle of champagne in an ice bucket and two glasses. He poured the wine and left the room. Price was uneasy about drinking champagne when he had deliberately omitted taking his hypertension pills, but he understood ritual. He lifted his glass, stared into Julia's eyes and said, "To your loveliness."

They sipped the champagne, staring at each other. It wasn't that he was suddenly overcome by her beauty, she thought, more likely Charley's *Time* cover was bugging him. And there was her father's near admission that someone had been watching her as she spent time with Charley. She became certain that it was Price who had paid to have the snooping done; therefore, put all together, he was going to try to get her into the sack so he could try to make close claims upon her, perhaps even going so far as insisting that she stop seeing Charley.

She decided that she had held out on him long enough if she was going to nudge him upward toward the chairmanship of Barkers Hill, leaving her to run the operation as CEO; they needed to be a little closer.

Staring at him, she moistened her lips with her wet, pink tongue and stared at him longingly and just lewdly enough to urge him to put into action what was so clearly in his mind. He responded instantly.

"You are the most desirable woman I have ever known," he said.

"Oh, Edward!"

He took her glass from her and placed it with his glass upon a nearby table, then placed his hands on her waist. "I adore you," he said. The fact that he had not taken the hypertension pills had definitely had the desired effect. He had an urgent need to adjust his clothing.

Julia took his right hand in her left hand and led him off toward her intimidating bedroom.

TWO WEEKS LATER Edward S. Price was facing his father on the top floor of the Victorian mansion at the foot of Brooklyn Heights. The don, wearing a gray woolen sweater over long winter underwear and a pair of blue jeans, offered him a cookie. Eduardo refused.

"How can you drink a cuppa coffee without a cookie?"

"I didn't know we were having coffee."

"It's coming. What's on your mind?"

Eduardo took a deep breath and exhaled slowly. "Mrs. Asbury wants to be named CEO of Barkers Hill at the next directors' meeting," he said.

"What about you?"

"She thought I might like to be Chairman of the Board."

"It figures," his father said. "Now that she has a lock on her billion four and has twenty percent of all the Asbury profits, she wants a shot at all of it."

"What am I supposed to do?"

"Tell her you'll think about it."

"I told her that."

"This woman has been more trouble for me than any other man or woman in my life and I am eighty-seven years old. Send her to me. I'll convince her that there is no possibility of her having anything to do with Barkers Hill."

"The thing is—well, I may have compromised myself."

"How?"

"I am sleeping with her."

The don stared at him, shocked out of his skull. "*Sleeping* with her?????? Did you lose your mind? The one sure way for a woman to take a man over is to let him go to bed with her! What came over you? With all of the women in New York City you had to go to bed with the biggest schemer I ever met?"

"Poppa! I thought that was our game plan."

"Our game plan was to keep her under control, not to put her *in* control! I gotta find a way to get around this."

"We could marry her off to Charley Partanna."

"Have you forgotten that he is engaged to Vincent's daughter?"

"She is still seeing Partanna. I know that."

"Sixteen months ago this Asbury woman was a simple housewife, now she runs 137 companies and wants to take over the biggest conglomerate in America. It's that goddam woman's movement that puts these crazy ideas into their heads."

"What can we do?"

"So you'll marry her!"

"I'm not saying she wouldn't marry me—eventually. But right now is just a bit early on. I've got to get her much more involved."

"Then there is only one thing *to* do—we gotta run her for the U.S. Senate. That will tie her up, she'll have her hands full campaigning and your people can make sure her picture is always in the papers and on television so she'll be bit by the celebrity bug and we'll be rid of her for once and for all."

"But who'll run the Asbury companies?"

"The brother."

"He's on his honeymoon in Europe."

"Honeymoon? When did that happen?"

"He married the woman who wrote all those stories in the newspaper."

"What kind of a family are they? The sister wants to take over our action and the brother marries our enemy! Is this some kinda practical joke?"

"Running Mrs. Asbury for the Senate is a wonderful idea, Poppa. Which party is scheduled to win this year? Who won the toss-up?"

"It's gonna be a Democratic year."

"Right. Then she'll go in as a Democrat."

"How are you gonna break the news to her?"

"I'll have to think about that."

"Whatta you have to think about? You make a list of your biggest charitable and religious donations. That gets you names that'll convince her. You talk to the *capos* at the Democratic Party. You round up the Cardinal, the bankers, the news media owners, a buncha feminists, eight or ten business leaders from your companies, a coupla housewives, and maybe Magic Johnson. They go to her—a citizens' committee. They plead with her to run for the United States Senate as the most successful woman business leader in the country. How can she refuse them?"

"Yes! She'll be swept off her feet," Eduardo said excitedly. "She'll come to me. She'll ask me how she can serve the nation but still not neglect the Asbury companies. I'll tell her how, but I will also lay out the possibility of her becoming the first woman President of the United States and she will forget all about the Asbury companies and devote all her time to the Senate so she can have a springboard to the White House in '96."

"Lissena me—handle it right and this woman will be grateful for giving her the big chance. Lay on the romance and when you ask her, she'll be gladda marry you and we'll sew up the whole proposition."

"We are home-free, Poppa."

"Just be careful, Eduardo. This is a very, very tricky woman."

THE NEWLYWEDS, Nuala and Allan, came home to a prodigy of interior decoration in the apartment that Julia had given them as one of her wedding presents. She had had four of the country's most fashionable decorators, working independently of each other, create the ambience for four separate living areas of the duplex apartment she had given the bride and groom. She had had the decorators work apart from each other in such wholly feminine rooms as Nuala's boudoir, her bedroom, her bath, quite distinctly away from such distinctly masculine rooms as Allan's study, his bedroom and bath, and his spa, from such neutral areas as the music room, the dining hall, the main salon, the library, and the guest rooms, into areas to be designed by each of them without the knowledge of the other designers. Styles ranged from all glass and Aubusson tapestries to heavy Jacobean with hi-tech overtones. Color was either rampant or invisible. There was a small figure skating rink in Allan's mini-gymnasium. The effect was startling. Nuala told Allan that she had the feeling that she should change clothes as she moved from room to room.

"I don't see what we can do about it," Allan said dazedly after Julia had taken them on a tour from room to room. "Perhaps, after ten years or so, she won't notice it if we change a few things."

"But it's so *int*eresting," Nuala said. "I feel like some kind of explorer."

Allan told Julia when she asked him how he and Nuala liked the effect that it wasn't actually an apartment but more an infinite measure of the distance he and his sister had traveled from President Street. "You'd better believe it," Julia told him grimly.

But nothing could bring the radiant couple down from the high of expecting a baby in three weeks' time. The elation that had carried them from North Africa to Rome to Paris to Kilmoganny in Ireland, where Nuala had presented Allan to her aunt.

As the Asbury Industries legal counsel, Allen met with his sister at the Asbury offices on the fourth day after their arrival. Julia was waiting for him.

"Things have gotten a little heavy since you left," she said. "Price wants me to run for the Senate."

"The *Sen*ate? The United *States* Senate?"

"Price pretends he doesn't know anything about it, like it was all news to him."

"Why should he know about it?"

"It's all a snow job, Al. It happened like three weeks after I had suggested to Price that he move up to chairman and have me take over as CEO at Barkers Hill."

"You did?"

"Price is almost sixty-seven years old. There is no successor and it's Corrado Prizzi who has the vote, not Ed Price."

"But, Jesus, Julia—"

"I can bring Corrado Prizzi in on my side—not right away, but more sooner than later—because I am the only one in his life who ever scored him for important money. Nothing like that ever happened to him so he listens when I talk and waddles when I walk."

"Who offered you the Senate? Price or the don?"

"They're too slick for that. A committee came to me. Would you believe Wambly Keifetz, the Cardinal, a network television head, a woman who was more feminist than Joan of Arc, and the state head of the Democratic Committee?"

"They asked you to run for the Senate?"

"Wambly Keifetz got tears in his eyes when he told me how much the country needs me."

"Who would run the Asbury operation?"

"You."

"*Me?*"

"I knew the answer but I asked Price the same question. Then, from the way he answered about the Senate, I twigged to what they were trying to do to me. Price began a spiel about how American big business money and influence would get behind me to make me the first woman president of the United States."

"No shit? He gave you that?"

"Straight-faced. Didn't blink an eye."

"So what are you going to do?"

"I'd have to be out of my head to give up a two-million-dollar-a-year job with stock options and bonuses, protecting my own interests, to take some dinky $135,000 job in the Senate in Washington, plus my share of the PACs, and he shouldn't hang by his nose until they put up a woman for President, not that I would take it if a miracle happened."

"You told him that?"

"Not straight out. Corrado Prizzi wouldn't respect me if I showed them anything in my hand. I told him that whereas I would certainly think about it, that I had a little too much on my plate just then to be able to give it all my consideration."

Corrado Prizzi was pale with anxiety. "You are telling me that she not only turned down the U.S. Senate," he said to Eduardo, voice trembling with indignation, "but that she showed no interest in being President?"

"Maybe not in so many words, Poppa, but that was the absolute gist of her attitude."

"This is a dangerous woman. What am I supposed to do? I can't have her iced because she already blew the whistle on me about that. How am I supposed to protect myself? Everything I try to do she turns against me."

"It's very difficult."

"One thing is for sure—we can't let her take over as head of Barkers Hill—she could leave me penniless."

"Don't worry about Barkers Hill, Poppa. I have everything well in hand."

"You are past retirement age! Two more years and you'll be seventy."

"Three."

"Please—I happen to know your real age. Anyway, that's a multibillion-dollar bidniz. It must go on, and on, and on. Someone who is as young and as smart as the Asbury woman would be exactly the right one for the job if I only knew she wouldn't take over the lion's share."

"There must be a solution, Poppa."

"Of course there's a solution! You gotta marry her and she's gotta sign a contract before the marriage which guarantees that she gets something like—oh, whatever—ten million—as her share of your estate but not a penny more."

"I'm working on that, Poppa."

"So? What's happening?"

"I thought I'd give it perhaps sixty days more so she could have a chance to become physically dependent on me."

"Physically dependent."

"Sex is like opium to women, Poppa. The better it is, the more they want, and the more they get, the more they have to have."

"I don't get it, Eduardo."

Eduardo coughed diffidently; a slight abrupt cough. "I have certain powers which women find irresistible," he said with quiet pride. "I turn them into volcanos. I think we can say that, within sixty days, I'll have Mrs. Asbury hooked and in the net."

Angelo stopped in for a visit with Corrado Prizzi later that afternoon.

"We been making good progress on checking out the people who work for Mrs. Asbury."

"What have you got?"

"They're all clean except the butler. He did time in France eighteen years ago."

"What for?"

"Get ready. Attempted murder. He did fifteen months."

"*Fantastico!*"

"He's been clean for seventeen years but I gotta say he's a real live one."

"Every spittoon has a porcelain lining, like an old cop used to say. You done good, Angelo."

VINCENT PRIZZI was so concerned that Charley might be exceeding his authority as Acting Boss and getting into a lot of unorthodox scams that could possibly make Vincent look bad that he had himself lifted out of the bed where he had lain for weeks trying to focus on things such as the ceiling light. Since the installation of his new all-Dacron aorta he had not been able to summon up the concentration to be able to look at television and had fallen behind on seven episodes of his weekly *The Eternal Light*. Attempts to read newspapers had made the columns of newsprint blend into a black-and-white omelet. He had grave difficulties in changing his facial expressions.

When Vincent decided that he had to get back to the laundry he had to be dressed by a male practical nurse. With difficulty and much cursing he had to be seated in a rented wheelchair, then be driven off to Flatbush, pale and shaking. In his office at the laundry after enforced resting, much damp sweating and heavy breathing, he summoned Charley and the three *caporegimes*. When they had assembled he was able to murmur hoarsely, "I'm back. Whatsa score?"

Word of his return immediately got out to the house in Brooklyn Heights. Don Corrado sent Angelo Partanna to tell Vincent that he was not back as Boss until he was able to meet with his father which meant when he would be able to climb the three flights of stairs to Don Corrado's room. Until he could climb the stairs and take a meet he could not assume his duties as Boss. Until then, Don Corrado decreed, Charley was going to run things.

Vincent didn't have the strength to protest his father's ruling. He was barely able to whisper "Take me home" to the nurse. When they got there, there was considerable difficulty in getting the wheelchair up the eleven steps to the entrance to

Vincent's brownstone house, which entailed having to telephone the laundry to send two muscle workers to carry the
chair up to the front door. This hiatus left Vincent in the chair,
sitting on the sidewalk, staring blankly at passersby, one of
whom tossed a quarter onto the blanket that covered his lap.
The *shtarkers* arrived at last, carried the chair and Vincent up
the steps, and got him to a sofa in the front room, where he
lay for more than an hour, humming a medley of "Yes Sir,
That's My Baby" and "Sonny Boy" while he plotted how to get
even with Charley.

Vincent blamed Charley for the humiliation that was patent
in his father's decision to keep him away from active management of the family's business. The word was probably out to
every corner of Brooklyn that the don had taken his son's balls
away. He believed that Charley and Angelo had conspired
against him to influence his father, to maneuver him to cause
him to hand down such a ruling. Then he fell into a long sleep
while the nurse pulled off his shoes and socks and loosened
the belt around his trousers.

The don's ruling confirmed Charley in his own power. He
became brisker. He set up an appointments schedule to hear
grievances and approve new rackets, to order hits, to hand out
favors at the laundry and at his thrice-weekly appearances at
the store-front Monongahela Social Club, where the Prizzi elite
liked to meet and greet.

Mystically, to Charley, the don's renewed vote of confidence
confirmed his right to a relationship with Mrs. Asbury. He no
longer felt (entirely) inferior to her while at the same time he
felt a greater sense of freedom and openness about visiting
Maerose twice a week. Once, he actually took Mae out to dinner and to the movies, startling her.

He was unable to admit to himself that he was being more
considerate of Maerose because he was getting in deeper and
deeper with Mrs. Asbury. He had tremendous feelings for
Maerose, of course. She had jilted him and that had shocked
him so badly that, even though they spent most of their time
together in the sack, jilting was such an alien action to a man

who, all his life, had done the dumping and, excepting for this
aberration of Maerose's, had never been dumped by a woman.
Not only that but the entire environment knew she had
dumped him and that if it weren't for the bullheadedness of
her father they might never have seen each other again. But it
hadn't worked out that way. They had been engaged to be
married for nine years and had become very close.

Charley accommodated Mae in the sense of seeking her com-
pany when he needed comforting, but he was in love with Mrs.
Asbury, whom he no longer thought of as ever having been
The Plumber's daughter. If someone had told him that Mrs.
Asbury had some kind of blood relationship with The Plumber,
Charley would have insisted that the man see a good psychia-
trist. The Plumber was a hulk, a sweater, who still hadn't
learned how to speak English without sounding like Henry
Armetta. Connecting a slob like that with such a refined, elegant woman would have been anomalous with everything she
stood for: wealth, culture, admirable ethereal femininity, and
class. She wore gloves!

Charley knew they could not continue as they had been
doing, grabbing a quick dinner than racing off to the sack at
her place, his place, or in the back of the panel truck. Once,
late at night, they had done it between trains, standing up in
a De Kalb Avenue subway station phone booth.

They were in love, as much has Charley detested the tran-
sience of that phrase. They loved in the way the great ones
had loved, Charley insisted; the way Bogie and Ingrid had
loved, and Ingrid and Bogey. With all his heart he knew that
he and Mrs. Asbury were one being. They made cosmic music
together. Why else, Charley asked himself, did he always wear
a jacket and a necktie when he saw her?

The heavenly music they were making was growing so loud
that it was deafening Charley. Something had to be done. She
had to be his, forever, into eternity. Somehow, he had to get
up nerve to ask her to marry him, but even with his confirmed
authority as Acting Boss, he could not imagine what he would
do if she put him off, or refused him outright. Each time he

saw her (the meetings were happening twice a week), he was on the verge of asking her to marry him but each time the fear of her possible refusal held him back. Also, he wondered if he should talk it over with his fiancée, Maerose, but one thing was for sure, if he was going to marry Mrs. Asbury at all, he had better do it while Vincent was in terrible shape.

Julia, on her side, was coping with the ardor of Edward S. Price on two other nights a week and at one "business" luncheon every Tuesday. Price, on his part, was coping with the impatience of his father who, more and more, imagined that Mrs. Asbury would somehow get away with his money. He pressed Eduardo to bring more density to his courtship. "Make believe you are a young man," he said. "Think with all the passion of a young man. I cannot wait! is what you feel. You must make her yours."

At last, one Friday night in the intimacy of his dining club high above the city, Eduardo leaned across the table, covered Julia's hands with his hands, stared into her eyes for a long moment, then said, "I love you. I cannot conceive of a life without you close to me, a part of me. Will you marry me, Julia?"

Eduardo had had to write the essence of that short speech on lined paper and to play it back over again and again through the intimacy of the mouthpiece of his Dictaphone until he was convinced that it had the right ring of sincerity. Even after listening to his father's urgings he had never dreamed that he would be capable of falling into the manhole of marriage again because he could not conceive of himself asking any woman again, anywhere, to share the cool intelligence of his mind, his uncountable wealth, his wit, his warmth, and his charm. But for all of his life, his father had trained him to put duty first. His clear duty was to marry this woman and to gain control of the enormous plunder she had looted from his father.

Julia's eyelids fluttered. She had been expecting the proposal for several weeks, ever since she had consented to allow him to bed her. She had converted all of her hard-won cash into U.S., German, and Japanese government bearer bonds, all of them safely held in anonymous accounts in secure banks throughout the world. She did not want to seem to give in to the Great White Whale of his egoism at his first asking. As though she were taken by utter surprise and gratitude that such a marvel of manhood would bless her with the ultimate seal of approval, an offer of marriage, she said, "Oh, Edward!" She said it in a manner so unbelieving that such an enormous boon should be offered to her, that she could read the intense gratification in Edward's eyes.

"Yes. It is true. I want you to be my wife," he said as humbly as his *amour-propre* would allow. "But I shall not rush you. I shall be awaiting your answer at this table, one week from tonight."

ON THE FOLLOWING morning at 2:18 A.M., because the father had said human gestation took exactly ten lunar months, twins—a boy and a girl—were born to Nuala and Allan Melvin. Allan called Julia from the hospital at seven-thirty. Steiner sent Curry in to awaken her to take the call.

"Twins! Allan, how fateful. But are you sure?"

"Am I *sure*?"

"Twins are always passed through the female line."

"Then Nuala must have some twin cousins."

"What are you going to call them?"

"God knows."

"When can I see Nuala?"

"Why don't I come over to your place for some breakfast, then we'll both go up to see her."

"Where is she?"

"Lenox Hill."

The babies were beautiful, the women both said so. The father thought they looked great but he wouldn't have said beautiful. Allan took pictures with a Polaroid camera and Julia said she would commission Richard Avedon to photograph mother and twins as soon as they were home from the hospital.

Julia sprang her surprise. "I spoke to Ed Price about having him ask the Cardinal to baptize the babies at St. Patrick's. He did and it is all arranged."

Nuala was ecstatic. "The right start means so much to children," she said happily.

On the way downtown Julia told her brother she was going to deed Bent Island to the twins so that they could have the chance to get out of the city whenever they needed to and that would include the use of at least one of the helicopters, of course.

"That's really generous, Jule. Nuala will weep."

"Not that generous. I will have full use of the place throughout my lifetime. But will you draw up the papers?"

"I sure will."

"I suppose that will force you to name the children, to keep the deeds legal."

"Well, we did decide on that actually. We're going to call the girl Julia."

"Allan! How sweet! And what will you call the boy?"

"We thought—Corrado."

She whacked him over the head with a folded newspaper.

Allan had taken an indefinite leave of absence from the law firm to take over as Julia's second-in-command at Asbury Industries. Julia was so distracted temporarily by the men in her life that she leaned on her brother more than ever before. The due date on Edward's marriage proposal was getting nearer and nearer but more than anything else, she had Charley on her mind, thinking every minute she was awake how she could get him to ask her to marry him before the night when Price expected her answer.

There was no question about where Julia's heart was. If Charley had asked her to marry him, she would have flung her arms around him, pulling him to her and devouring him. But she knew that she and Charley were powerless to change the one implacable fact of their lives no matter how much they loved each other: Charley was engaged to marry Maerose Prizzi and, if that solemn fact were denied, then every known law pertaining to the honor of a *mafioso* would be invoked, beginning with the violent murder of Charley by his fiancée's father. She could not bear that thought.

She knew that and Charley knew that, which was why she despised Maerose Prizzi. Mae had met Charley before Julia had met him and therefore had been able to take unfair advantage of him. Julia railed against the injustice of having been born in the same environment as Charley and brought up within streets of him to have fate determine that it was Mae who met Charley first and Mae who had tricked him into an impossible and ludicrously extended engagement. She could never forgive Mae for that.

But, after she and Charley had packed away two full portions each of *salsiccia alla Siciliana* with its fulsome pork and coarsely ground fat, fennel seeds, hog casings, red chile pepper flakes, and chopped caciocavallo at La Festa, a combination that Julia enjoyed beyond measure but found difficult to digest, Charley suddenly defied the danger of offending a Prizzi right at the point where Prizzi sensibilities rested.

That night, on their return from La Festa, two nights following Edward Price's proposal, a perfect night in June with a full moon almost filling the sky, as they sat on Julia's glass-enclosed terrace on the thirty-first floor of the building, beneath its hugely romantic weeping willow tree rising to the glass ceiling three storeys above where the idyllic waterfall began its descent, Charley proposed marriage to her.

It was so *different* from the manner of Price's uncontrollably haughty offer of marriage. Charley was abject, almost apologetic, heartbreakingly in love with her, unable to help himself despite all of the enormous hurdles that would rise up before him if she accepted.

"But—Charley, darling," Julia said huskily, "how can we marry? Everyone, particularly Vincent Prizzi, knows you are engaged to marry Maerose."

"You know Maerose?" he asked with astonishment.

"We went to school together, all the way up to Manhattanville."

"Listen—one thing I know. Mae will understand."

"But will her father and her grandfather understand?"

"There are some things that are none of their business."

"Oh, Charley."

"All right. One thing at a time. If there were no Prizzis, would you marry me?"

"Instantly. Totally."

"Then that's the way it's gotta be. Nothing means anything to me, except you. Will you marry me?"

They rose together. Julia put her slender arms around his neck and stared up into his adoring eyes. He moved close to her, his arms enfolding her. Breathing shallowly, he waited for her answer as if nothing else had ever happened in the world. "With all my heart, my dearest," she answered.

His head came down toward her mouth but, just before they could kiss, a volcanic eruption rose from deep inside Julia, a rumbling belch that shot upward from those sausages exploding like nuclear missiles within her. As Charley's panting lips almost reached her mouth, a tearing, reverberating *GrrraaaaAAAACK!* which stopped all time, tore out of Julia.

Charley stared at her, dumbfounded. His hands dropped to his sides. He stepped back, his eyes as blank as glass. Something had snapped inside him in the presence of that volcanic burp. A woman whom he had considered perfect had turned out to be just like any other woman; just like that girl with the crooked stocking seams and the manicurist who had dirty fingernails. That one coarse burp had erased Charley's feelings of love as if a giant hand had appeared with a damp cloth and had wiped all of it away from the slate of his life forever. He stared at her for an instant as if she were a stranger, some unkempt panhandler who had tugged at his sleeve on a wintry night. He turned away abruptly and strode away from the terrace. Julia could see him moving across the room toward the front door. She cried out to him in confusion. "Charley! What happened? What have I done?" But he was gone. She heard the front door slam as he left her behind forever.

*   *   *

She gazed around at all the unfamiliar objects on the terrace, each in its turn, recognized none of them, then tottered across to the bar where she poured out a large shot of cognac and knocked it back, large tears falling down her cheeks.

JULIA telephoned Charley nine times in the next two days: to the St. Gabbione Laundry, to the Monongahela Social Club, and to his apartment at Brighton Beach, but not only was she unable to get him on the telephone, he never called her back. She could still hear that awful deeply subterranean belch as it had accumulated force, building to a 1.2 reading on the Richter scale. She could have done nothing to repress that natural force, no more than King Canute could have stopped the tides. But Charley's abrupt desertion had left her embittered. *He* had belched for hours every time after they had left La Festa, after wolfing down those sausages. She had never denied him his right to burp; stentorian, thundering, guttural, rotund belches, some of them so strong as to make the chair he was sitting on tremble and sway. *She* had never shown any disapproval whatever whenever his reverberating burps had startled dozens of people seated around them in restaurants or passing on crowded sidewalks. She had always accepted that if you ate *salsiccia alla Siciliana* you burped, for it followed as night the day. He knew that. He had been raised among barking, burping, eructing people who enjoyed the occasional *salsiccia* and who had never been known for delicacy. She imagined that being around Vincent Prizzi, as both Maerose and Charley had been, must have been like being trapped in the timpani section of a great symphony orchestra.

Her despair was wasted. Her grief lost all meaning. Charley

never relented in his abandonment of her. By the third day she had to stare at reality; it was over. A dream had been shattered. All that was left for her was to negotiate a marriage with Edward S. Price.

On the night before she was to dine with Price and to give him her answer to his invitation to join their lives together, she stayed up quite late with yellow pads, making analytical notes on either side of a dividing line as Henry George Asbury had taught her, as she reached conclusions upon her computer. She worked out the basics, haunted by the loss of Charley, the man she had coveted for all of her life and whom she had almost attained. She vowed that if Barkers Hill Enterprises had a single corporate entity that manufactured or sold any kind of sausage she would make certain that such threats to happiness were stricken from their lists.

She dressed carefully the following Friday evening. She wore the sapphire and diamond choker, a simple but breathtakingly expensive little scarlet dinner dress by Chanel, and a rope of emeralds that hung to her navel, to point out silently to Price that he was hitting in the big leagues. She sat quite alone in the cavernous library, sipping chilled Blagny '61 and counting the ecstasies that would have been hers had she not been racked with that ghastly burp as she and Charley had (almost) plighted their troth.

The telephone call came in: Edward S. Price had left his building and would be at the entrance to her building in 11:43 minutes. Her shoulders accepted the chinchilla wrap that Steiner placed upon them. She allowed him to press the button that opened the door to her private chinoiserie elevator and was dropped to the main floor. The colossally long, large Price limousine was pulling up at the front door as Julia swept out, crossed the pavement, and entered the car.

"You have never been so beautiful," Price said. "You have the radiance of the first bride at the first wedding in all history."

"How charming you are, Edward," she replied.

The identity check at the dining club seemed interminable

to both of them. Julia refused champagne insisting that they produce a good Blagny, demanding a '67. "It is one of the long-lived whites," she said distantly to the street-level *sommelier*.

They did not discuss her decision regarding marriage. They spoke of soybean futures and of two of the national football teams that Barkers Hill owned. Julia noticed that Price's hand was trembling slightly as it held the wine card.

After twenty minutes the identity check was completed and the armed guard led them to the express elevator which was equipped with telephones, two-way television, a fax machine, and radar.

Safely inside the dining club, they were escorted to Edward Price's table. Each member had a fixed location that protected him from having to glance at fellow members whom he might have attempted to ruin or perhaps even attempted to cheat in one business arrangement or another. Importantly, it was the table at which Edward S. Price had proposed marriage to his guest one week before.

After the meal (Julia had ortolans' wings sautéed in sterlet caviar and served on a bed of daisy petals, Price had the cheeseburger), he leaned across toward Julia, covered her hands with his hands just as he had when he had proposed to her, and said shakily, "What is your decision, my dearest?"

"There is the matter of my place at your side."

"Of course, my darling. That is what marriage means."

"I meant—our children. If there will be any."

"Yes?"

"We would—both of us—want them to be protected. And we would want them to be proud of both of their parents."

"Of course, yes."

"There would be such actual and symbolic unity, Edward dear, if you took over the helm of Barkers Hill as chairman and I served as your handmaiden, the president and chief executive officer."

"But as attractive as that sounds, do you think it is really necessary? And what has that got to do with the protection of the future of our children?"

"Well! I would need to merge my 137 Asbury companies with Barkers Hill, wouldn't I? I know that is hardly a drop in the bucket compared to Barkers Hill earnings, but I would be sacrificing Asbury Industries in order to consolidate our children's rightful shares in our worldly goods."

"My father owns a considerable number of those companies."

"Ah, yes. But so do I."

"I can assure you, dear Julia, that our children's share in what I own will never be in jeopardy."

"You are older than I am, Edward. It is remotely possible that you might go first."

"But I will leave a will!"

"Ah, yes. But if I go first, what will I have to leave if I have to merge all my Asbury interests with what is yours and yours alone at Barkers Hill. No, Edward. To protect our little ones we must each draw wills which will leave everything we own each to the other."

"But what about the billion-odd that you extracted from all those companies at the time of Henry's death? And the seventy-five million which was the ransom money which was never required."

"I don't follow you."

"My father is particularly keen on recovering that money. My God, Julia, a billion, four hundred million not even counting the ransom money."

"Recovering? How recovering? It was never his money. Henry and I owned the Asbury companies and put them into a stock speculation pool."

"It was my father's intention to earn that money in the same way you acquired it, excepting that you took advantage of the situation. In his view."

"Well it seems to be that we will need to agree on a waiting period, sort of a cooling-off period."

"How do you mean?"

"I mean if you accede to the joint wills, each in the favor of the other, and if I am elected as president and chief executive officer of Barkers Hill under a twelve-year contract which will give me most favorable stock options to a ceiling of fifty or sixty million dollars, a salary of three million three a year and expenses, as well as the Barkers Hill agreement to pay for the taxes and upkeep on my houses and staffs in various cities, I don't see why, after such a cooling-off period of eighteen months, his two-thirds share of the billion four can't be made available to your father."

"Eighteen months?"

"After all, he did take down a billion three out of all those pension funds. He is hardly hurting."

"But it seems so inequitable."

"How, Edward? The billion four can be part of my estate and, should anything happen to me, you would inherit that. I would say, all in all, that it is a very generous offer on my part."

"Then what you are saying, my dearest, is that you will marry me?"

"Yes, Edward," Julia said demurely.

CORRADO PRIZZI, wearing his steel-rimmed eyeglasses to validate the seriousness of the meeting, sat in a tobacco-colored plush chair facing Angelo Partanna on the top floor of the Victorian mansion in Brooklyn Heights. "You will not believe the deal the Asbury woman has put over on Eduardo," he said.

"Eduardo?"

"My own son. A Harvard man."

"What did she do?"

"She agreed to marry him."

"But you wanted that."

"But what she wants! She keeps the billion four for another eighteen months! That's like a hundred million more in interest she socks away. Next, she is made the *padrona* at Barkers Hill for over three million plus expenses plus stock options worth sixty million dollars! On top of that we gotta pay the taxes and upkeep on all her houses and the army of people she has. A twelve-year contract plus a clothing allowance! The whole thing could cost me two hundred million!"

"This is serious."

"She's gotta go."

"Sure—but how? Anything happens to her she's already set it up that we did it to her."

"There's always another way."

"You figured another way?"

"The butler. The one who did time on the murder charge."

"Yeah?"

"After the wedding—which is set for six weeks from now—the Asbury woman and Eduardo are gonna take a honeymoon in Rio at the same time the President invites Eduardo to be one of his backups at the big economic summit they're gonna have."

"So?"

"So the butler and the secretary and the maid all go with Mrs. Asbury on the honeymoon and, while they are in Rio, thousands of miles away from Brooklyn, the butler slips the special drops into whatever Mrs. Asbury drinks and in like three minutes she is dead from heart failure. The beauty part is that the stuff, whatever it is, can't be traced even with autopsy. The heart attack will look strictly natural so nobody including that newspaper can blame us."

"That is world-class thinking, Corrado."

"But you ain't heard the *real* beauty part. Part of the deal when she agreed to marry Eduardo was that they make out wills in favor of each other so when she goes, Eduardo gets back my billion four and the seventy-five million ransom which she wouldn't let go of plus all that interest on so much money."

"Sensational!"

"So lean on the butler. Then, after you have him scared, tell him he's gonna get a nice piece of money in a Swiss bank."

An assistant muscleman named Aldo Brancuso picked up Arpad Steiner at 7:20 the following morning as he came out of the Sixty-first Street exit of Mrs. Asbury's apartment building to do his daily household shopping. Brancuso walked him smoothly across the pavement into a large car that drove up Park Avenue to Seventy-second Street, then turned left to ride serenely into Central Park.

Steiner protested angrily so Brancuso dislocated his thumb, a painful move. "You want me to break botha your legs?" he asked Steiner testily. The car rode inside the Park until it reached the Ninetieth Street exit. It didn't make the turn out to Fifth Avenue but stopped at a park bench about thirty feet from the exit. A small, nattily dressed man wearing a brown Borsalino hat and a large nose was seated on the bench reading the business section of the *New York Times*. Brancuso delivered Steiner to the empty space beside Angelo on the bench.

"Good morning," Angelo said.

"What is this?"

"We don't know each other. This was a good way to meet."

"To meet? What for? That man broke my thumb."

"I wanted to talk to you before we tell Mrs. Asbury that you are a convicted felon."

Steiner stared. All color left his face. It was many seconds before he could speak. "But that was eighteen years ago," he said weakly. "And I was wrongly accused. The man insulted me and I assaulted him. He died but there was no question of murder. The autopsy proved that."

"The charge was attempted murder. You tried to strangle him. You went to prison."

"What do you *want*?" Steiner pleaded.

"You have a very good job, Mr. Steiner. It is a position of trust."

"Tell me what you want."

"I want you to be able to work at your job, if that's what you want, for the rest of your life. But if you refuse to cooper-

ate with me, we will follow you from job to job wherever you
go and you'll be finished for any kind of work."

"What kind of people are you?"

"We are generous people who are not asking something for
nothing."

"What something?"

"I want you to have time to think, Mr. Steiner. We will talk
again." Angelo got up from the bench, walked to the car, got
in, and was driven away.

THE PREPARATIONS for the wedding were pressing
because the groom had been named as one of seven American
business leaders to accompany Osgood "Goodie" Noon,
President of the United States, to an international economic
summit meeting in Rio de Janiero, departing two days following the date that had been set for the wedding. The wives of
the national leaders from eleven countries would also attend,
for the theme of the meeting would be "The Year of the
Woman," a phrase that the President had decided would be
apt for an election year. Trade agreements, excise taxes, and
parameters of pricing would be discussed at the Rio summit,
for knitwear, sportswear, women's accessories and shoes as
well as aprons and housedresses. Osgood Noon had said, in
announcing the meeting of the leaders of thirty-seven nations,
"Particular attention will be paid to establishing uniform sizing
for all pantyhose. We will return with a victory for the
American woman."

While Julia got her trousseau together, thinking morbidly of
Charley Partanna and what might have been, while Nuala

nursed twin infants, and Maerose felt a flood of relief in a welcome renewal of Charley's attentions to her, Angelo Partanna sat on a park bench near the Ninetieth Street exit in Central Park and laid out his demands to Arpad Steiner.

"All you have to do," he said persuasively, "is to pour about eight drops of this oil I will give you into Mrs. Asbury's tea or perhaps a glass of wine."

"What will the oil do to her?"

"It will put her to sleep, requiring that she be returned by air ambulance to New York, or, say, the Mayo Clinic, so that countermedications can be used to awaken her. Our people at the conference will cause such a commotion that the wives of all other delegates will see that they, too, are in peril and will beat upon their husbands to abandon the summit meeting and return to their homelands."

"Why do you want to do that?"

"We represent an enormous Taiwanese cartel of ladies' ready-to-wear and mass-market lingerie. We must disrupt the summit meeting at any cost and bring it to a close so that no decision can be reached which will bring about high prohibitive tariffs on these items. It is a matter of life or death for our people."

"And a matter of a considerable amount of money as well, I would say," Steiner said shrewdly.

"I do not deny that. I realize that the laborer is worthy of his hire. You will be paid well for the work you do for my clients."

"How much?"

"Fifty thousand dollars. Twenty-five thousand payable in advance."

"When?"

"Now, if you accept the job. But I must have a receipt for my people."

"I accept," Steiner said.

Angelo produced a flat white envelope. He opened its flap to reveal a thickness of twenty-five thousand-dollar bills. "Count it, please," he said.

Steiner counted the money rapidly while Angelo removed

another sheet of paper from his breast pocket and unscrewed the top of a fountain pen. "This paper says that, in return for placing not more than ten drops into a beverage to be drunk by Julia Asbury Price-to-be that you accept herewith the sum of twenty-five thousand dollars representing one half of a total payment of fifty thousand dollars to be made on your return from The Year of the Woman summit meeting at Rio de Janeiro in Brazil. It is fully dated, et cetera. Sign here, please."

Steiner pocketed the envelope containing the money, signed the document, and accepted his copy. Angelo got up from the bench, extended his hand, then walked to the waiting automobile to drive off.

As he tried to sleep on it that night, something about the arrangement bothered Steiner. He finally put the poultice on the canker that was gnawing at him. The United States women's ready-to-wear and popular lingerie industry was enormous. If a man who was hailed to be as canny as Osgood Noon, the American president, had called a meeting to regulate tariffs and trade practices for, among other items, women's ready-to-wear, then every other manufacturer of every other country would be accepting such conditions for the good of their industries, therefore why should Taiwan take such an undoctrinaire stance? Something was decidedly fishy here, Steiner cautioned himself and since, at the very least, the dignity of his employer/benefactor was at stake, he resolved to talk it over with Mrs. Asbury when he, not Curry, would take in her breakfast tray.

He took the tray to Madam's bedside. She propped herself up on pillows, saying, "Is Curry ill this morning?"

"No, Madam," Steiner said, placing the tray on her lap upon the bed. "A rather urgent matter has arisen which I need to bring to your attention."

"Ah. And what is that, Steiner."

"After you have had your breakfast, Madam. I shall wait for your ring."

He withdrew from the room.

Julia enjoyed the breakfast at her usual pace. When she had

quite finished she rang the small silver bell. Steiner appeared at once, removed the tray, placed it on a small table, and said, "I feel that you should know, Madam, that an elderly Italianate gentleman had a ruffian abduct me as I left the building at Sixty-first Street on two subsequent mornings. The ruffian dislocated my thumb on the first journey, causing this unsightly bandage as you may have noticed, then, at the second meeting the elderly Italian gentleman, wearing a *brown* fedora made out of rabbits' fur, bribed me to place drops of this solution"— Steiner removed a small vial from his pocket and held it up— "into your afternoon tea while we were at the conference in Rio de Janeiro."

"Let me see that, please, Steiner."

He handed her the vial.

"What did the man say would be the effect of these drops?"

"He said it would put you into a deep sleep, Madam, requiring that you be flown back to New York—or to the Mayo Clinic, he said—disrupting the conference."

"And they offered to pay you for this?"

"Indeed yes, Madam. Twenty-five thousand dollars on account and twenty-five thousand on my return to New York."

"I deeply appreciate your loyalty, Steiner."

"Thank you, Madam."

"Was the Italianate gentleman rather short, with a pronounced widow's hump and a quite large nose?"

"Yes, Madam. That would describe him accurately."

"If it weren't for the sum of money involved, it would all seem to be an elaborate practical joke."

"What they have done to my thumb rather belies that possibility, Madam. Will that be all?"

"Yes. Thank you, Steiner."

The perfect servant took up the breakfast tray and left the room.

Julia went to the small desk in her room, took up an electronic Rolodex, and dialed the home telephone of the chief chemist at Asbury Pharmaceuticals. After a short conversation with the chemist she rang for Curry to draw her bath, canceled her massage and her martial arts workout, brushed aside Curry's explanation of why she had not brought the tray in that morning and, within twenty minutes, was fully dressed and in the study talking to Richard Gallagher, her security chief.

". . . therefore, please take this small package to Mr. Gumbiner at the pharmaceuticals labs, see that he analyzes it immediately and wait for his written conclusions."

"Yes, Mrs. Asbury."

"I have sworn Mr. Gumbiner to secrecy and I must ask you to reveal nothing about this conversation to anyone."

"Yes, Mrs. Asbury."

"I will be waiting for the lab analysis at my office. Please ask Mr. Gumbiner to complete his written report by noon today. When it is ready please bring it to my office. I have instructed Laszlo to drive you in a staff car."

❻❸

THERE WERE a great many things to do, but Julia took time to gloat as she was driven to her office that morning. Perhaps it hadn't been entirely fair to have taken advantage of two old men like Corrado Prizzi and Ed Price but they had risen to the bait like trout and had swallowed the hook greedily. She had known she would be taking a risk when she had insisted that she and Price exchange wills in each other's favor and by putting the billion four out of their reach for another eighteen months, but holding it out had sharpened their greed and offering to write her will in their favor had been something that Henry would have been proud to have thought of himself. They couldn't have her hit, so they would poison her and figure, because it would have happened so far from Brooklyn, no one could accuse them. It was all really too delicious.

There were just less than four weeks until she and Edward would be leaving for Rio and she had a lot to get done. She had a meeting with her father to have him get her a forged French passport in the name of Evelyn Cacciatore. She told him that he owed her without saying exactly what she meant but The Plumber had aced her husband, the adviser to presidents, and had always felt a little sheepish about that, so he figured that she had found out when she was hanging around with Charley. To equalize the guilt he had made a deal with the best forger in the business, an artist who turned out a perfect French passport carrying eleven visas and an old Photomaton picture of Julia that looked more like her cousin twice-removed; a work-of-art for only two thousand dollars, a present from Dad.

There were other things to do, almost too many, what with the money arrangements, the fittings for the bridal dress and the bridesmaids' ensembles, the invitations to the wedding reception at the 7th Regiment Armory, the merger of Barkers Hill with Asbury Industries, the transfer of all of her houses to Allan, Nuala, and the twins, and her underlying melancholia over the loss of Charley, but the time between the grim reading of the chemist's report on the "few drops of oil" and her wedding day went rapidly.

The contents of the vial were analyzed in a conclusive report from Mr. Gumbiner. "Five drops of this substance, *diorolgeum trichide*, will paralyze the muscles and the chambers of the heart within eleven seconds of ingestion, sooner if administered in a hot solution. Furthermore it is so instantly soluble throughout the physical system that it would be virtually untraceable as the cause of death. Death by heart failure would need to be the coroner's verdict."

Julia marveled at Sicilian ingenuity. An old man who had never as much as attended school had had the resources to find this marvelously arcane chemical substance but, she reasoned, that was what had made them great; great enough to have accumulated several billion dollars so that she could clip them for a billion four.

Using the one copy of the deed she had asked Allan to draw

so that she could bequeath Bent Island to the twins, secretly she had other copies made with the effect of legally transferring her properties in Gstaad, Rome, New York, Paris, London, Maui, and Aspen to either Allan and Nuala jointly or in the case of Paris to Nuala, and London to Allan, separately. She had decided long before that Allan was in no danger of being trashed by the Prizzis, if they could ever make any connection between what she had done to them and what Allan had done for her, because Nuala's newspaper was his insurance. If anything happened to Allan the publicity would finish the Prizzis no matter how solid their connections. She deeded the house in Bali to Arpad Steiner. That should be far enough away, she thought.

On the day before her wedding Julia chose one hundred of the companies she had been carefully building up within the Asbury Industries conglomerate and she withdrew $2 million against each of the companies' accounts and had the money transferred to her own account in Zurich with instructions to redistribute it to her numbered accounts in eleven banks around the world, with specific instructions to open an account with the Banco de Argentina main office in Buenos Aires in the name of Evelyn Cacciatore in the amount of $750,000. Why else, Julia wanted Corrado Prizzi and Ed Price to remember, had she been made chief executive officer and CEO of Barkers Hill Enterprises? These final transfers would bring the score up to a billion six. That should remind Corrado Prizzi and his ice-assed son to think twice before they double-crossed their next partner and dumped him into the sea.

JULIA ASBURY and Edward S. Price were joined in holy wedlock at the little church of St. Philip of the Wounds in the West Thirties. Because of the maturity of the groom and the combined number of their marriages which had preceded this ceremony, it was not the splashy sort of wedding that it might have been. The papal Nuncio performed the marriage. The Chairman of the Federal Reserve Bank was best man. Nuala Melvin was matron of honor and six reigning stars of screen and television were, in all their thunderous beauty, maids of honor, since Barkers Hill owned the two principal Hollywood talent agencies and one major film studio. Four television networks recorded the wedding ceremony itself and the sound bites of the wedding guests as they entered and left the little church: the mighty, the great, but very few near-great, taking time away from their conquests in the worlds of sports (Barkers Hill owned two football franchises, three big-league baseball teams, two national basketball teams, and three boxing champions); industry and finance (CEOs of forty-one leading Barkers Hill companies); politics (vast numbers of Senators and Congressmen whom Barkers Hill owned); and crime, although that was not an entirely separate category.

The bride wore a pale-blue afternoon dress, the signature sapphires and diamonds at her throat, and was, beyond any doubt, the most beautiful woman in the church; striking, glossy, radiant, poised. The groom, utterly distinguished, with his blue hair by Albert of Warsaw, his gray stock, his somber frock coat, and his utterly aristocratic features that told of centuries of breeding, was a few inches shorter than the bride but so prepossessingly distant in his bearing that his presence dominated every man in that holy place.

The congregation, as successful and as famous as they all were, were cowed by what was estimated to be the combined worth of this examplar bride and groom because, if some of them hadn't known it already, the published wedding announcements in the news media had mentioned quietly that the groom was a member of the world's most unattainable dining club and that the bride was president and CEO of Barkers Hill Enterprises.

A choir of *castrati* imported from Florence sang thrillingly. The organ pealed Gounod and Mendelssohn.

Angelo Partanna, seated at the rear of the church, represented the Prizzi family at the wedding.

Two days after the wedding the newlyweds flew to Andrews Air Force Base in Washington aboard the bride's *Gulfstream IV*. Price was taken by a Marine Corps helicopter to the White House to join the President's party, which would fly out that afternoon to Rio. Julia continued on to Rio immediately, flying with Steiner, Miss MacHanic, Curry, and her *wha-rang-do* instructor. She slept most of the way so that she could look her best at the official reception the following evening.

Before retiring she sent for Steiner. "Did they give you instructions as to when you were to administer their potion?" she asked him.

"The drops were to be administered at teatime on the afternoon of the second day, Madam," the butler replied. Julia consulted the official schedule of the summit meeting. Edward would be busily engaged as an adviser to the President until seven o'clock on that evening.

The Prices were settled in a large suite in the small but elegant Ouro Verde Hotel on the Avenida Atlantica on Copacabana Beach. Edward, who had no opportunity to sleep aboard *Air Force One*, was worn out. The honeymooners didn't have a proper reunion until breakfast the next morning, which had to be early because the President was a man to be up and about.

"There will be the usual opening ceremonies with a fashion show today and an official luncheon. I'll be back at about four for a shower and a quick nap so that we will be ready for the welcoming cocktail party at six o'clock."

"I'll be ready, dearest," Julia said.

Edward had an official breakfast with the European delegation on the morning of the second day and would be in committee meetings all afternoon after a luncheon with the Pacific Fringe group of nations, but he said he hoped Julia would be able to fill out her day with the various wives of the delegates, promising that they would have a quiet dinner in their rooms that evening.

"You must promise me that you will return here for tea this afternoon," he said gently, "so that you may have some rest from your busy day."

"Don't give me a thought," Julia said. "I shall have lunch with the Canadians, do some shopping, then come back here at four or so for a relaxing cup of tea as only Steiner can prepare it. You are so thoughtful, darling."

Edward smiled benignly, patted the top of her head, took up his briefcase. "I can't wait to see you this evening," he said.

After Edward left, Julia put a little check for fifty thousand dollars made out to Arpad Steiner with the deed to the house in Bali into an envelope, addressed the envelope with Steiner's name, sealed the envelope and left it on her breakfast tray. She thought of Henry for a moment. She knew that it was Henry's lifelong belief in himself, how it would have been impossible for him to make a mistake—it was that granite-hard faith that had carried her through. Then she packed a small bag with her jewels, some cosmetics, and a spare pair of shoes and left the hotel, taking a taxi for the nineteen-mile ride to the Galeo airport, where she bought a Tourist-class ticket to Buenos Aires, producing her French passport. She flew off to a total reincarnation by Dr. Mitgang, wondering if someday, with her new face, she might ever meet Charley again.